HIDDEN TREASURES
An Erotic Romantic Suspense

by
George A Bernstein
#2 Best Seller at Amazon "Crime Thrillers"
#5 Best Seller at Amazon "Suspense"

GnD Publishing LLC

GnD Publishing LLC
Palm Beach Gardens, Florida 33418
www.GeorgeABernstein.com
info@GeorgeABernstein.com

Publisher's Note: This is a work of fiction. Names, characters, and incidents are a product of the author's imagination. Locales and public names are sometimes used for atmospheric purposes and may have been altered to meet the demands of the story. Any resemblance to actual people, living or dead, or to businesses, companies, events, institutions, or locales is completely coincidental.

Cover Design by Paradox Book Covers

Ordering Information: Quantity sales. Special discounts are available on quantity purchases of print copies by corporations, associations, bookstores, and others. For details, contact the publisher.

Hidden Treasures/George A Bernstein

ISBN: 979-8-9871607-1-8

**Other Steamy Romance novels by
George A Bernstein**

Trapped
A 5-Star, parapsychological Romantic Suspense
**Winner in "The Next Great American Novel"
contest**
An Amazon Top 100 Novel
Available in e-book, audio book, and print at:
www.amazon.com/dp/B00GLX1EKU

A 3ʳᵈ Time to Die
A 5-Star paranormal Romantic Suspense
Available in e-book, Audio book, *and print at:*
www.amazon.com/dp/B00D962DL6

See also George A Bernstein's
Seven, 5-Star **Detective Al Warner suspense novels**
Starting with the riveting *Death's Angel*
#2 Best Seller at Amazon's *Crime Thriller*
#5 Best Seller at Amazon's *Suspense Category*
Followed by:
Born to Die
The Prom Dress Killer
White Death
Sniper
Taken
Cold Vengeance
All 5-Star rated

DEDICATION

To my critique team, Sharon and Fred, who insisted I use my talents at writing love scenes to write an erotic romance. I hope you've found it was a worthwhile task.

HIDDEN TREASURES

~ 1 ~

Derik Brand's eyes swept the western horizon—what was visible of it. Black clouds roiled like tumbling boulders for as far as he could see. He glanced again at his chart as he struggled to hold his Choy Lee 36 sloop quartering south-by-southeast on a reach for Martinique ... and safe harbor.

He won't make it. Tropical Storm Chico churned into a hurricane, plowing into the Eastern Caribbean a full day ahead of schedule. Against the surge of the storm, he may not be able to beat east enough to even make Dominica, much less Martinique. Derik turned up his marine radio, set on Coast Guard advisories. His teeth clenched as he listened, a pained groan rumbling in his chest.

"This is a weather alert. Hurricane Chico has fed on the warm waters of the Eastern Caribbean, blossoming quickly from a tropical storm to a category two hurricane. It is expected to further strengthen, moving west at twenty knots, and may approach Category Four strength when it arrives at the Winward Islands tonight. All marine vessels should immediately seek safe harbor and batten down. This is a weather alert. Hurricane Chico ..."

"Tonight, my ass!" Derik snapped off the radio to conserve battery. "The outer bands are here now," he growled. "If I can't make Dominica, where the hell can I go?" He snatched off his cap, ran fingers through soaked, shoulder-length blond curls and peeked at his chart, plastered to the custom panel secured at the side of the helm. It was a struggle to hold the sloop's head up as the storm drove them relentlessly west. He scanned southeast and made out tips of peaks on the small island of Dominica, midway between

Puerto Rico and Venezuela, but no way, in this wind, he could get there.

He hoped to reach some sort of uncharted cay before the full brunt of the storm descended on him. This leased thirty-six-foot sloop would surely founder, taking him down with it.

"Shit!" *Andrea dumps me for some rich dude just as I get my MBA, so I take off on my bucket-list trip of a six-week, solo cruise of the Caribbean, and that's going down the tubes.* "I might just follow it there if I don't find shelter, and quickly!" he grumbled.

He'd planned this last fling after getting his Master's Degree at Northwestern, and before beginning his career as a second assistant controller at Wall & Baker. He'd rejected the NFL draft, despite being one of the three top college quarterbacks in the nation, to pursue an advanced degree in finance because he loved the idea of working with the little guy to build their dreams. No big NFL signing bonus at the greedy bitch moved on, which was probably lucky for him.

Derik raised binoculars from around his neck. *If I don't find a safe place to hunker down fast ...* A spoke of the wheel wedged under an arm, he struggled to hold course in the shrieking gale while peering west over the roiling sea. Plumes of foam and sheets of cold spray drenched him and partially occluded his view as he swept the surface out to the far horizon where lighter sky still prevailed.

Nothing but towering waves and ... wait! Was that ...? He wiped his eyes, blinked, and peered again through the glasses. The pitch and slew of the yacht made focusing dicey.

Yes! A bulge of land—a largish hill. No, *two* hills. And there, a second one, maybe a half-mile east of the first. Two tiny cays, unlisted on his charts! Struggling for a bearing, he lost control of the helm. The wheel spun hard, the spokes thumping his hands. The boat skidded across an eight-foot wave, healed hard starboard and sliced through a mountain of water, towering above and about to swamp it. Derik snatched the whirling helm, jamming two fingers, but was able to bring her about. The sturdy yacht popped out of the canyon of water collapsing around it with a thorough but not fatal dousing.

He spit out a mouthful of seawater, steadied the yacht, still healing hard to starboard, and found again through salt-blurred eyes, those fast-approaching hills of possible safety. If he could gain a heading of five degrees easterly and not get tossed overboard, he should make the western one. He snatched up a rope and lashed himself to the helm with a quick-release knot and studied his rigging, straining in the gale: full jib and half main-sail. He had to increase the main sheet or he wouldn't have enough speed to reach the isles before the storm drove him past them.

Derik murmured thanks to the outfitter who'd installed a retrofitted aluminum mast and upgraded the sloop's auto-furl to modern standards, as he cranked up a bit more sail. The yacht healed even more onto its starboard hull as it surged ahead, its railing nearly awash. It plowed through eight-foot waves, battered by powerful winds. Sheets of salty spray crept past Derik's yellow slicker, sending rivulets of cold water down his spine as the Choy Lee sloop staggered toward a growing vista of green hills and, hopefully, a protected cove where they might snuggle in lee waters until angry Chico fled west. Twenty minutes later, his Perkins diesel at full throttle, his sail and jib reefed, the sloop sloshed through troughs and cascades of seawater, and motored into relatively lee waters provided by the little isle's two low hills.

A tiny niche in the shoreline hardly qualified as a cove, but it would have to do. Derik snuggled the sloop as tight to shore as possible and dropped the bow anchor, then hurried astern and threw a grappling hook. It took three tosses, as he struggled to keep his wiry 6'2" frame from going overboard, before the pronged anchor snagged rocks. Derik drew it tight, nosing the sloop into the wind, and wound the line across two cleats. He threw open the hatch door and staggered below to retrieve necessities—a change of clothes, a sack of dried rations, bottles of water, his portable marine radio, and as an afterthought, his Colt .45. Just in case something or someone unfriendly was on this tiny patch of land. All went into a waterproof boat-bag. He had to get off the yacht, which may still founder as the wind shifted. He hoped he'd find some sort of shelter ashore.

Back on deck, he stumbled to his knees as he fought to lower a ten-foot dinghy with its 9.9 hp outboard and a six-gallon fuel-tank. He slithered aboard the bucking skiff, teetered, and lost his balance, pitching over the side. His knees caught the gunwale with a painful smack, his gut slamming down on the railing and his face catching a full wave, but he was saved from a complete dousing. His boat-bag wasn't so lucky, going overboard and floating away. Derik struggled onto a seat, swiped saltwater from his eyes, swore, and gave a yank on the starter cord. The stubborn little engine required CHOKE and six pulls on the cord before it chugged to life. Two minutes slid by as he tried to release the davits, confounded by the bucking sloop and heaving waves. Freed finally and fighting smaller chop, he sped after his floating bag, catching up to it at the mouth of the cove.

He snatched a boat hook from under the seats, but heavy wave action were a serious hurdle. Twice he nearly went overboard while trying to grapple the bag's strap. Luckily, waterproofing kept it afloat, and he finally managed to snag a strap, but a hard wave broke it free, and he flopped backward, skinning his back and bruising his butt. Derik swore as he scrambled to his knees and peered over the side. The sack now bobbed within arm's reach. He snatched it, took a full wave in the face, and spit water as he hauled it aboard. He collapsed to the floorboards, gasping for breath and tried to quell his pounding heart. Not even his toughest game as quarterback while at U. of Miami had fired such exhaustion. *Those were just games. This is life or death.*

That thought got him back on the dinghy's rear seat, and at full throttle, was drenched by chilly spray as the skiff pitched and slewed across growing waves, back into the relative shelter of the cove. Derik beached the little boat and hauled it across the rocky shore, his face stung by wind-driven sand. He headed for two sturdy palms, dancing in the wind. With the outboard and gas tank removed, he upended the boat, covered them, and lashed the bow and then stern between the two trees. If he couldn't find better shelter, he may have to hunker under the skiff and hope for the best.

The boat bag over his shoulder, Derik groaned at aches in his back and right hip. He'd taken a worse beating than ever inflicted by any blitzing linebacker. Derik shielded his eyes from rain pelting him by the driven wind, and slogged toward the nearest hillside, seeking shelter. A large rock outcropping would be nice. A cave would be even better, but not likely.

~ 2 ~

Any real cover was scanty. No large boulders to wedge behind and very little growth along the base of what was more a cliff than a hillside. Derik stumbled along the nearly vertical base searching for something … anything to provide some measure of protection. The full strength of a possible Category Four storm would be upon him very soon, and if he didn't find …

Hey. A large clump of shrubbery clung to a slight slope of the cliff's surface, about four-feet up. If it grew there, there should be some sort of indention for it to root into. He hoped so, because he was running out of steam. Derik secured the strap of his bag with sturdy twine he'd brought, hooked the other end to his belt, and tested one of the limbs to see if it would hold his weight.

It seemed secure. He was half-way up, reaching for more when the greenery pulled loose. He plummeted down, slamming hard on his back, his right leg awkwardly twisted.

"Shit." He rolled over, flexed the leg and grimaced. Sprained but survivable. Sand brushed from his hair, he limped back to the cliff's base and glared at the green promise of possible limited safety. Derik groaned, reached up to gather two branches this time, and using his last reserves, hauled himself up. He grasped other limbs as he worked to the end of the patch and wriggled behind the growth. Surprised, he found a larger opening than expected. His bag, still suspended from his belt, was retrieved, and he pushed into the niche.

More surprises … he kept going.

Wow! A cave. Black and dank, he sneezed at the musty odor, and his eyes watered. He struggled slowly to his feet and felt for a roof as his eyes began to adjust to the gloom. A sigh hissed between teeth as he flexed his aching back, then he shoved his arms full stretch above his head, meeting no ceiling. He sank to the ground, found soft earth not rocks, and sighed again.

Safe, at least for now. So tired ... He dragged over his boat bag, stretched out, used it as a pillow, and despite being chilled and wet, slept.

~ ~ ~

Derik lurched awake, startled by loud booms of thunder, confused by the blanketing darkness and musty smell. He shivered.

"Where the hell …?" Then he remembered. The hurricane, and a cave to hide in. He sat up, stymied, unable to make out anything around him. He scrambled for his boat-bag, found two light-sticks, and snapped one on, finally able to scan his nearby surroundings. He lumbered to his feet and winced at a dart of pain across his right knee.

"Sprained the sucker during that fall, but I've had worse," he mumbled. He swept the area within the limited range of the light-stick's green glow, and looking up, was unable to see the roof of the cave. It was huge. He shined the green light across the floor and noticed scattered piles of twigs, small branches, and larger pieces of what looked like driftwood. Plenty for a fire. He dragged piles of wood and kindling close to the cave's entrance, hoping any smoke would be drawn outside. Wind howled, and rain pelted the island with almost solid sheets of water. Hurricane Chico had settled in and was making itself known. He shivered again, still wet and chilled. He needed that fire. The tangled brush at the cave's mouth shimmied and shook but repelled most of the storm's fury.

Derik set about building a flame, and eight minutes later a nice blaze crackled, lighting up more of the cave. Thunder cracked and he spied lightning flashes through the screen of leaves. As he'd hoped, smoke was drawn out as the wind whistled by. His yellow slicker shed, he sat and warmed his hands, then turned, hoping to dry his back and chase away the chills. Soon he rose and limped to the center of the cavern, seeking more driftwood. By the flickering firelight he spotted two piles, bleached white branches, near the side wall, but as he got nearer, he jerked back.

"Holy crap!" Not bleached driftwood. Bones! Skeletons, actually. He retrieved his light-stick from near the fire and returned, kneeling for a better look.

The two skeletons appeared mostly intact, laying feet to feet, as if they'd been facing each other when they died. What little clothing that remained was rotted leather boots, belts, and a few tatters of cloth. Maybe some sort of tri-corner hat for the one on the left. And—wow—an old black powder pistol near the guy on the right who also appeared to have a sword … looked like a cutlass from old pirate movies … jammed into his ribs.

"Jesus. Were these pirates fighting over treasure?" He rose and stroked his chin. *Coulda been over two hundred years ago, hiding in this cave all this time.*

Treasure? He wondered as he moved around the bodies. *Totally undisturbed all these years.* He's probably the first to discover them, since these tiny cays would never attract tourists … or even explorers. The cave's mouth was invisible until he climbed behind that scruffy outgrowth. Derik stumbled, barely avoiding a fall and grimaced at a bolt of pain lancing his knee. He sucked in a couple of breaths to quiet his heart and glanced down. Something near the bodies glinted in the green light. He leaned over and brushed away the dirt.

A three-foot-long spade. Rusted iron blade but the oak handle was still solid. *A spade? Something to bury treasure with? Something to fight and die over?* He knelt, the ancient tool in hand, and examined the nearby dirt floor. He tested the surface with the point of the shovel. Firm, but diggable. Had they buried their loot here and then, filled with greed, died over who owned it?

Derik moved around the two, jabbing at the ground. If that were it, it should be close … He paused, then dug again at the spot he'd just tried. Appeared softer, but after all these years that seemed unlikely. He struggled to his feet, and ignoring a pained knee, began to dig. If it were there, it shouldn't be very deep. He searched methodically, working away from the two skeletons. A few minutes later he struck something hard. Furious shoveling, dirt flying everywhere, produced nothing more exciting than a three-foot long, flat boulder. He moved on.

A half-hour later, he sunk to his seat, sweating and exhausted, with no chest of gold discovered. Was this wishful thinking? No, there had to be something there. Those two hadn't fought to their deaths for nothing. He struggled wobbly to his feet and studied the many holes he'd dug. No results other than the small boulder … He cocked his head, then limped back to his first dig and studied the partly uncovered rock. It was the only one he'd run across, which now seemed strange.

"Had they …?" He began digging and found the edges of the three-foot wide rock. He cleared away the earth surrounding it, worked the blade of the shovel under one edge, and pried. The stone, a slab really, rose, then slithered off the iron blade and dropped down, making a resounding thump.

A resounding thump? Not the sound of hitting dirt. More vigorous digging beside the rock showed something else hard under it. A chest, obscured by the rock? The slab was too heavy for him to lift, especially with a damaged knee, but twenty-minutes of digging cleared away a large area to one side, and levering with the still sturdy spade, spilled the rock into the hole. A quick brushing of the surface where it had sat produced the top of a copper-banded, oaken chest.

Derik gasped, hands fisted on his hips. A feral scream burst from his lungs.

"Pirate-fucking-treasure." He sank to the ground, rolling back and forth with breathless laughter, suddenly quelled. He sat up and caught his breath. *Who do these cays belong to?* Unless these were international waters, they surely had laws about ownership of treasure discovered under their purview. And what, exactly, had he found, and of what value? He scurried back to the chest and began digging away at the sides to free it up. No need to hurry. The storm still raged outside and would be at least another day before things calmed down. The painful knee ignored, he worked methodically and soon had the three-foot-wide chest fully exposed.

He grabbed a brass handle but could barely lift one end. Pausing to ponder for a moment, he retrieved the cutlass from the duel of death and used it as a ramp. At twenty-four, he was still ripped from a rigorous workout routine he'd continued after his four years as quarterback for national championship runner-up, Miami Hurricanes. It still took everything he had to work the chest out of its tomb and onto the cave's floor.

Panting, he regarded the large, padlocked hasp. *At least two-hundred-years-old, it should be easy to break.* He was wrong. Several resounding smashes with the spade were useless. He sat, spread-legged, and glared at the offending lock. Then he remembered his pistol. He retrieved the Colt .45 from his bag and standing well back, took the shot. His ears rang as the boom echoed throughout the cave, but the lock hung free.

Derik dropped the gun in his bag, knelt in front of the oaken box, removed the broken padlock, and raised the rusty iron hasp. Breath held, he grasped the lid, but it didn't budge. The iron hinges were rusted. He rose and tugged again but there were no lid-handles to grip, and it refused to oblige. Scowling at the age-stained top, he had an idea.

Retrieving the cutlass, also corroded by time, but still keen-edged, he forced the blade under a corner of the lid. Using it as lever, he managed to open a gap. Repeated at the other corner with the same results, he now had handholds. He crouched, fingers under the top's lip, and ignoring a painful knee, used the strength of his leg to raise the lid, screeching it as it swung open.

Panting for breath, he stepped back, and his eyes flared at what he saw. Gold, silver, diamond rings and broaches, a huge emerald pendant, rubies mounted in a gold neckless … and gold coins. Piles of coins, loose and in sacks. He plucked up one bearing the image of what was probably a king. Flipping it, it was engraved with Spanish and the date 1688.

"Jesus!" *Taken by pirates and hidden here over three-hundred years ago. This is worth millions!* He knelt again, pawing through the treasure, his mind numb. Then he noticed paper—parchment, really—fastened to the underside of the lid. He removed it with care, worried it may disintegrate from age. Some sort of document, in Spanish, and penned with flourishes. He started to lay it aside when he noticed a scrawled sketch on the back. As he studied it, his brow creased, realizing it was a rendering of these two tiny cays. It depicted the one he was on with a rough likeness to the cave, and a large "X," right where he found the treasure.

His heart pounded when he understood what he was looking at—a treasure map. And the sketch of the other island, about a half-mile east of where he was hunkered down, showed another cave with *another* X.

"Holy shit," he muttered. Was there another chest like this, just a half-mile away? He shivered and plopped back on his butt, his laughter so intense he fell over, rolling back and forth on the dirt.

When the storm abated, and if his sloop was intact, he'd sail up there and see if he were really that lucky.

He chuckled, rocking back and forth, hands cupping his cheeks. *Looks like Andrea made the wrong move after all.* Lucky for him he learned where her cards lay before she discovered he was one very rich guy.

~ 3 ~

Two days passed, and angry Chico was long gone, bringing its fury to Cuba, and expected to move into the Gulf Coast. Old Sol peeked from behind billowing white cumulus, and the breeze was not yet hot, wafting gently across rippled, sparkling water.

The Choy Lee sloop had survived the storm largely intact, thanks to the retrofitted aluminum mast and fiber-glassed decking. The tiny cove had provided enough lee protection to keep her safe.

Derik spent half a day cleaning her up and getting ready to sail. He'd motored the dingy to the second island as soon as conditions allowed, and used his new-found map to uncover a second, slightly smaller chest, equally laden with incredible treasure. All he had to do was figure out how to tote it off the two cays without alerting the local governments. He sure as hell didn't want to share his new-found loot with some greedy pol who'd probably line his own pockets.

He needed a full day and part of an evening to transfer his loot from both islands to the boat. He filled backpacks and boat-bags with as much as he could carry, making dozens of trips. Once everything was aboard, he restocked each chest and secured them as deep in the hold as he could, covered with a tarp. Without cell phone service, he hailed the boat's owner in Miami on his ship-to-shore radio.

"You survived the storm, Mr. Brand? I worried we'd lost you. Over." his static-laced voice reflected his concerns.

"I was lucky enough to find shelter west of Martinique and

hunkered down. Weather's cleared, so I'm gonna sail to Fort-de-France tomorrow. Can you extend my lease for a month? I'll wire payment as soon as I reach port. Over."

"Of course. Thank God you're alive. That was some surprise storm. Over."

"A beast, but with your upgrades, this Choy Lee is a tough little babe. Thanks. Over and out." The radio turned off to conserve battery, Derik prepared to depart, but first he was going to get a good night's sleep.

Derik sailed for Martinique the next day, entering the Fort-de-France harbor on the island's east coast under power of his Perkins diesel. He wove his way around three sunken vessels, probably curtesy of Chico's power. As he headed for a mooring, he spied piles of debris being cleared from the shoreline. No buildings he could see were damaged, a surprise, considering the power of the storm, but Martinique had survived many such hurricanes and apparently learned to build secure structures. Once dockside in Fort-de-France, now with cell phone service, he called a professor he knew at Northwestern University. The man was an avid numismatist, especially well-schooled on old coins. Guidance was required as to the value of these coins. The Northwestern switchboard transferred him to the man's office, and it took some wheedling to get his secretary to put him though. That he was calling from Martinique was the clincher. Two clicks, and the man answered, uncertainty in his voice.

"Dr. Beadle, it's Derik Brand. I was in your Global Monetary class last year."

"Oh, yes. I remember you. My most inquisitive student. You're calling from the Caribbean, I understand. How may I help you?"

"I've come across some old, Spanish gold coins. Absolutely mint condition, and I wondered if you'd have some idea of their value?"

"Doubloons, huh. Can you describe them? Are they dated?"

"Yeah. A bust of what I presume was the king of the time, some Spanish I don't understand, and the date 1688."

"Really? 1688 King Philip doubloons? Mint, you say?"

"Yes, sir. Bright and shiny. I presumed they may be valuable—"

"That's an understatement, my boy. Any 17th Century Spanish gold doubloons, if pristine, could fetch well over $5,000 each from any collector, but King Philip gold doubloons dated 1688 are extremely rare and had been known to sell for as much as $20,000, and occasionally even more, at auction." He paused. "Do you actually you have possession of such coins?"

"Yessir. I did some diving after surviving Hurricane Chico and found several in the sand." The story he'd concocted as a start. "Musta been stirred up by the storm. I guess I got lucky."

"Lucky, indeed. When you return, I'd love to see them, and possibly buy one from you for my collection.

"I'd be happy to, sir, if and when I get back to Chicago, and thank you for your help. I'll send you photos when I return to Miami."

"Wonderful. You've made my week, young man. Good luck." And they disconnected.

A grin split Derik's face as he perched at the dinner table in the sloop's salon, hunkered over his inventory notes, struggling to get a handle on the enormity of what he'd stumbled upon.

Thank you Hurricane Chico. Who knew fighting to survive the earliest Cat 4 storm ever to batter the Caribbean in June would turn out to be my lucky day. Most of the doubloons were in sacks of five-hundred, and there were four of them … ten to twenty million dollars in doubloons alone. No wonder they were rare. He probably owned most of the minting. Of course, he couldn't cash them all at once, or the market value would drop. The rules of supply and demand, a check on his laptop showed the current prices of pure gold at about $1,100 per troy ounce on the Commodities Market, or about $16,000 per pound. So, just for its gold, the coins alone were worth about two-million.

Plus, he had twenty-four gold ingots, about twenty-five pounds each, worth roughly ten-million dollars. And stacks of diamond, ruby, and emerald jewelry, and several gem-encrusted crosses and other religious items. Some of the diamonds were huge—maybe ten carats—and to his untrained eye, looked perfect. A few emeralds were even larger. If he could get all safely back to the States, the whole collection was worth many tens of millions, if properly managed. Luckily, he *did* have a master's degree in finance.

A quick visit to a marine hardware dealer near the dock provided two substantial hasps and padlocks, and the tools with which to mount them. Three-hours later, the hatch to the cabin was well secured with two, through-bolted locks. The side windows were way too narrow to admit even a small child, so he felt his treasure was safe from the usual dockside thief. While the big locks suggested something worth stealing inside, it would take a protracted effort, and the dock was regularly patrolled by armed security. His treasure was reasonably safe.

So, he pocketed eight doubloons and set about finding a coin dealer in the island's busy marketplace. He'd repeat his claim to have found them diving off the southern beaches after the storm passed. Three hours later, and after some vigorous horse-trading, Derik was ninety-three-thousand US dollars richer. Funds were wired to the yacht broker for an extra month's lease payment. He kept ten-thousand in cash, and opened an account at Banque Nationale de Paris for the balance. He'd figure what to do with it later. *An offshore bank may be handy when I began liquidating some of my new-found assets.*

It had been a full day and he was bushed, so he grilled his last steak, fried some diced potatoes, opened a can of baked beans, and ate in his galley. Early to bed, some errands to do in the morning, and maybe a relaxed day at the beach before heading home. He *was* eager to get started in something other than second financial officer of an equity investment firm. This new, unexpected wealth made everything possible ... provided he could safely sneak it ashore in Florida. As he drifted off, he smiled at the thought that greedy Andrea had hooked onto the wrong guy. Good to know before things got serious.

The next day he provisioned for the long haul home. Sails and mast were checked for damage, and the sloop put shipshape. Then a day for rest and some release of tension. That meant a modicum of drink and an excess of women. French women ... something Martinique was noted for.

Tall, tanned, with shaggy blond hair, his broad-shouldered and a lean but muscular body made him a babe magnet ... and he spoke passable French.

Beautiful women littered Martinique's beaches, savoring the storms aftermath. French babes were seldom bound by Western cultural norms. He headed for the boardwalk, eager to see what developed.

~ ~ ~

Gisele Dumelle, sprawled on a beach towel spread across the warm sand, glanced up from the pages of her novel and pursed her lips. She rolled her luscious five-foot-ten body to one side and poked her twin, redhead sister. "Coline. Look who just arrived."

Her sister, sprawled on a blanket, raised her head and clucked softly. *"Bon homme.* And tall enough," she continued in French, "not to be intimidate by my gorgeous sister." She looked at Gisele. "American?"

"Probably." Gisele sighed. "But, am I ready for a frolic, after so soon dumping that Spanish lout, Raul." She snickered. "Sex, sex, sex. He had no interest in who I am, as a person."

Coline sat up. "Yes, but the sex *was* great, wasn't it? I was almost jealous." Said with a chuckle. "Anyway, it's time for a new start, and a new lover." On her feet now, a hand offered to her sister. "I'll join you, my darling, and together we'll seduce that hunk. It may be fun as a threesome for a change, if he's up for it."

Gisele rose, brushed off sand, and glanced down the beach. "You think it'll be so easy? I see many other lovely women here."

"French, twin, redhead beauties like us?" A soft chortle. "It's not vain to say we're every American man's dream." She took Gisele's hand. "Come, we'll ask him to join us in that volleyball game," nodding up the beach. "They need players."

Derik's eyes widened at the approach a pair of tall, lithe, green-eyed, redhead twins. They were magnificent in their tiny bikinis—long, shapely legs, tiny waists, and well-filled out bras.

"American?" Her ruby-red lips danced in a saucy smile.

He nodded, and noted the other's lips and nails were pink … the only way to tell them apart.

"I'm Coline, and this is my sister, Gisele." Her English was perfect, with that slight, sexy French lilt. "Would you care to join us in that volleyball game?" glancing up the beach. "We need a tall player on our side."

"I'd love to." He stepped off the boardwalk and followed as the moved across the sand. "I'm Derik, just arrived today and in need of some fun time."

Gisele took his hand as they walked. "You were on that sailboat that docked earlier?"

"Yeah. Lucky to be alive after surviving that nasty boy, Chico." He chuckled. "So, I'm up for a celebration."

"You must tell us about it, and maybe we can help you celebrate," Coline said.

"Sounds good, if you have no plans for later."

"I suspect you may be our plans for later," her turn to chuckle, "but only if you are any good at volleyball." She nodded at a blond Amazonian woman watching their approach. "We need to put that German bitch in her place for a change." Both redheads laughed, then made introductions.

The contest began, and although the twins were graceful and consummate athletes, considerable touching ensued as Derik showed them the overhand serve. Their freckled skin, surely pale under their bikinis, gave authenticity to their hair color. An hour later, after twice drubbing the blonde and her two male partners, Derik and the twins headed for the surf.

"You are a wonderful athlete, Derik," Gisele said, her hand in his as they entered the water. "Did you play volleyball in college?"

"In high school. I was quarterback for the University of Miami Hurricanes in college." He barked a scoffing laugh. "The Hurricanes. An appropriate name, huh, after what happened the past few days?"

"You must tell us how you survived that storm in such a small boat," Coline took his other hand and pulled him down.

"Maybe later. I just want to relax in the water right now." Floating on his back, he pulled pink-lipped Gisele on top of him, her head rested on his shoulder as they hung in the mild surf.

They swam and floated together for the next hour, and ensuing teases and caresses were no longer subtle. He caught Gisele by the waist when a rogue wave tumbled her. As he drew her back onto her feet, her arms snaked around his neck, and she planted a tongue darting kiss on his lips.

Coline bodysurfed up to them in chest-deep water and plastered her nubile figure against his back with a sensual hug, her fingers trailing through the blond hair of his chest as she nibbled on an ear. All laughing, he took each by a hand and towed them to shore where they dried off and reclined on towels to absorb the last of the afternoon sun.

He glanced at Coline. "Will you join me for dinner, girls?"

"Both of us, Derik?" Eyes twinkling, a saucy smile tickled her lips.

"Of course." He pushed up onto his elbows, and his eyes swung from one to the other. "How could any sane man choose just one of such a magnificent duo?"

They giggled as they rose, and as Derik helped brush off sands from their bodies, especially their firm butts and sculpted legs, his heart thumping his ribs. Then each with a hand in his, they entered a beachside café, clad in their swimwear and thin cover-ups. A light ocean breeze cooled the evening as they perched on a plank bench at a driftwood table. The auburn-hair beauties flanked Derik and snuggled close as they supped on oyster on the half-shell, three-pound southern lobsters, and a magnum of champagne. Hands and bare feet were busy explorers under the table as they ate. Finished, they rose to leave.

"That was delicious, Derik." Coline leaned against him, the touch of her hip and breast sending electric tingles down his spine, and she kissed his cheek. "Thank you for a pleasant evening."

"It's still early." He cupped her cheek, drowning in those glistening, emerald eyes. "I've booked a suite at the Omni. I'd love to serve you both dessert there, if you care to join me."

"Dessert, huh?" Gisele grinned. "You have something especially tasty in your suite?"

"Yeah." His heart again tumbled, and he licked parched lips. "I promise I'll do my best to serve something special ... to both of you." His grin was impish. "Hopefully, multi-courses."

A silent signal passed between the women, and Gisele nodded. "I think we're definitely up for that dessert, *mon cher.*" The twins each took a hand and started out the door for the short walk toward the Omni Hotel, just down the beach. "I believe we are as eager," Coline tugged at his hand, "as I suspect you are, to see what is there for us."

Barely out of the café, Coline grabbed an arm and spun Derik into a heated embrace, her mouth consuming his, her pelvis pressed against his. As their tongues fenced, Gisele molded her erotic form across his back and kissed his neck and ear, fingers briefly grazing his crotch where she noted the expected response. Derik's hands caressed Coline's firm butt, groin undulating against groin, as Gisele's fingers teased his sides. After several passionate minutes, Derik leaned back, and drew Gisele around for a sloppy kiss, her fingers still busy, firm breasts pressed against his chest.

Panting, he said, "C'mon, you gorgeous creatures." His tongue swiped her delicious saliva from his lips. "We can do this better in my suite."

"*Oui,*" whispered in breathless unison. "*Allez.*"

He grabbed each by the hand as they hurried down the path, eager for a protracted finish to what they'd started. He was thankful his beach coverup hung to his thighs and covered the bulge in his bikini trunks.

Mon Dieu, Giselle thought, *quell homme. Can this man be more than a brief fling?*

They scurried down the boardwalk, her bikini bottom once again damp, but not from the ocean.

~ 4 ~

Derik, an arm around each beauty's waist, staggered down the hallway, their progress impeded by the 5'10" girls' teasing assault on his body. He fumbled with the key, succeeding on the third try to open the door.

They tumbled inside, kicked the door closed, and shuffled across the carpet to flop onto the sofa. Coline hung behind him, clawing at his open shirt. Gisele sat across his lap and attacked his mouth, eyes, and neck with her pink lipstick mouth. Coline's red lips and nails were the only way to tell them apart. He soon also learned Coline was the more passionate kisser.

He gently pressed Gisele back. "Easy, *mon amour.*" He gasped for breath, his heart hammering his ribs. "We have all night. Let's not rush this." He gathered her in his arms and rose, his lips brushing her eyes, nose, ear, and lips, and set her on her feet. She pressed against him, arms around his neck, swaying body to body, shining eyes locked on his.

"You are so handsome and strong, *mon amour.* I need to ravish you." She glanced at her sister, wrapped tightly against his back, her arms circling them both as she blew on his ear.

"*We* need to ravish you," Coline whispered, hands venturing down his sides, across his hips, and finally, his crotch. "It would be a shame to waste what I just found here." She nipped his neck.

"I agree," he chuckled between panted breaths. "And I believe I have enough for both of you." He reached back and slid fingers inside Coline's bikini bottom and found moist, open lips. "But it'll be best explored in the bedroom."

Coline slithered against him and moaned. "Ah, *oui.* We must go there now. I am already about to cum." She pressed tighter as his finger found and tweaked her very wet, engorged pleasure button. Her breath came in short, hard gasps.

Derik spun out of Gisele's grasp and scooped Coline against him, freeing luscious, firm breasts from her bikini top and casting it aside. His lips circled her extended nipples, his tongue sucking and tweaking them. She squealed with pleasure and wiggled out of her bikini bottom. Gisele stripped away his suit, dropped to her knees, and stroked his considerable erection.

Coline rose on her toes, arcing her pelvis. "Fuck me, Derik. Fuck me *now,*" and with Gisele's guidance, he was inside her tight, wet, and pulsing pussy. He grunted, legs spread for balance and surged against her, quickly building toward a climax.

"Oh, baby. You're so hot I can barely hold it." He gripped her butt cheeks and they quickly developed a rhythm. Gisele still knelt behind him, her fingers busy, urging him on. He snatched Coline at the thighs and lifted. Her legs locked around his waist, long arms circling his neck, they thrust together with growing urgency.

"Oh, *oui, mon amour. Oui.* Do it, *beaux homme.*" She crushed him to her, their lips and tongues tangled, then leaned back and uttered a breathless moan, hands in his hair. Her vagina pulsed and squeezed his cock, and he ejaculated hard as she let loose a protracted wail.

Derik and Coline hung together, catching their breath and peppered each other with kisses. He withdrew his shrinking organ, set her down, still against his damp skin, and turned to Gisele.

"Now to the bedroom?" He chuckled through panted breath, drew her in with his other arm for a kiss, and unsnapped her bikini top. "And, why are you the only one here still dressed?"

"No, *mon amour,* no reason at all." She shimmied out of her bottom, and twirling it on one finger, cast it aside. "We will retire to the bed, and I'll do my best to rekindle your ardor." Her fingers trailed down his stomach and lightly teased what hung below.

"I doubt that will be a problem." He grinned, his hand venturing over her up-jutting breasts. "And I'm betting your sexy sister will help that along."

"But of course." She dragged him after her. "We share all, and the night is still young."

Moments later, he was sprawled across the king-size bed, Gisele snuggled against him. His hands explored her erotic curves as they kissed with growing heat. Coline massaged his back and neck, her lips and tongue teasing his ears. Her fingers ventured across his butt and between his legs. As promised, he had again become aroused.

It portended to be a long night, probably without much sleep, but he hadn't been with a woman for over a month, and this *was* every man's dream ... making it with gorgeous twins. These two confirmed the rumor that redheads were fiery and passionate.

After initial lust was slaked, he savored that the evening became an adventure in true love-making, often slow and tender before fiery completion. It was, at that point, one of the best nights of his life ... maybe second only to that in the cave, finding treasure beyond imagination.

~ 5 ~

Sleep came, finally, just as the golden disc edged above the blue twinkle of the riffled Caribbean. Covered only by silk sheets, redhead nymphs in each arm, nestled close, they slept until almost noon. Though once eager to return to Florida with his treasure, Derik had no schedule and was in no hurry to leave this passionate duo. He awakened to tiny kisses and fluttering fingers and found Coline atop of him, her green eyes holding his.

"Ah, *mon amour.*" She laid her head on his chest. "This no longer seems a dally in passion." Her tongue tweaked his nipple and drew it into her mouth. She sighed and sat back, straddling his groin. "You are much more than just the *beaux homme* Gisele and I found for a night of pleasure."

"I gotta admit," a smile tilted his lips, and he pulled her down for a gentle kiss, then held her close, "you two are also far more than I expected."

"I cannot get enough of you." Coline slithered out across his body, her velvet skin caressing his, igniting yet another inferno. Her kisses were intense, the best he'd ever known, fused simultaneously with passion and tenderness, teasing, then attacking. She drove him crazy. Slowly, she inched down his body, lips and fingers in a maddening voyage.

"I love the taste of sex on you." A wiggle of her hips, and her engorged and very wet pussy lips surrounded his again turgid cock, sliding up and back, begging for entry, then coyly refusing that act, until Derik was inflamed almost beyond control. Only then did she draw him inside, rising to her knees, beginning a slow, deep ride. Despite the previous evening's frequent parties, Derik could barely control his orgasm, finally cumming with thrusts of his pelvis. Coline continued her ride, and the intensity of it kept him hard until she shuddered with her own release and collapsed against him, mewing softly, their mouths engaged in a gentle, protracted kiss.

After a brief pause, red lips and nails were exchanged for pink as Gisele took her sister's place and began her own trek into mutual ecstasy. Derik was amazed that these gorgeous and loving creatures could continue to fire his arousal, even after so many previous trips to the well. He'd never before experienced consuming passion like that. How could he possibly leave this behind?

~ ~ ~

Three hours later, the threesome finished a sumptuous brunch in the Omni's posh dining room, and Derik took them to the hotel's high-end boutiques to shop for elegant evening dresses with matching shoes and handbags.

"You are too generous, Derik," Gisele said, pulling him to a halt outside the store. "This is a very expensive shop."

"I know. I want to see you two gorgeous creatures in clothes for a change." He winked, and they giggled. "And my new loves deserve the very best. I can afford it, my darlings." New found wealth was, as is said, burned a hole in his pocket, and he couldn't think of a better way to spend it at that moment.

Coline zipped up the side of the strapless, slinky black evening dress, her delectable thighs erotically exposed by side-slits, and pivoted before the dressing room's mirror. "What do you think?" she asked her sister, who was wiggling into something equally sexy, in white.

"Do you mean, what will *Derik* think?" Gisele chuckled. "He'll love you in it, and he'll certainly love you *out* of it." They both laughed, and then Coline paused, her face now serious.

"Do you feel it, Gisele? Do you sense something *different* here?"

"Kismet?" She sighed. "The storied lightning bolt?" She turned to pose in front of the mirror. "I don't know, my darling. This is a very unusual man."

"Yes, he is." Coline slipped on black stilettos adorned by jeweled bows. "We started this in search of a much-needed night of carnal pleasure, but for me, at least, I feel in my heart something not felt for a very long time." She turned, her eyes glistened as she searched her sister's. "Derik is both passionate and tender, keyed to our needs," she waived a hand at the several outfits strewn across the room's chairs, "and certainly generous. I sense an honest and caring soul there,"

"I, too." Gisele selected red, four-inch stilettos to try on. "Not like so many of the lecherous men on this island who think we are only here for their pleasure." She straightened and took her sister's hands. "So, dear sister, what are you saying?"

"I think, incredible as it seems, I am in love." Moisture shone in her eyes. "And you?"

Gisele nodded. "Me, too. Is it really possible? We barely know him but ..." She dabbed a tissue at her own pooling eyes and sighed, accompanied by a shrug. "Can we find a way to keep him here?" She chuffed softly. "And if he stays, in the end, only one of us can have him." She smiled, cupping Coline's cheek with her palm and thumbing away a tear. "If he were to select you to spend his life with, I promise not to be *too* jealous."

Coline pulled her into a gentle hug and kissed a cheek. "I'm not sure I can also make that promise, but I'd try." She stepped back. "So, let's go out there and knock his eyes out." She grinned. "As they say in basketball, a full court press."

26

They picked up Chanel evening bags, Coline's black and Gisele's red, and hand-in-hand, exited the dressing room to find Derik awaiting their appearance.

Derik had sighed as he watched them select a variety of outfits, giggling like teenagers. They were twenty-seven, three years older than he, but that made little difference to any of them.

Amazingly, neither had boyfriends, and they'd admitted their fling with him was impulsive, the first time they'd indulged in a threesome. Gisele confessed shyly, that when she pointed him out to Coline, they shared an uncommon feeling of connection, and an undeniable urge to hook up. Was this just lust, or Karma, rearing its head?

They were much more than just hot lays, and if he stayed, he could easily fall in love. Brow wrinkled, he grunted. "Could fall" had already happened. Two days and he was in love—with both girls! But how could that be real, and if true, how to choose one and not the other? He especially loved Coline's passionate kisses, but also relished Gisele's amazing Kegel control as she rode above him. But those physical hooks were only part of who these lovely women were.

Can he really cast all that aside? He shook his head. Staying there with them wasn't an option.

Or was it?

Somehow, he seemed compelled to get his treasure safely home, establish his position as an upstart mega-millionaire, and build a new life in South Florida. He had formulated an idea of starting a venture capital firm to help small businesses succeed. Was that sufficient reason to draw him away from the intense lure of these two sirens? The swish of a curtain swept aside drew him from his musing, and glancing up, his face split into a lopsided grin.

"Wow! You girls are amazing." He rose and took a hand of

each. "How the hell did I get so lucky?" A gentle kiss for each. "I'm definitely in love." He missed the look Coline gave Gisele as they pirouetted in front of him.

"You like?" Coline asked, one thigh gracefully exposed through the dress's slit.

"Like doesn't qualify?" He laughed. "*Love* barely works, but I can't think of anything stronger. So, these are what you've decided on?"

"If it's okay with you, *mon amour?*" Gisele said. "This is all very expensive."

"Nothing's too good for the two most fabulous women on Martinique." He nodded toward the dressing rooms. "Change back into your day duds while I pay."

"All right," Coline said, "and then we're going to give you a tour of the island. But first we must stop at our offices to check on the day's schedule." She kissed his cheek. "Promise to have you back at the hotel in time for dinner." She winked. "And will you be here for another night? We'd love to spend it … and many more … with you."

He grinned and nodded. "Me too." *Many more? Wow!* "Anyway, at this point, if I'm leaving, the best tide for me will be mid-day tomorrow." He watched as they swayed across the room, sensuality in motion, back to change clothes. What did another day's delay matter? Or two? *Or a lifetime?* Shit, how could he tear himself away from these redhead sirens, who revealed much more depth of personality and character as the day progressed.

Their first stop, with Coline driving, was the visit to their real estate office, Island Reality. "You are the sole owners?"

"*Oui,* for the last five years, as co-brokers." Gisele's hand swept the room. "You like?"

"Lovely, which at this point, shouldn't surprise me." It was elegantly appointed, staffed by three agents and two clerks. A very tanned couple rose from one of the agent's desks and turned to Gisele, kissing her on both cheeks.

"We've just finished closing on the villa, Gisele." Clearly a Germanic accent. "Luckily, undamaged by the storm."

"*Ja,*" the man said, and turned toward Derik. "If you are buying here, there are no better than these to women." Gisele blushed as the man raved about the service they'd received, and the great deal she'd engineered, with a low interest, seller-financed mortgage.

Derik nodded, and followed his new lovers to their co-office, where they sifted through several notes and two active files, all business. Instruction given to their staff, they then led the way back to Coline's Toyota Avensis station wagon.

They toured Martinique, Coline driving, with brief visits to the pottery village, the vast, ocean vista from Diamond Rock, and time to meander through a local market. As they drove, the girls discussed island business and finance. They had informed and opinionated world views, including a good sense of American politics. No airheads here.

Returning to the Omni at six, Derik again treated them to cocktails and dinner, each girl magnificently decked out in the lovely, and very sexy outfits he'd bought them. Many heads were turned, both male and female, as they entered. It was an evening of sumptuous food, alcohol, and dancing late into the night at the hotel's lounge.

All a bit tipsy from two magnums of champagne, they once more retired to his suite. Derik made a quick trip to the john, and when he returned, both women were naked, Coline sprawled on the queen-size bed, and Gisele perched on its corner. Derik stripped, climbed aboard, and laid diagonally across Coline, their lips instantly tangled, tongues darting, and teeth nipping. His fingers trailed across her curves, a firm breast cupped and nipple tweaked, then strolled, lightly raking her skin, until they found moist, lower lips open, begging for attention.

He sucked in a breath with a soft grunt as Gisele, kneeling beside the bed, licked and sucked his balls and turgid member, her hands teasing his back and massaging his thighs and rump.

Coline coiled her arms around his back, crushed him to her, and intensified her kisses, murmuring, *"Mon amour. Je t'adore."* She rolled them over, settling astride his groin.

"I need you now, my love," her voice a hoarse whisper. She rose on her knees and guided him inside her pulsing pussy, leaned forward as she began her ride, and smothered him with delicious kisses. Poised above, her breasts teased his chest, snatching the air from his lungs. Gisele remained below, hovered between his legs to tease and fondle his balls as her sister, building into a soft wail, increased her thrusts, emitting, finally, a feral growl as her orgasm was quickly followed by his. She collapsed atop of him, their sweat-slickened bodies still tingling with fire, her tongue busy with his neck and eyes. Gisele slid alongside, her arms and legs binding both to her, her lips making a tender voyage across Derik's face and neck.

Several minutes skipped by before they disentangled, and Coline collapsed to Derik's side, mewing with content. Gisele edged on top of his body sucking in the pleasant warmth of the contact and not immediately seeking anything more erotic. That changed as they voyaged into foreplay and tender arousal, segueing into passionate completion. Afterall, Gisele was due her equal time.

Both women seemed committed to pleasuring him, but showed little interest in stimulating each other. That delicious task was left to Derik, something he continued well into the wee hours, filled more now with tender loving rather than purely carnal passion. When they finally slept, he was totally drained.

Mid-morning sunlight slithered past the edges of their blackout curtains as Coline stirred and snuggled beside him. Red-nailed fingers caressed his chest, lips teasing his ear as he awakened.

"Why must you leave us, Derik?" she whispered. "Gisele and I have had dalliances, but somehow, this is—different." She glanced at her sister, draped across his other side, who nodded. "Our hearts are pierced. Stay. We could be so happy here." She propped up on an elbow. "You'll see we are more than just passionate lovers."

"Oh, baby, I believe that." He pulled her in for a kiss, his hand skipping across her back to pat her taut butt. "This began as every man's fantasy—making it with two gorgeous and passionate babes, but somehow, in just two days, you've snared my soul. You two fill my heart, and I can't imagine leaving you behind." He groaned. "I'm so conflicted, because I'm also compelled to get back to the States." He cupped Coline's face between his hands. "I don't suppose either … or both of you would consider coming with me." He chuckled. "And if that actually happened, how could I pick which of you to spend my life with? You can't share me forever."

"Oh, but we can." Gisele slid atop of his groin, wiggled her rump, and leaned forward, offering a lovely breast to his mouth. "We *always* share everything, and see where that goes. But our lives, our friends, and our business are here. How could we leave that for something so unknown?"

Coline had an earlobe in her mouth and a hand venturing between his thighs. "Can you really leave all that we offer you, Derik?"

He was amazed that after two protracted sessions with each vixen during the night, he was again becoming aroused. Her lips crushed against his, he muttered, "We'll talk about it later." He may not be able to come to completion a fifth time, but he'd give these incredible beauties as much pleasure as he could. Their multiple orgasms *were* an incredible aphrodisiac. It *would* be tough to forsake this Nirvana, but what was there for him, other than the love of a beautiful woman? He was nagged by his need to return to Florida with his treasure and establish his new financial position. Trading the promised treasure of beauty and love for the known comforts of home and all his new-found wealth would bring.

The previous evening's romance made leaving more difficult by the minute, but after a late breakfast, he packed his meager belongings with a nagging reluctance, and with Gisele and Coline on his arms, checked out of the Omni. Then, in Coline's Toyota, they chauffeured him to his sloop.

They lingered on the dock, a beauty in each arm. Protracted kisses and fierce hugs made it still harder to leave, but he had an ebbing tide and a fair wind for his northwesterly track, and so he finally left two weeping lovers—and part of his heart—at the Fort-de-France dock. The Perkins diesel drove the sloop out of the harbor to begin his journey home.

He dared not look back at two teary-eyed redheads throwing kisses, or he might say "fuck it," and return. An ache swirled through his chest. What started as a casual sexual fling had morphed into something a lot more emotional. Can one really fall in love so quickly and completely? He'd heard of the "thunderbolt," and he'd been struck ... twice ... squarely in the heart.

He groaned. Florida and his new life beckoned, and that future loomed on an exciting horizon. Teeth gritted, he solidified his resolve, and cranked up full mainsail, the white sheet snapping as it bloomed in the brisk wind. He was headed home, making nearly seven knots. The Choy Lee listed to port, slicing the modest sea, the proverbial, foaming "bone in her teeth." Two weeks at sea, with a stop in San Juan and a call to Chick Radford to arrange for his arrival. His best friend and most frequent target as his tight end at University of Miami was the only one he'd trust with the secret of his new-found treasure—both financial and emotional. And Chick's Master's in Computer Science would be integral in legitimizing his fortune.

He hoped that would eventually quell the ache currently surrounding his heart.

~ 6 ~

Derik's diesel puttered quietly, making two knots up the narrow canal, southwest of Everglades City. He'd fished in the Cypress National Reserve extensively with his grandpa as a youth, catching sea trout, small redfish, snapper, and the like. He knew these waterways intimately. Canals and "rivers" crosshatched this desolate Everglades park, and an inexperienced boater could soon be lost, with no sense of where he was, or the way out.

But not Derik. This particular canal was deep enough at high tide to accept the Choy Lee's keel, and it led to a rutted Indian path, where he hoped Chick would be waiting. He'd draped his mast with mesh, strewn with grasses plucked from the shore. Colombian drug smugglers may have used this route to offload their cocaine, and he didn't want to be spotted by Customs, mistaken for a drug mule. What he ferried was just as illegal, though not in any way deadly, but the U.S. government would love to collect duty on his haul. Maybe even confiscate it.

So, sliding along, shielded by tall grasses and stunted, gnarled live oaks, he hoped to be invisible. Chick would arrive with a trailered, fourteen-foot, flat bottom pram and be fishing as cover. The small boat would aid in ferrying his treasure to his friend's Chevy Suburban. There was more than enough to offer Chick a partnership in the wealth. If all went well, Derik would be out of the park and under sail, circling the tip of Florida for a legal entry in Miami.

"Almost there," he muttered aloud. "Another ten—" He paused, head cocked, and powered the engine down to a quiet idle. The whump-whump-whump of a helicopter's rotor, coming fast. Derik sped up, rushing toward a small clump of oaks and tall sawgrass. He powered the bottom edge of his keel through the soft bottom, hoping to do no damage and prayed the Coast Guard chopper would miss him. Even if spotted, and if Chick were on time, they'd probably be long gone before any Customs agents might find them.

He spied the 'copter, cruising along the outer shoreline, weaving back and forth. Searching for drug runners for sure. His relatively slow yacht was an unlikely carrier, but would still seem involved in nefarious activities. He held his breath as the chopper moved in across the park, sweeping back and forth, no higher than five-hundred-feet above. Derik used a machete to hack off some sawgrass and tall fronds and strew it across his deck, hoping to create camouflage.

He slipped inside the cabin, the hatch cracked open to provide him a view, and crossed his fingers. The chopper passed a hundred-feet south, an angle from which the sloop was invisible, then circled and flew by, two-hundred feet to the north. It never slowed, nor returned, and in six minutes it was out if sight, moving up Florida's southwest coast.

Derik released held breath with a quiet gasp.

That was close. I gotta get moving. Unfortunately, the keel was mired in the soft bottom, unwilling to release. Full diesel power, and his efforts to rock the boat had little effect.

"Shit! I gotta get outta here." No guarantee that pilot hadn't seen him and called in the Feds. Hands on hips, he considered going over the side and diving down to dig out. Too bad he left that ancient spade on the little Caribbean cay. That may be his only …

He cocked his head, then strode across the sloop's deck and peered up the narrow canal.

The purr of a small outboard motor, so not likely Coast Guard or Customs, who favored big engines and fast boats.

A small skiff, driven by a single person puttered into view.

Chick!

"Hey, pal," he hailed. "What'cha doing, hanging back here? I got worried."

"Hiding from a Coast Guard chopper, and now I'm stuck in the mud. Come astern and I'll toss you a line. Maybe with you towing and my Perkins, we can pull free."

Three hours later, the booty offloaded into Chick's SUV, Derik motored down the river of grass, back toward the sea and a trip around Cape Florida for the Port of Miami, where he'd clear Customs before finding a place to dock the sloop.

Hurricane Chico had thrust an unexpected curve into his life, creating opportunities he'd never expected.

He just needed some time to figure that out.

~ 7 ~

Eight Years Later

Derik Brand sprawled back on his black leather executive chair, ankles crossed and angled across the corner of his refinished oaken captain's desk. His interlaced fingers rested upon what were still six-pack abs, even at thirty-two, as he gazed through his tenth-floor Bayshore Drive office's picture window. The rippled waters of Biscayne Bay sparkled like thousands of tiny mirrors, ignited by the westerly sun. This was where he often lingered when his mind swam with new ideas ... or old memories.

It was the latter filling his head that May afternoon as he reflected on the events eight-years past. A tall, shapely redhead, lunching at a table across the room at Spiro's Café opened the door to that time.

He'd often thought of Gisele and Coline those first few years after returning from the Caribbean, nostalgic, but usually peppered with regret. Had the grip of the fortune he'd stumbled upon so colored his mind that he let Nirvana slip away? He'd resolved never to contact them, or even follow them through social media. Keeping the memories fresh would be too agonizing. Before leaving, he'd suggested they do the same, and in fact, he'd never heard from them, which was strangely disappointing, despite their pledges.

But eventually the glory of those two amazing days worked its way to the back of his consciousness. He chuckled quietly and shook his head. If he had really pushed them so completely away, why was he still single and without even a significant companion? He'd dated and had brief affairs, but no other woman ever measured up, and his new career became his obsession.

Work? Yes, that's what crowded his time and thoughts, once he could openly display his fortune. After Chick Radford met him at that desolate beach, just below Everglades City, and helped him unload the two chests of treasure into his SUV, Derik needed a way to justify a source for this newfound wealth. So much found treasure would pose too many questions he didn't want to answer.

It was Chick who thought to create a bogus and distant spinster aunt who parlayed the fictious purchase of a 1950's IBM's stock into stacks of cash, horded piles of jewelry, and collectibles. All had been gifted to Derik at her death, as she had no family and, according to their fiction, had babysat him many times in the 1990's.

Chick created a sufficiently full and rich digital history to satisfy all but the most rigorous examination. Derik was free to sell a portion of the gems and some of the coins to pay federal gift taxes (not, of course, disclosing the true value of the entire cache) and establish himself as the new rich guy on the block.

A canal-front ranch house in Bal Harbor filled his need for a place to moor the Choy Lee sloop he acquired from the lease broker, after getting settled in Florida. He could afford a much fancier yacht, but the sturdy sloop held a sentimental spot in his heart.

As did fantastic, redhead twins. How did a three-day tryst affix barbs in his heart that seemed unshakable?

He'd departed Martinique in 2014 shackled by the painful promise not to contact Gisele and Coline, and the closer he got to the United States, the stronger became that resolve. It wasn't that he didn't care enough, but strangely, that he cared *too much*. No way to foster hope for a possible future with one of them, which seemed extremely unlikely. And *that* was the conundrum, because it would have to be with just one, if something serious were to develop. How could he possibly choose? And how unfair for the other.

So, he opted for time to mitigate desire, certain such an outstanding pair, melding beauty, brains, and passion, would move on with their lives and find adoring mates. That would render their memories of two fantastic days into no more than fond reminiscences. Unfortunately, many lusty, sex-filled one-night-stands never dimmed what those three days had become. In eight years, only once was he compelled to see a woman twice, and even that affair never progressed beyond that.

He knew he was kidding himself, but he plowed ahead with his life, and the new purpose he'd discovered there.

Derik shook away his thoughts, dropped his feet, and scooted up to his desk to answer a buzzing intercom.

"Mr. Lithgow is here for your three o'clock, Mr. Brand." Ginny, his executive assistant was only formal in the presence of clients.

"Put them in the conference room and offer coffee or whatever. I'll be right there." He gathered a file binder from his desk. "Ask Chick to join us." He added and clicked off.

"Yessir, Boss."

He grinned. It took two years to wean formality from his staff. He wanted them to feel part of a team, not just hirelings.

A quick check on his computer of current balances in the bank, and he rose and headed out. If all went well, this would be their sixth management deal since he started this business. He'd lingered a bit too long between the first, second, and third, determined not to make the mistake of many of his clients—taking on more than they could handle.

Homestead Rod & Tackle was a perfect example of that problem.

Now he had created an efficient team ... two actually, with Chick heading one and he the other ... so he was eager to have both operations running simultaneously. Homestead Rod would be Brand & Radford Investment's second in play at that moment, if he made the sale. If not, he'd identified two others as possibles.

He strode into his conference room and found Callum Lithgow, CEO of Homestead Rod, another unknown man, and Chick, gathered beside a red teak chart table Derik used for serving guests. He'd appropriated it from a derelict, long-range trawler about to be scrapped.

A grin ticked the corners of his mouth. The source of his wealth impelled him toward nautical themes wherever he went. The table was adorned with a basket of donuts, another of a variety of bagels, and bowls of nuts and fruit. The odor of Jamaican coffee drifted from a large urn, flanked by colorful ceramic cups.

His entry drew their attention, and he gestured toward the oval mahogany dining table, rescued from the same sixty-eight-foot trawler, now used as his conference table. Eight cushioned, mahogany-slat deck chairs surrounded it.

"Looks like you're all stocked up with goodies, gentlemen, so have a seat." He settled at the table's head and placed his file in front. Chick brought him a cup of steaming coffee, *"Martinique"* emblazoned on its side, and perched beside him.

"Love your nautical theme, Mr. Brand," Lithgow said as he dropped onto a chair opposite Chick. He nodded toward his associate. "This is Jake Witt, my chief operating officer."

"Famous big game fisherman. Seems appropriate." Derik waved a hand at the furnishings and smiled. "This all keeps memories alive from a pleasant time." He glanced at them. "And it fits right in with your business … saltwater fishing."

"True. But of course, many of our fly and spinning rods are used in freshwater as well. Pike, musky, salmon, and such, and we're about to introduce a line of lighter flyrods, aimed mostly at trout buffs."

"Right." Derik flipped open his file. "I was reading about that." He raised his eyes to the man. "And according to this, that's why you're here. Seeking financing for that. Correct?"

"Yes." Lithgow and his companion, who sat beside him, opened their own files. "We've been contracting with Akron Graphite for our rod blanks. We want to begin our own fabrication department."

"Well, there are a lot of pros and cons in doing that." Derik lifted a page from the folder, scanned it, then looked at Lithgow. "I presume you understand how we work?"

"I believe you offer collateralized financing—assets like equipment and receivables."

"In a sense, correct." He closed his file and held Lithgow's eyes. "But the asset we require is stock, and it's not a loan."

"What?"

"We purchase fifty-one percent of your shares— controlling interest—and give you the option to buy it back any time after three years at the then market value. That's based on a price/earnings (P/E) ratio, then and now, at fifteen times earnings."

"You're kidding!"

"No, I'm not." Derik eased back on his chair and issued a

soft sigh. "I hope you won't take this personally, but many companies—companies like yours—succeed at first, then get afield from what made them successful."

He leaned forward and gave a wry smile. "Sometimes it takes hard decisions to set things right, and we need to be in charge to make them."

Lithgow glanced at his companion, who shrugged and gave a small head shake. The CEO slouched back and rubbed his eyes, then stared at Derik.

"I'm not giving control of my company to anyone, despite your good record. We can ..."

"Keep losing money," Derik interjected. "Stay on your current path, and I suspect you'll be out of business in two or three years." He folded his hands atop the table. "Look, I know it hurts, but your profits the last two years have dropped to zilch. We're prepared to pay a half-million dollars for fifty-one percent of your stock, and that's very generous. Eighty percent of the money stays in the company to finance what needs to be done to right the ship. I'm the CEO and chairman of the board. Chick here is also on the board. You guys continue to run the day-to-day, but we set policy."

He sat back. "Take it or leave it. We won't be offering this again a year from now." He glanced at Chick. "We'll leave the room, if you want time to discuss this."

The man sighed, rose, and gathered his papers. "Nothing to discuss. I appreciate your time and consideration, but no deal."

Derik pushed up from his seat and offered his hand. "I understand. Nothing was lost here except a few hours of time. I wish you good luck."

His hand was shaken by both men as they moved toward the door. He paused and laid a hand on Lithgow's shoulder. "I don't usually offer free advice, but I have some for you, if you're interested."

"Of course." Lithgow turned, briefcase in both hands.

"Your business suffers from what many do after a successful startup." He shoved hands into his pockets. "Over expansion. You've created an excellent line of standard, mid-range graphite rods. Those took off so well, you began expanding into custom designs, plus you started marketing reels manufactured by others under your name."

"We are trying to expand our market." Lithgow glanced at Witt.

Derik leaned against the open door's jamb. "I understand, but your custom rod department has too many people producing too little profit, and the cost of marketing the reels heavily outweighs their benefit. Just too much competition."

He opened his folder and withdrew a page. "The proposed new fly-rod line makes you an also-ran, competing with legacy companies like Orvis and Sage." Derik handed him the sheet. "It'll be the proverbial 'last straw' that will break you. This is a freebee because I'd hate to see you fail."

They exited the conference and he ushered them to the door. "If you cut forty percent of your staff and ditch custom rod-building and your reel line, you'll succeed and become profitable again." They paused at the exit. "Stay in the viable niche you've carved out, and be happy with moderate growth—and be rigorous at cutting fat. And, if you offer profit sharing for the staff you keep, you'll have a happy winner again."

Lithgow looked at Jake Witt, who grinned and said, "We can do that, Boss. I told you not to be sentimental about layoffs." Witt shook Derik's hand again.

"Thanks, Mr. Brand. I appreciate your input, which is pretty much in line with what I've been telling Callum."

Derik watched them depart, turned to Chick, and shrugged.

"Couldn't help myself. I'd hate to see those guys flounder. Besides, we got two more prospects and only one slot to fill."

"Yeah, I understand. So, who d'ya want to approach first?"

"I think the clothing designer seems most likely."

"Okay, I'll pull our files and we can work up a plan before you contact the owner."

"A woman, right?"

"Yeah. An ex-runway model. A real babe, from what I hear."

"Terrific." He grimaced. "I can hardly wait."

He hoped she could get over herself when it came to business.

~ 8 ~

Brita Kruger leaned her svelte, 5'11" frame over the mezzanine fence, forearms resting atop the railing, and scanned her busy shop below. The clack of shears and buzz of a half-dozen Singer sewing machines had lost some of their musical joy.

She'd loved watching the blossoming of one of her haute couture designs that made her a name in elite women's fashion. The skill she'd acquired in nine years as a runway model schooled her in what looked great, but was still wearable.

But now sales lagged. She'd met with her reps, but a three-hour discussion never identified the problem. A newly released line of frocks—evening dresses, semi-formal, and formal gowns—hadn't inspired buyers, who seemed less than enthusiastic. They loved the designs but were uncertain they would sell in the current market.

Brita's lips twisted into a scowl. She stood back and ran a hand through her blond pixie cut. Confidence had sailed her through growth and success in the garment trade, but this time it may have taken her over a precipice.

Flush with success, she'd purchased a luxury two-bedroom condo on Key Biscayne—twelfth-floor, ocean and bay views. Valet parking and concierge service for your every want.

The epitome of success.

Virtually all her remaining capital went into this new clothing line, and if it flopped, so may she. She needed funds—a loan or an investor—and she needed it *now*. Three bank visits had produced no joy.

"Fucking bankers," she muttered. All were eager to dine her at upscale bistros, but none had a loan for her. At thirty-two and no longer needing to starve to properly model flimsy garb down a runway, she'd blossomed into a modestly buxom, curvaceous temptress. Two bank officers hinted a loan might be available if she'd be "friendly" to them, but that was never going to happen. She wouldn't prostitute herself, and that's what it would be, prostitution, to raise funds. Besides, she'd seen others girls make that choice and get nothing in return but degradation.

Evette, one of the girls from her runway days, mentioned a private investor who sometimes made personal loans. The fact he was Russian or Ukrainian gave her pause. They were often mobsters. She made a cautious inquiry and then met one of them, Gorya, at the Hilton hotel bar. He seemed pleasant and offered her a one-year, hundred-grand loan at nine percent, which seemed quite reasonable. There'd be monthly payments, same as her mortgage on the condo.

It wasn't until he'd come by her business for the first month's installment that she realized it was nine percent *per month,* not per year. She'd used most of the loan for salary, late rent, and to bring month-old supplier bills current. There wasn't enough left to make the $9,000 payment and keep the shop running. Gorya, who'd come with his brutish brother, Alik, said they'd let it slide this time, but there was a 25% late fee. Next month's payment would be $22,500, and there'd be more than just monetary penalties if she were again late.

"Where the hell am I gonna get twenty-three-grand by

then?" she mumbled. She strode to her office and rummaged around her paper-strewn desk top.

"Aha!" She snatched up a letter from some guy named Derik Brand, a private investor. She'd originally cast it aside because he was not a lender, but someone who provided funds for an ownership stake in her business. That seemed unacceptable at the time, but now it may be the only way to bail her out. Maybe to keep her alive, too.

She glanced at the letterhead, *Brand & Radford,* then made the call. After speaking with Ms. Mendoza, Brand's executive assistant, she'd arranged an a.m. appointment in two days.

Brita scanned the Internet, something she should have done first, and researched Mr. Derik Brand. A blond hunk who'd apparently inherited millions and parlayed it into a massive fortune, partly through treasure hunting successes. That was weird. Been in business about eight-years with a partner from his college years, and had successfully resuscitated five companies during that time, making a tidy profit for everyone each time.

It appeared he was uninvested at the moment, which might give her some negotiating leverage. Of course, if he knew of her current straits, *he'd* have the leverage, not her.

She settled back in her chair and sighed as she studied the computer screen. This was her last option, so she'd better make it work. Her lips ticked into a tiny grin. At least working with a handsome ex-football star would be a lot better than dealing with the brutish Kolodenko brothers.

She exited the file and put her computer to sleep. Pushing from her chair, she began gathering any relevant papers she might need for her pitch. She considered what to wear—something conservative but that still accentuated her classic beauty—and maybe just a bit erotic.

It never hurt to play every card she had, because this may be her last chance to survive, both financially *and* physically. She had no doubts the nasty brothers wouldn't hesitate to hurt her... or worse ... if she were short again next month.

She shivered at the thought.

~ 9 ~

Derik exited the elevator at the Marriott Hotel with his arm circling Karen Matsu's waist. Holding her close, he found the suite he'd rented for the night.

He glanced at the twenty-three-year-old Japanese/American hottie he'd met two hours before at a noisy Brickell pub. She was a classic Asian beauty—silky, coal-black hair to her waist, alabaster complexion, ebony almond eyes, and a tiny physique accented by full boobs that he'd earlier discovered felt natural. Despite clear Asian ancestry, she was all American, born and bred in San Francisco but recently moved to Miami, fleeing that state's exorbitant taxes and rampant homeless invasion.

Ninety minutes of wooing and three scotches was what it took to get to this place, and they both were eager to see where it led. Once inside the door, they started with passionate, tongue-fencing kisses. A foot shorter than Derik, he grasped Karen's thighs and lifted her so her arms circled his neck as did her legs around his waist.

Her lips teased his as she nipped then slipped away, first eluding his, then returning for brief teasing of tongues before fleeing across cheek, eyes, ear, and neck. He'd never been so expertly played, and his heart was at full gallop. Finally, her mouth made a full-frontal attack, and passion so expertly kindled, boiled over. After several minutes, he broke free with a gasp and stared into the dark pool of her eyes.

"The bed now?" He struggled for breath.

She nodded, a pixie grin splitting her face as one hand trailed down to his crotch.

"Such a beautiful thing I found here, pressing so eagerly against my wet pussy." She too was panting. "I need to have it."

"Nothing it wants more than that, you sexy siren." He strode toward the suite's bedroom with her still wrapped around him, that skilled tongue in full tease mode.

They reached bedside where he sat her on the edge and started unbuckling his belt.

She slipped to her feet and brushed his hands away. "Let me." Their eyes linked, her face filled with a saucy smile. "Though I'm an American, I was raised in the Japanese tradition." His belt loosened, she started on the buttons of his shirt. "Let me play geisha for you." She chuckled as she undid his cuffs. "You'll never want anyone else after tonight."

It was Derik's turn to chuckle. "You hardly know me, Karen." A fleeting vision of a redhead duo flashed across his mind. He never knew much more about them, but they still had their hooks in his soul.

"I know more than you think." His shirt off, she lowered his pants, pushed him to sit on the bed, and removed his shoes and socks. "I Googled you on my phone when I went to the john. Had to know who you were before I trusted my life to you. Turns out, you're just the guy I'm looking for."

She pivoted. "Unzip me, please." Easily done by herself, but this was hotter.

Derik complied and she shimmied out of her mid-thigh length dress, back to him, arms raised and intertwined over her head.

The view was stunning. She wore no bra, and a silk thong split a small, round and very tight butt, above gracefully tapered legs. She rotated to him, her firm breasts jutting out, eraser-size nipples extended from prominent dark circles.

Karen brushed his seeking hands aside as she stepped in. "And now, the last of it." She pulled down his boxers and freed his iron-hard erection.

"So lovely." She knelt, her blue-nailed fingers in a tantalizing voyage down its shaft, followed by a magic tongue, licking and tweaking its head as she wiggled out of her thong.

Derik grunted. She was driving him mad. He snatched her arms and hauled her onto his lap where once again their mouths and lips engaged in wonderful warfare. Hands under her thighs, he raised, then lowered her with him inside a very wet, tight pussy as he laid back.

Her mouth still enveloping his, she began her ride, the fall of ebony hair tenting her head and teasing his chest. He was amazed at how firmly she gripped him with pulsing Kegel action. They thrust together with urgent heat, her breasts teasing his chest.

"Oh, I'm gonna cum," she moaned and attacked him more vigorously with her mouth, sucking and biting his lower lip.

"Fuck me, Derik, fuck me hard." She surged against him, and her vaginal muscles grabbed his cock. "I'm cum-m-i-n-g *now!*"

And he was soaked by a rush of her juices, triggering his own orgasm.

"Oh, yes, baby, yes." Karen slumped against him, slick with sweat, and continued a slow ride, sucking him dry. "Give it to me, Derik. I want it all."

His arms circled her and stroked her back and butt, while he nipped and kissed her ear and neck. They laid together for a full minute before she leaned back, those dark eyes boring into his.

"That was one amazing fuck, Karen." His tongue swiped his lips, still filled with the taste of her. "How did you get so good?"

"I was an early teen when I discovered the wonders of self-help orgasms." She chuckled. "I read everything I could find on Geishas and the Kama Sutra." She wiggled free of his shrunken cock, straddled his lap, and planted a kiss on the tip of his nose. "I intended to be the ultimate lover, so when I found my man, he'd never want to leave me."

She leaned forward and offered a damp breast and still-erect nipple to his eager lips. "How am I doing, lover?" She wiggled her rump, happy to see by his reaction he was more than a one-shot guy. "Can you ever tear yourself away from this?" Her fingers slid between his legs, teasing his balls. She gave a wicked smile. "I see my new best friend loves it here."

Derik was amazed at his quick recovery. This woman was a succubus, and he was clearly in for a long night. Karen was on of a dozen or so women he'd slept with over the past eight years, but none of them had kept him hooked for more than a few trysts, and the encounters always centered around lusty sex. Each had quickly lost their luster against his persistent memory of the twins.

It wasn't inadequate sex. Some of the women were very good, and Karen was beyond exceptional. But he knew in the long run, that wasn't enough. Something magical had struck him with the two redheads, and until he found that same hook in a new woman, no relationship was destined to last.

He sighed to himself as he lifted Karen onto the bed and began a second voyage into sensual oblivion. He'd enjoy the night immensely, and maybe even have a repeat or two, but the rest of the relationship, he knew, was doomed to go stale.

When that occurred, he'd try to find some gentle way to

let her down. Karen was someone to be treated well, and Derik had a high moral code about not abusing women.

In the meantime, he'd enjoy what may be the best sex of his life. Sex that he was right in the middle of at that moment. He returned his concentration to the writhing woman under him and was soon rewarded with—

"Oh, baby, I'm coming!" And she did, quickly followed by his own release. He collapsed atop of his Asian lover and knew this was only the beginning of a long night of pleasure. That was good, because he had a few busy days looming.

Derik stepped back from the vault's entrance, scanned the interior once more, and swung the massive steel door closed, spinning the handle to lock it. He patted the cold, gray metal with affection.

When he arrived in South Florida with two pirate chests overflowing with treasure, he realized he couldn't chance stashing it in the usual public storage areas. He needed somewhere much more secure, and there was way too much to stuff into even several bank's safety deposit boxes. He needed his own, private vault. Chick found a small, two-bay service garage which Derik bought for cash. An Internet search produced two vault manufacturers, and after a lengthy negotiation, Derik contracted for a small, walk-in vault capable of withstanding vigorous attempts at cracking. It had both combination and eye-reading technology, and they actually had one in stock due to a previous cancelation.

The vault was delivered in a week, fully customized, and installed in a steel-reenforced concrete bed inside the garage. The building's rollup repair-bay doors were sealed by a brick wall. The only entrance to the bays containing the vault was through an inside office door—solid steel with a combination and facial-rec lock.

When completed, Derik spent just under two-hundred thousand on the project, not a lot considering the value of its contents, now estimated at over a hundred million dollars.

Only Derik and Chick knew of its location and had access to its interior.

Derik turned and left, six hardened-steel bolts setting as the outer door closed. He fingered the small bag in his left pocket containing three, five-carat and a seven-carat diamond, and one larger ruby, which he planned to sell on diamond row to one of the many, mostly Jewish, dealers. They already knew him well, a fact that reduced the most spirited negotiating. Derik's right hand curled around his pocketed 9mm Smith & Wesson carry gun, for which he had a permit. It was often holstered on his right ankle, but when he visited the vault, he kept it more ready.

Just in case.

Derik strolled into his office just after lunch, having completed the sale of the five gems, all to Solomon Herzog, for $723,000. The larger stone proved to be vvs2 quality, reducing its value a bit, but overall, he was pleased. A half-mil was wire-transferred into his account at Grand Cayman. The balance, which he'd declare for capital gain income, went into his local bank. One more large, blue-white diamond, along with eleven others from three to five carats still remained in storage. Plus, seventeen blood-red rubies and twenty-two emeralds, all fully faceted and mostly flaw free.

More value there than he could ever spend, so he'd been contemplating starting a charitable foundation. He hadn't, however, decided what that would fund. He needed to find a place where he could make a difference.

Climbing out of his contemplation, he spied Chick approaching, two folders in hand.

"Hey, pal," his partner said, "everything go okay?"

"Perfectly." Derik laid a hand on Chick's shoulder and

steered him toward his office. "The big stone proved to only be vvs2," he whispered, "but I got an excellent price for everything. All wired into the accounts."

He gestured toward the files. "Got some new prospects?"

They entered his office and Derik settled behind his restored oak desk, purchased from a salvager, taken from a sunken 18th Century French frigate found off the coast of North Carolina. His love of nautical themes persisted throughout his offices.

"Yeah, I've whittled the list down to two: the couture fashion designer, and a large, custom machine shop, specializing in aviation." He settled opposite Derik and laid the two files on his desk. "Both are in trouble and may be willing to accept our terms for financing." He eased back in his chair. "I've spoken to each and have set up appointments for tomorrow. Take a look at those," waving at the folders, "and decide which you want to interview, and I'll take the other."

Derik nodded, flipped open the red folder, and quickly scanned its content. A moment later, he repeated the action with the blue one. He leaned forward, fingers steepled.

"Hmm. The woman's business is much smaller and seems in imminent trouble." He chuckled. "I like the idea of helping the little guy—gal, in this case. You okay with taking the machine shop?"

"Actually, that's my preference." He ran a hand through his wavy brown hair. "Figured you'd go for the woman, too."

"Tomorrow, huh?" He rose. "What time?"

"Ten-thirty. She sounded real eager, pard, so keep an eye out for tiger traps. She's a looker, too, so ..."

"Not to worry, buddy." He watched Chick start for the door. "You know that stuff doesn't get to me."

"Yeah," Chick glanced over his shoulder as he exited.

"But, it's about time that changed. Eight years is long enough." He pointed at the file in Derik's hand. "Check out her social and business media. All the info's in there," gesturing at the red folder.

Derik nodded, returned to his desk, and read the file's contents more carefully. Then he woke up his desktop and pulled up Brita Kruger's website; Allure Attire. He whistled softly. She was one hell of a classic beauty.

Someone to take his mind from the twins? Maybe her? Not a good idea to mix business with pleasure, though. He began scrolling, and gained further appreciation for this tall, blonde knockout. She'd created one hell of a fine line of rags, but hadn't taken any steps to diversify.

That's where he would come in, if they made a partnership. He set the folder aside, eased back in his chair, arms crossed, as his mind began considering what the gorgeous Ms. Kruger needed to accept to save her company.

He intuitively knew the answer.

11

Gorya Kolodenko glanced up as his brother, Alik, lumbered into the room. The 6'2" bearish Ukrainian plopped onto a chair and tossed two envelopes onto the utilitarian blue steel desk.

"Only two?" the shorter, slim brother asked.

"Yeah. And bistro guy was grand short." He stroked his drooping, black mustache.

"So, we collect grand and 25% late fee next month." He leaned back and interlocked his fingers. "You provided incentive, I presume?"

"Sure. His left arm'll be in sling for week or so." He stretched forward, planting both hands on the desktop. "How's it going with girls?

"About as expected. Gotta get Gracie and Char their fix today, or they won't be any good for weekend." He fingered his Van Dyke beard. "Desirée's gone to pot. Gotta be replaced." He eyed his larger brother. "You'll take care of her?"

"Yeah, I do it tonight after one last party. Just more trash to take out." Alik chuckled. "So, we're gonna need new girl for airport area. How about hot blonde who was short last month?"

"No way." Gorya rose from his desk. "That babe'll bring big money as high-end escort. We gotta take her first, though."

"Okay. When? I wanna be first with her." A wicked grin

creased his unshaven face. "Show her how ta handle big guy."

Gorya grunted and glanced at the calendar on his desk. "We seeing her in six days for next payment, which she can't make. We do it then."

"We gonna shoot her up at her place?" Alik's brow creased. "Kinda risky, bro?"

"Nah. No one gonna say nothing when we cart her out." He snorted. "One look at you will shut 'em up." He patted his brother's broad shoulders. "So, now get us new chick to cover airport. You aughta find someone at bars or titties lounges." He poked Alik as he came out of his chair. "Someone nice-looking with decent bod. Not like last pig."

"Shit, bro," Alik grumbled. "Some guys like meat on bones."

"Not this time, Alik." He gestured toward a closed back room. "We got two hypos of H in the fridge. And take some ruffies, if ya meet someone at lounge. Even if ya grab one today, it'll be week before she's fully hooked and back on feet, ready to work for next fix."

"I'm on it. I still get to break in newbie, right?" His tongue swiped full lips.

"Yeah, yeah. Have her often as ya want, once she's hooked."

Alik nodded, a grin tilting his lips. This was his favorite job, and the more the girl struggled at first, the better he liked it. That tall, blond babe, Kruger, filled his head. He was going to really enjoy playing with that one. He could hardly wait.

12

Brita slouched in her chair and studied the image of Derik Brand on her laptop's screen.

"A real storybook hunk," she muttered. Tall, handsome, a fit, college football hero, and an unusually successful treasure hunter. The guy had scored millions from sunken ships.

And now he was interested in becoming her partner and rescuer. Saving her from financial collapse, but not realizing—not yet, at least—also from physical trauma, and maybe even death at the hands of the Kolodenko brothers.

How did a smart, cautious babe like you do something so dumb, Brita? Alarm bells went off when she first met them, typical Russian hoods. Ukrainian, actually, but with little difference. She was so desperate to save her business, she ignored her usually sharp assessment of people, and took money from *loan sharks*.

And now they wanted to collect a payment she didn't have. She had no idea what penalty they'd seek, but whatever it was, it wouldn't be pleasant. She needed Brand to save her. No one else was in the wings if this fell through, but she was reluctant to cede control of her business to outsiders.

She glanced at her gold Piaget watch, then closed her computer. Her appointment at their offices was in thirty-minutes, so she'd better get going. Better to be early than late. She'd see what they offered and if he was open to negotiations. In any case, she'd reserve a decision until later, having learned from her mistake with the Kolodenkos not to rush into anything this big.

She strode to her office closet where many of her latest designs hung. She wanted something classic and sexy without being obvious. Feminine wiles should never be wasted, and while she rejected all the lecherous bankers, Derik Brand might be different. She pictured herself nestled in those strong arms, and chills on tiny mouse feet skipped down her spine.

Quit it. This was business, and the fact she hadn't had a "significant other" since Klaus in high school had no bearing on this meeting. She needed a bail out to escape the clutches of the Kolodenkos, and that was her focus. If her looks and sex appeal aided in that, so much the better. At least, it shouldn't be a chore with tall, blonde, and handsome Derik Brand.

An hour later, Brita relaxed on a yacht-type deck chair in Brand's office. All very nautical, including his lovely oaken desk. She'd outlined her needs, and they'd discussed his offer: the purchase of 51% of her stock and absolute control of operations. He emphasized he would always consider her positions on how they were to proceed, but in the end, the final decision was his.

She was careful not to come on to him sexually. They agreed each side needed a day to consider their options, and they set an appointment to meet for drinks at a mutually convenient, upscale tavern on Brickell Avenue the next afternoon. That's when she planned on using her charm and the implication of intimacy to sway him into something more acceptable.

Giving up control of her business to this guy, no matter how successful he'd been in the past, seemed a bridge too far.

She rose, and they shook hands.

"I'll see you tomorrow at four," he said. "This has been a good start. I believe we can do good things together, but I've got to discuss the opportunity with my partner, who is also interviewing another prospect."

He escorted her to the exit, a hand on her waist, sending delightful tingles across her back.

"We're only able to accept one new project at this time, and we never proceed unless we're both on board with the client."

"I understand." She pivoted toward him at the doorway, their bodies brushing lightly, which set her heart dancing to the chase music from "The William Tell Overture." Hi-yo Silver!

"I understand." She took his hand. "I, too, must consider what this will mean to me and my business."

He nodded, his fingers lightly squeezing hers. "So, tomorrow, then."

She smiled, and left him watching her depart, doing her very best runway stroll.

~ 13 ~

Derik lounged at his desk and skimmed his notes from his meeting with the lovely Brita Kruger. He chuckled softly, thinking of the sexuality she exuded. Derik appreciated that she'd dressed in an understated, but clearly intentionally sensual manner. He sighed. She was the first woman since Martinique for whom he'd felt any interest, and he had to admit it was exciting.

His eyes swung toward the door at Chick's knock. Derik slid forward and waved him in, gesturing toward a side chair.

"Your interview finished?" He settled behind his desk.

"Yep." Chick laid a blue folder on the desk. "And I saw yours leave a few minutes ago." He grinned. "That's one hot, classy babe."

Derik nodded. "Agreed, but that doesn't affect the fact she's got a legit need and seems to know what she's doing." He leaned back and folded his arms. "What about your guy?"

"Also in need of funds, but I doubt he'll go for our 51% deal." He flipped open his file. "I suspect he can get bank financing and was just prospecting for something better."

"Yeah, well I don't think that's an option for Ms. Kruger." He glanced at his notes. "Looks like three banks have turned her down, and I get the impression she may have snagged funds elsewhere that she needs to pay off soon." He glanced at Chick. "Seemed pretty edgy, but wants a day to think it over."

"So, you got a meeting set for tomorrow, then?"

"Yeah. Drinks at four at some bar on Brickell. She's gonna text me the address later."

"Nice," Chick chuckled. "Drinks, snuggled away in a shadowy booth, with a gorgeous blonde who needs your help." He grinned. "What could go wrong?"

"Yeah, well, she seems more than just a beautiful woman. She's got brains and drive. I gotta admit, she's the first lady since Martinique that's perked my interest."

"It's about damned time. Just don't let that influence your judgement about her deal, if she wants one."

"Not a chance. Don't even know if the attraction is mutual." Derik pointed at the blue file. "What about him? Does Kruger have competition for our services?"

Chick rose, the blue file in hand. "Like I said, I don't think so. Even if this guy wants our help, my gut says he'd be a struggle to work with." He nodded at the papers in front of Derik. "If you don't make that deal, I think we'll have to look elsewhere again." He held Derik's eyes.

"That shouldn't influence your decision, partner. If you don't think that'll work, there's plenty of other fish in the sea."

He turned toward the door. "It's not like we gotta have someone new, or else," said over his shoulder as he left.

Derik's eyes followed Chick's departure, then settled back in his chair, and sighed. His friend was right, but for the first time in eight years, he trembled with anticipation over an intimate meeting with a woman. His lips tilted into a tiny smile.

Chick had said it.

It's about damned time.

~ 14 ~

Derik perched on a stool, back to the polished oak bar. He glanced at his Rolex Submariner ... six-fifteen. She was running late.

He gazed up at the swish of the pub's door opening and spotted Brita standing in the entrance, a halo of light from the westerly sun igniting her graceful figure like an angel descending from heaven. Derik swallowed, his tongue flicking across suddenly dry lips.

A snug, mid-thigh, sky-blue leather skirt and sleeveless, robin-egg silk blouse were offset by a wide, royal blue leather belt. He grinned. Interesting outfit for a business meeting, but she was, after all, a model at heart.

He slipped off the stool and waved as he moved to join her. Her bow-shaped lips arched into a sweet smile as she waved back. They met and he took her offered hand.

"Sorry I'm a bit late."

"Not a problem." He nodded at a row of booths along the back wall. "I've got a table where we'll have some privacy."

Taking an elbow, he guided her toward their seats. He noted she carried a small briefcase.

She slid into the booth and touched his hand as he entered the opposite bench.

"Do you mind sitting next to me?" She gestured with her file case. "It's easier to read documents when we're both on the same side."

He shrugged. "If you wish," and began to rise.

"Sit." Said with a waved hand. "I'll move." She exited her side, adjusted her skirt, which had hiked higher on her thighs, then slipped beside him as he scooched left against the wall. Brita drew her folder in front of her.

"Thanks. This is better."

Derik gulped as their hips grazed on the bench seat. It was a narrow booth, but two wasn't a crowd. Still, he found himself enjoying the contact.

She opened her leather case on the epoxy-coated oak table, swiveled toward Derik, and their shoulders touched as she laid a hand atop of his.

"Thank you so much for seeing me again so quickly."

Her electric smile and glistening cobalt eyes sent a cascade of tingles skittering down his spine. The warmth of her fingers and the delicious aroma of her perfume fired a stirring in his groin the likes of which he hadn't felt for ... what? Eight years, he realized. Derik swallowed hard and blinked.

Brita withdrew a stack of papers from her case—the contract he'd offered her the previous day, spread the documents out, and plucked up one of the sheets. She leaned in, her firm thigh now pressed heatedly against his, and one clearly unfettered breast caressed his arm.

"I appreciate your generous offer, Derik." Her voice low with a sultry edge. "And I shouldn't admit this, but I really need the financing quickly."

Her face inches from his, moist, ruby lips begging for a kiss. He struggled to ignore an erection grown to its fullest glory. *Shit. Let's keep this professional, Derik.*

"I'm just not comfortable giving up control of my business." A pink tongue-tip swiped slightly parted lips. "It's not that I don't trust you. Your company has an impeccable reputation. It's just that—well, what do you really know about the garment industry?" Her left hand found his thigh, gently squeezing. "I'd be *so* grateful if we could do this without that clause."

Derik's light-blue eyes found hers, and his lips tightened into a hard line.

She's trying to seduce me into changing our deal.

His hard-on began to sag as he leaned against the wall and brushed her hand away. He shook his head.

"You disappoint me, Ms. Kruger."

The formal use of her name caused her to flinch, her eyes flaring, and fingers covered her lips.

"You're a bright and attractive—no, *gorgeous* woman, but I didn't think you'd stoop to sexual inuendo to try to sway me." He sighed. "And the funny thing is, all this," waving a hand across the table, "wasn't necessary. I've gotta admit, you're the first woman in maybe eight-years who actually lit my fire again."

He shoved the papers back toward her. "I would have thought this was beneath you, but I guess I misjudged your character." A backhand flip urged her to exit the booth so he could get out. "That also seems to apply to my potential interest in you, other than in a business way."

"Oh, Derik, I'm so sorry." Tears puddled in her eyes as she slid out and rose. "This is so—so unlike me. I don't know what I was thinking. I'm so desperate—"

"Enough to prostitute yourself?" He gritted his teeth and shook his head. He had no right to be so cruel to this beautiful and apparently fraught woman.

"I'm sorry." He exited from the booth. "That was uncalled for." He sighed again. "However, this requires a reevaluation of our offer, even if you now decide to accept it."

"I ... I don't know what to say." Mascara-stained tears

trickled across her cheeks. "You were probably my last hope."

"Not a position I like to be in." He tentatively took one of her hands. "I dislike a potential client coming with us because they have no other option."

Brita withdrew a tissue from a small purse and dabbed at her warpaint-like, black streaked cheeks. She clutched her briefcase against her breast and sniffled.

Shit. I hate to think I made this lovely babe cry. "Look, I'll discuss this with my partner. We have standards I'm unwilling to compromise, but—well, we'll see. You go over our offer and decide what you want to do. Chick and I will see if we're still willing to go ahead if you are." He paused and studied her. "I'm not sure we'll be able to make that happen, even if you do, but we'll talk."

He took her elbow and eased her toward the door.

"Can I call you?" She squeezed his hand. "I've never really told you why this is so imperative for me."

"Of course. I'll speak to my partner today, so our position will be set by tomorrow morning." She had the look of a deer in headlights.

Is there something else terrifying her besides the possible loss of her business?

They tarried outside. "Would you like me to walk you to your car?"

"No. I'm just in that lot," gesturing across the street.

"Okay. Then we'll talk tomorrow, I suppose." He turned to walk to his car, parked up the street.

"Derik."

He paused and turned. She was backlit by the setting sun, a gorgeous seraph sent to Earth to mess with him. A third sigh. Messing with her seemed so appealing less than an hour ago.

"Please, believe me," she called. "I've never done

anything like that before. I feel so embarrassed and cheap. Life or death desperation, I guess, but it's no excuse."

He nodded and gave a small wave, not knowing what to say. *Life or death? That's pretty extreme.* He turned back toward his car and growled softly. *If she hadn't had ulterior motives, I might have found my first real relationship with a woman in years. Fuck! I suppose a woman like her expects to use men at will. Life or death?* He shook his head.

Brita watched him depart, tears again in full flood. *Damn, you idiot! I let desperation drive me off a cliff. That's the first guy I could see building a life with, and I screwed it up.*

She paid the attendant in the little booth as she exited the lot and headed for her office. Gotta get her ducks in a row and find a way to resurrect this deal. The Kolodenkos were going to show up any day now, and if she didn't have their money, she suspected they'd do more than charge her another late fee. She'd been self-sufficient all her life, but for the first time, she was really scared. These were the kind of guys who easily did bodily harm.

How the hell was she so stupid as to borrow from loan sharks and not realize who they were? Desperate people do dumb things. Her only hope was Derik Brand. She needed to be on her best, professional behavior, and plead a persuasive case. No sexual innuendos. Just a good argument.

She sighed. Such a handsome, intelligent, and really *nice* guy. It would have been lovely if something had happened, with no strings attached, but she'd blown that out of the water. Well, business first, and who knew what might develop down the road.

Of course, if they declined to invest with her, that road promised a very unhappy ending. She shuddered, picturing that scenario, then gritted her teeth as she pulled into her parking lot.

Somehow, I gotta find a way.

She stepped from her Beamer sports coupe and hurried to her office. She needed to prepare the best pitch of her life, because she suspected that life depended on it.

~ 15 ~

Derik strode into his offices and found Ginny Mendoza, his executive assistant at reception.

"Hey, Derik. How'd it go with the bombshell?" A grin tickled her lips.

"Not as expected." He glanced into the open office bullpen where his two other employees sat in glass-topped, blue wall-portioned cubicles.

"Chick in?" He glanced back at Ginny.

"Yep. Just returned. He's in his office." She studied her clearly agitated boss. "Didn't seem any happier than you do."

Derik shrugged. "Thanks." He started for his partner's office. "Hold any calls for a while, Ginny."

"Gotcha," said to his quickly disappearing back.

A moment later, he entered Chick Radford's office and spotted his 6'4" friend and partner behind his oak executive his desk, scribbling notes in a file.

"Hey, Chick." Derik settled on one of two chrome-frame, canvas deck chairs. Nautical themes permeated the entire office.

"How'd your meeting go with the manufacturer?"

"About as I expected." Chick eased back in his wine-colored leather chair. "They're not gonna give up control of the company, so they've found some short-term bridge financing."

He slid the file to one side. "Okay by me, 'cause I feel

they're not the fit we first thought. So, how'd it go with the blonde beauty?" He grinned. "I'd love to see you two working together."

"Yeah, not likely." Derik crossed his arms and gave a small head shake.

"Why? What happened?" He leaned over his desk. "I thought she was perfect." He chuckled. "Ignoring her looks, if that's possible, she needs our investment, and like we talked earlier, it's a business we can turn around."

"True, but after today, I'm not sure I could work with her."

"Christ, Derik, how could you *not* want to work with her?"

"Yeah, it seemed right." Derik sighed. "I think that's what she thought too."

Chick scratched his chin. "I don't—"

"She came on to me, Chick." His brow wrinkled. "And, I don't mean just flirting. Rubbing against me, hand on my thigh. Hell, she was almost in my lap."

"Damn, I wouldn't mind that babe on my lap." He leaned back again. "So, ...?"

"It was all an effort to wiggle out from us buying controlling interest." Derik's palm slapped the desktop. "The implication was, she'd be mine if we'd scratch out that clause."

He lurched from the chair and began pacing. "Shit! She's the first woman to take my mind off Martinique, and it took just five-minutes for her to trash that." Derik spun and glared at his partner.

"It was plain prostitution—sex for a favor. I ain't buying it."

Chick rose and joined Derik. He squeezed his shoulder. "So, how did you leave it."

"She was in tears, apologizing, saying she was so desperate she'd done a stupid thing." He shook free of Chick's grasp. "Pretty sad to watch, actually. Even invoked life or death." He slumped onto his chair. "Begged for another chance, and I said I'd discuss it with you."

"So," Chick dropped onto his chair. "what do you want to do? You think she's really in danger?"

"Don't know, but, I'm here, and we're discussing it, aren't we?" his voice muted.

"Okay. So, if she comes back and agrees to our terms ...?"

"Do we want to chance working with a manipulator?" Derik massaged the back of his neck, eyes locked on Chick's.

"Well, you said she apologized up and down. You think it mighta been a one-time thing, based on her apparent desperation?"

"Maybe. I get the feeling there *is* something else— something more than just the business—that's got her scared." He paused and stroked his chin. "The 'life or death' thing came up as I was leaving, so we never got into it." He sighed again and massaged tired eyes. "So, what d'ya think? Go or no-go, if she agrees to 51%?"

Chick stared off, then nodded. "I think we should do it. I believe we can make a go of her business and profit for all. And, what could be better than rescuing a gorgeous damsel in distress? You can be her white knight, and I'd love to see you shake off the eight-year doldrums as a bonus."

Derik chuckled, tension seeping away. He rose and gave a thumbs-up. "Yeah, I think you're right on all counts. The ball's in her court, and I *did* leave it open for further review." He turned to leave. "Meanwhile," said over his shoulder, "keep researching other ops in case this one falls through. I'm heading for the gym to work off some of this stress."

Habits of an athletic youth had stuck with him: eating right and staying fit. Maybe he'd even visit the dojo after dinner to polish up his black-belt skills. He was finally getting to where he gave the sensei a pretty even challenge, and it was a great way to settle his soul.

He started for his office when Gina flagged him down.

"Call for you, Derik." She waved the phone. "It's Miss Kruger, I believe."

So soon? "Okay. I'll get it at my desk." He perched on a corner of his desk and plucked up the phone.

"Hello?"

"Mr. Brand?" Gone formal, has she? Possibly a good sign.

"Yes, Miss Kruger. What can I do for you?"

"First to again apologize for my shameless behavior this afternoon. I don't know what got into me."

"Water under the bridge. Where do we go from here. The ball, as they say, is in your court."

"I appreciate you saying that, because I am willing to accept your terms of investment. If you can work some magic, we'll both be the better for it." She paused. "Can we meet and finalize things tomorrow?" She continued to sound desperate.

"Sorry. I'm taking a bunch of inner-city kids sailing and camping tomorrow and Sunday. Trying to give them a reason to stay clean and a way to get out of the slums." He glanced at his schedule on his cell phone. "Monday work for you?"

"It'll have to do." She sighed. "Nine a.m.?"

"Fine. I'll come to your place to give me a chance to plan our approach. See ya then." He hung up the desk phone.

Derik settled at his desk, drew out her file, and scanned its meager contents. Her voice was filled with tension.

Something else *was* going on here, and he needed to discover what it was before he finalized anything.

He smiled softly. Despite what had happened earlier, or maybe partly because of it, he *was* eager to see her again.

~ 16 ~

Gorya Kolodenko found his brother at their in-house gym. He was sprawled on his back, bench-pressing 280 pounds. Not a soft spot anywhere on Alik, as a few ambitious guys had discovered to an unhappy ending.

"You take care business at airport, Bro?" Gorya perched on a nearby bench.

"Yeah. Desirée's gator bait in in 'glades." He secured the barbell on its hooks and sat up. "Put her down with heavy dose H after one last party. No fuss, no muss, nice 'n quiet."

"Too bad. Was hot little piece once, but job wore her down." Gorya studied his brother. "So, you found replacement yet?"

"I gonna hit bars in Little Havana. Find hot Spic babe, slip her roofie, and bring to our hooker haven. Will be hooked on H end of week." He rose "That work fer you?"

"Sounds like plan, so do it. We been Ubering girls in. Airport's always hot for travelers." He patted his larger sibling on the butt. "Took crew whole day clean up apartment, once Desirée gone." He shook his head. "What a pig."

"She was hot, but drugs ruin her. I keep new one hooked but not over done this time."

"Good. So, get babe tonight, will ya. Remember, we visit blonde cunt tomorrow at ten, and set her up, 'cause no way she got bread for next payment."

"You plan grab her then, Bro? I'm sure eager for piece of tight little pussy."

"Yeah, me too, but we see how it plays out. I not dabble like you, big guy, but that cunt's real special." Gorya turned to leave. "If ya pick up hot gal for airport tonight, Alik, we need fresh hypo of H ready for morning, in case we get lucky with blondie." He gave a wicked grin. "If not then, soon, and I got best service to hook her up. A grand an hour, easy, and free pussy any time you want. Just don't mess her up. Got it?"

"Yeah, yeah. I know, don't damage merch. It's just so much hotter when it's rough."

"Take out on our local cunts, but not her." Gorya glared at his brother with flinty eyes. "You know what happens if ya make me mad."

"Don't' worry." Alik mopped newly formed sweat from his brow. "I not mess her up." Despite being much larger than Gorya, Alik feared his brother's rage.

Then he thought of the Kruger dame and licked his lips.

Brita disconnected her call to Derik and laid her cell phone on her desk. She groaned softly. *I've got to be on my best behavior with him. Strictly professional. If I can't swing this deal* ... tears flooded her blue eyes. She'd been so stupid, trying to use sex to get her way. How desperate!

The really foolish thing was, she really was attracted to this guy. Not only because he was a handsome hunk, but because he exuded a certain ... what? Solid character and strong morals, that's what. Not many men with those attributes in the modeling and couture profession.

Who knows what those loan sharks will—she glanced at her buzzing phone. Speaking of the devil, literally. Couldn't ignore them, though."

"Hello?" She held her breath.

"Hey, blondie. Just checkin' in. We come early next week, collect our payment, and late fee from last month. Ya have cash?"

"I'm working on it. I didn't realize there was that big late fee."

"That's why read small print, babe."

"Well, I hope to have it all by Wednesday."

"We might stop by earlier. See how things coming." His chuckle had a nasty edge.

"But the payment's not due until mid-week." Tension raised her voice an octave.

"I know, I know. But we like make early visit. Ya know, impress client on need be prompt. See ya then." The phone went dead.

She stared at her cell and knuckled away tears. *If Derik backs out, I'm gonna die.*

She rose and squared her shoulders. She had to be her best sales person with Derik, and that was usually pretty damned good. One of the modeling agency honchos told her that not only could she sell ice to Eskimos, she could sell them a freezer to put it in.

She'd better be that good on Monday and close the deal right then. With the cash Derik offered, she'd be able to pay off the Kolodenkos and get on with her life.

She had no choice but to make it work.

Or else!

~ 18 ~

Derik pushed into his office, flopped on his desk chair, and glanced at his Rolex. Four-ten p.m. He ran a hand through his hair and grinned. The weekend with the kids turned out better than he'd hoped.

As expected, the office was empty on a Sunday afternoon, but he'd decided to come in after docking *Martinique* at home. Catch up on a bit of work and prepare for his visit with Brita tomorrow. He flipped open the red folder, centered on his desk, and leafed through the papers. All the contracts and disclosures seemed in order, which was no surprise.

The first person he'd hired for his fledgling business was Eli Adler, lured away from his position as legal assistant of the managing partner of one of West Palm Beach's top law firms. He was a savvy lawyer, despite no degree and license to the bar.

Derik closed the file and slumped back in his ocher leather chair. He was tired after two days of stewarding seven rowdy kids through the basics of sailing and camping. He swelled with a sense of satisfaction at the outcome. One of the Latino boys and a black girl really took to the sea, and three of the others—a Latina girl, a white girl, and another black boy, all were into it at the end, especially the camping.

They'd spent two nights tented on Elliot Key, baked fresh-caught fish, roasted marshmallows over campfires, and generally had a great time. Saturday they learned the basics, sailing to and from Key Largo. Derik was pleased five of them seemed to grasp there was a life other than in inner-city gangs, and that was the most he'd hoped for. He'd try for a repeat trip in a month or so to keep them hooked.

He sighed. It was years since he enjoyed a weekend like that, and it stirred warm memories. His thoughts drifted to Brita Kruger, and he wondered if anything would come of that? Business or pleasure—or both? While two redheaded nymphs still danced in his head, for the first time, they seemed to be urging him on rather than calling him back.

Well, tomorrow he'd see if Brita really wanted to go ahead with his offer. If so, where might that lead? He'd approach that with some cautious restraint.

He rose, left, and locked up, strangely eager to find out.

Brita hovered over her Baroque French mahogany desk, one of her few frivolous expenditures at Allure Fashions. In anticipation of Derik's pending arrival, she sorted papers into piles: supplier invoices due; operating expenses—rent, a/c, salaries, etc.; purchase orders to be placed for needed supplies; and customers' orders for her wares—unfortunately the shortest stack of the four.

From their earlier conversation, she knew Derik had a plan, and she wanted to show him what was at stake to continue operations. Of course, that paled next to the threat of the loan sharks, where her life might actually be on the line.

She jerked up when her office door opened. Julietta, her floor foreperson, paused in the entry.

"There are two men to see you, *Madam.*"

Ah, Derik must have come with his partner. They were early, but she was as ready as she'd ever be.

"Please show them in." She rose behind her desk as the woman departed without comment, other than a wrinkled brow. Why the obvious displeasure?

A moment later she had that answer as the Kolodenko brothers, not Derik Brand, strolled in.

"Nice little operation here, babe." The hulk called Alik leered at her.

"Thank you." A quavering, little-girl's voice was all she

could muster.

"Thought we'd stop by to check things out. Ya got our bread?" Gorya, the obvious brains of the two, scanned the room.

"Thirty K," the bearish brother said, lips drawn into a smirk.

"It's not due for two more days." Brita gnashed her teeth and forced herself to stand proud. "And it's $27,500, not 30."

"Yeah, but we add convenience fee," Gorya's smile was humorless, "making us come out here twice." He folded his arms.

"Ya got now, we don't come back."

"I'll have the $27,500 on Wednesday. I didn't ask you here today." She forced out a strong voice. "You did that on your own."

"Had to inspect investment." He studied her. "So, you have in two days, huh? Twenty-seven-five or thirty—it don't matter. How ya swing that, Missy?"

"That's my business. All you need to know is, you'll get your money."

"Ya better hope so, sweetheart." The brutish brother's face twisted into a scowl. "You don't got every penny, things not go well for you."

"Easy, Bro." Gorya glared at Alik. "We just investors, taking care of business. No need threaten sweet woman." He pivoted back to Brita. "Look, babe. Ya fall short, we work something out. Nobody gets hurt over few bucks. Okay?"

Brita nodded, but knew that was a lie. She was so petrified, her knees almost gave out. Her arms braced against the desk for support.

He turned as Alik tapped his shoulder.

"Some guy, Bro." He nodded toward the window. "Looks like he headed here."

"Okay, we don't want cause fuss." He returned his gaze to Brita. "There back way outta here?"

She nodded and breathed a sigh of relief. Derik to the rescue, she guessed.

"That side door," gesturing to the right, "and go right on the balcony to the end. Another staircase, and a fire exit at the bottom." She watched them scurry across her office toward the door and shuddered as she finally began to relax.

"See ya early morning, two days." Gorya said and smiled.

"After eleven." Would Derik be there by then? "I've got an early appointment and won't be back until about then."

"Fine. Eleven, okay." He glared, standing in the doorway. "You got bread, fine—and *is* now thirty K. Don't pay be short, twice." His dark eyes pierced her, then he pivoted and left with Alik close behind.

The door closed, and Brita collapsed onto her chair. She ran a hand through her hair and snatched up a small mirror. A quick dab of her eyes and hurried repairs to tear-streaked makeup. She hoped Derik wouldn't notice how disheveled she looked. Gotta make the sale, if he needed convincing.

Brita rose on still shaky legs and forced a small smile as Derik Brand knocked lightly on the door, and entered at her welcoming gesture.

"Hi." He strolled in and took her hand.

She shivered at his touch, unsure if it were tension release or excitement. She widened her smile and nodded at a chair as she settled in hers.

"You look a bit frazzled, Ms. Kruger." He perched on the edge of his seat and studied her face. "Everything okay?"

"Oh, yeah, sure. Just had some uncomfortable conversation with one of my—creditors." She leaned forward over the desk. "But, we're here to solve that now, I hope."

"Yes." He nodded, slid back on the chair, and opened his

attaché, withdrawing a sheave of papers. "I've discussed this with my partner, and despite getting off on the wrong foot, we're willing to go ahead if you are."

She sighed. "I'm afraid I'll never live that down, Derik." She knuckled away a tear. "Is it okay now if I call you Derik."

"I suppose so, since we're gonna be partners." The corners of his lips tipped up. "So, Brita, these are the contracts for the sale of 51% of your stock, in the amount of $625,000." He laid the documents on the desk in front of her. "That's generous, I think you'll agree, as it's based on fifteen times earnings from two years ago, when you were actually making a profit."

"That *is* very generous of you, Derik." She expelled a gentle breath. The use of her first name was promising, and the purchase sum should solve *all* of her problems, if the money were accessible by Wednesday.

"When will the money be available?" She studied her hands, folded on the table. "I've got a pressing bill to pay." Her words soft and choked.

"I'll open a joint, two-signature account today. Checks will have to be signed by both of us."

Brita looked away, edgy and clearly worried.

"What's the problem?"

"As I said, I have this one creditor ..." Brita paused and finally held his eyes. She sagged, slumped back in her chair, and tears came again. "Oh, shit. No sense in beating around the bush." She dabbed her eyes with a tissue. "I did a very stupid thing. My back was against the wall, and I needed funds, fast." A quick head shake. "Never even read the famous small print."

"Brita." He reached out and took both her hands in his. "What did you do?"

"I borrowed a hundred grand from loan sharks. Nine per

cent didn't seem too bad," she gave a short snort, "until I discovered it was *per month,* not annually."

"Wow! Have you made any payments?"

"One, but it only covered the interest. Now there's a big late fee—and they've threatened me." She groaned. "Next payment is due in two days. Thirty thousand, and if I don't have it—"

"But now you do." Derik sat back. "I'll convert a hundred-thirty-thousand to cash, and we'll pay them off in full."

"We, Derik?"

"Of course. I'll be here, and I'll bring Chick Radford, in case they cause trouble. We'll get them outta your hair so we can get on with turning your business around."

"Really?" Her eyes were in full flood mode, tiny rivers flowing across her arched cheeks.

"Look. It's part of our investment. Settling your debts and getting the company back on its feet. But we're gonna have to make some changes to get that done."

"Changes? I was afraid of that." She thumbed away the last of her tears. Her face would need "fixing," but she'd do that later. "I'm not great with changes."

"But they *are* necessary, and we *are* going to make them. I've prepared a list." He handed her a single sheet of paper.

~ 20 ~

"Okay, Chick, let me know when the funds are live and advise the bank we're gonna need 130K in cash." Derik glanced at Brita, perched on the edge of her desk. "I'll pick it up first thing in the a.m. I'll fill you in when I get to the office, but we've got our next project." He listened for a moment. "Right. See you later." He disconnected and turned to the lovely blonde.

"So, Brita, it looks like we're partners. Chick'll set up the account, and we'll go in together to arrange the signature cards." He settled on a side chair as she slipped behind her desk.

"It'll be dual-signature checking, with either mine or Chick's, and yours. That protects everyone so we all know where the money is going."

"Seems fair." Brita massaged her cheeks. "Once the Kolodenkos are paid off, I'll be able to breathe again."

Derik chuckled and didn't voice his concerns that payment in full may not end things with the Ukrainian hoodlums.

"So, let's put that aside for the moment and talk about what we need to do to start turning your lovely business around."

"You've got a plan already?" Her eyebrows knit. "That's quick."

"Right. Well, we do extensive research on a possible

partner before we make an offer. Not every struggling company has potential." He drew a sheet from the folder in front of him. "First, we're gonna cut unnecessary costs." His sapphire eyes caught hers. "That starts with selling your Key Biscayne condo."

"What?" She jerked back and her eyes narrowed. "That's mine—"

"No, actually your business holds title, so it's a company asset, or in this case, liability." He settled back in his chair. "Look, it seems you still own the three bed/two bath house in Coral Gables, don't you?"

"Uhh, yes. That's where I lived with my parents when we first moved from Germany while I pursued my modeling career in the States." She sighed. "But I've leased it out—"

"Yeah, but it's currently empty, isn't it?"

"Yes-s-s, but I have a new renter about to sign up."

"Apologize to him, but tell him something has come up and it's off the market." He leaned across the desk and touched her hand. "The condo is a black hole for you right now. You can't afford the luxury, and it's not a big step down to live in Coral Gables."

Brita drew her hand away, startled at the tingles assaulting her at his touch. Moisture coated her eyes.

"The good news is," Derik eased back and continued, "the housing market is hot, especially on Key Biscayne, and our company could net over a hundred grand profit on a quick sale to a cash buyer. Maybe even two, if there's a bidding war. You probably don't even need a realtor." He shrugged. "If you'd done this three months ago, you'd have the funds you needed, and never would have borrowed from those loan sharks."

Shit! She slumped back in her chair. *Why didn't I think of that?* Too damned cocky. This whole disaster could have been avoided. She studied Derik under hooded eyes. *But then I might not have met him, so fate works in strange ways.*

"Okay. Don't have much choice, do I?" She straightened up and leaned over the desk, elbows on the desk, supporting her face in her hands. "What else you got?"

"Something you may dislike more than selling the condo." He noted for the first time, a touch of Germanic accent, apparently more pronounced as she became agitated.

"Anything to dig out of this hole. Lay it on me."

"We used an AI algorithm to evaluate your industry. The demand for haute couture togs is fading. While your line came up as a leader, demand is switching to chic casual and especially, sport lines."

He offered her a printed report. "Women's golf, tennis, and pickleball attire are surging, and we feel you could be a major player in those fields if you move quickly." He rose and circled the desk, pausing next to her so they could scan the pages together. Her Black Opium perfume wafted seductively, causing a surprising stir in his pants. Derik felt the heat from her face, just inches from his.

He gestured at the graphs showing surging sales. "You could be especially well-fitted for this, Brita." He laid a hand on her shoulder. "We've noted that you're 4.0 rated at both tennis and pickleball, and a six-handicap golfer." Derik perched on the edge of her desk as she pivoted to face him. Her luscious bow-shaped lips slid into a soft smile, just awaiting a kiss. Derik clenched his teeth and tore his eyes away.

"My papa was a golfer, and Muter played tennis for a few years on the WTA." She shrugged. "Sports come naturally to me."

"Which is why I want to make you the face of your new sporting line." He slid off the desk and folded his arms, back in control ... mostly. "We'll run ads featuring you in the snazzy duds you are about to design, playing those sports and promoting your wares."

She also rose and ran a hand through her pixie cut. "Me, on the TV ads?"

"Why not. You strolled in front of cameras for years. Should be a snap for you." He grinned. "You'll hit a few balls, depending on the outfit you're wearing, and plug the line. You're a beautiful, classy woman that'll have guys salivating, and their ladies hoping your outfits will do that for them too."

They remained motionless for a few beats, taking each other in, and he kept his grin close-lipped, as he, too, was salivating. This was a gorgeous, down-to-earth woman that, despite her earlier misstep, he found magically alluring. But he probably scotched anything developing between them after his cruel comments in that lounge. She'd snatched her hand away at his earlier touch.

She nodded, finally, the tip of a pink tongue venturing across ruby lips. "Yes, I can do that." She chuckled as subterranean tension sluiced away. "Actually, I've been doodling with designs that fit in with your idea." She sighed. "I'll get right on it after we pay off those gangsters. They'll be here to collect Wednesday at eleven."

"Right." He edged back to his seat. "Chick and I will be here to do that, but you should stay away. We'll make the payment after getting written proof it was completed, and things may get a bit testy."

Brita's eyes widened. "You think they'll still come for me?"

Derik shrugged. "Bullies like them don't like losing control. I've never delt with loan sharks before, but I've known plenty of bullies. They only respond to force."

"But won't that be dangerous for you?" She circled the

desk and took his hands, igniting lightning bolts, and rekindling the stirring in his pants.

"We're two big guys." He squeezed her fingers. "We can handle it, but I want you safely out of the way. We'll be here Wednesday before ten with the cash, and I'll call when it's over." *Damn, I blew it. This is the first woman—*

He turned to leave, angry his rash condemnation of her made any romantic relationship unlikely.

~ ~ ~

Damn, why did I blow this? He was here, just taking care of business. That's what this was to him. *I really want to kiss him. My white knight.* He was a rare man—smart, warm, honest—the first to interest her in years.

They said their good-byes as she followed him to the door, where she planted very European kisses on both cheeks. Brita watched him depart, a film of moisture in her eyes, before returning to her office, pausing en route to inspect production of a new evening gown. Sales dead in the water.

She settled behind her desk, her face in her hands, and sighed. A small head shake, and she drew over her sketch pad. A graphite pencil tapped her lips, eyes rolled toward the ceiling, as images flooded into her head. Then she began to sketch.

"Out with the old, in with the new," she mumbled, filled with sudden confidence. Derik Brand may never be her lover, but she suspected he was going to be one hell of a great partner.

~ 21 ~

Chick Radford parked his black Chevy Suburban in an off-street lot a half-block from Allure Attire. Derik shouldered the canvas duffle bag and patted his holster containing his S & W 9mm, concealed under a light sportscoat.

He glanced at Chick. "Ready?"

He nodded and opened his door. "Got my Glock .40 locked and loaded." He watched Derik exit the other side. "You really expecting that kind of trouble, Derik?" He paused as his partner joined him. "I'd expect they'll be happy to be paid off, but you're not so sure, huh?"

Derik squinted at the golden disc, rising in the robin egg blue sky. "Gonna be hot early," he muttered, then looked at Chick. "You'd think that's what they're after, but I got a sense Brita's afraid of something else."

They strode toward the store. "I did some digging into the Kolodenko's history. My guess is their main gig is prostitution. Not a pleasant duo, for sure."

They were met by a smiling receptionist as they entered, recognizing Derik.

"Miss Kruger is in her office." She rose and moved toward the entrance to the shop.

"Thanks." Derik waved her off. "I know the way." He nodded at his companion. "This is my partner, Chick Radford. You'll be seeing a lot of us for now on."

"Nice to meet you," the woman said. "Brita said she had some new partners." She settled at her desk. "Go on up."

They entered the shop and were met by the hum of Singers and the quiet clack of cutting machines. Brita proved clothing could be produced in the USA and still make a profit. They ascended the metal staircase and Derik rapped on the half-glass door. Brita, hunched over her sketching table, rose, and waved them in.

"Hi." She gave a strained smile and gestured toward two side-chairs. "Everything okay?"

"Got the cash," Derik hefted the duffle, "and persuaders," patting his hip, "in case there's any misunderstanding." He nodded toward his companion. "I believe you met my partner, Chick Radford at our office."

"Yes, briefly." Her eyebrows arched. "You think they may become violent?"

"Just a precaution, should they have some other agenda." He held her eyes for a moment. "Which is why I want you to leave before they arrive."

"Leave? But why—?"

"Just in case they try to get rough." He reached across the desk and took her hand, surprised at the sudden heat that touch brought. *Damn!* He swallowed hard before continuing. "There's no need for you to be here. We're the majority shareholders now and can negotiate for the firm, if it comes to that." He smiled. "I think we'll all feel safer that way."

"Yes," she sighed, and obvious tension sluiced from her face. "I'm due for a visit to one of my cloth suppliers anyway."

"Good. Something to keep you occupied while Chick and I handle this end." He glanced at his partner. "I believe we'll feel easier, too, without worrying about your safety."

"Okay. They should be here within the next thirty minutes, so I should go now." She squeezed his fingers, still holding hers. "Be careful. I don't want anything happening to my new partners either."

"Not to worry. We're big boys and know how to handle bullies."

Brita nodded, gathered up a sketch pad and some charcoal pens, and hurried off.

Derik and Chick traded looks, then Derik took Brita's seat behind the desk and Chick settled on a nearby chair.

They fidgeted, a damp mantle of tension hanging over them.

~ ~ ~

Derik was clearing old messages from his cell when Brita's desk phone rang. He glanced at Chick, who'd been resting with his eyes closed. He was upright and awake now.

Derik lifted the receiver. "Yes?"

"Two men here, asking for Ms. Kruger." The woman's voice raspy with tension.

"Send them up, and don't mention she's not here." He hung up and nodded to Chick. "Sit in the far corner, so you'll be behind them when they enter."

"Right." He rose, drew his chair after him, and settled down, his pistol in his lap, hidden under some file folders.

Derik retrieved the duffel from under his feet and plopped it atop the desk. He sucked in a slow, deep breath and steadied his nerves. He twitched at a rap on the door, which opened before he could respond, and the Kolodenko brothers strode in. Derik's fingers curled around the handle of his S & W.

The two men paused at seeing Derik, and the smaller one's eyes swept the room.

"Who are you, and where's Kruger?" His face twisted into a scowl. The larger brother's brow knit, and he balled his fists.

"She's away on business, but I'm her partner, here to end our relationship."

"What you mean, 'away?' We here to collect—"

"Right." Derik rose and laid a hand on the duffel. "And I've got all she owes you right here." He patted the bag. "Paid in full, including your so-called late fees." He unzipped the sack and showed the cash. "All nice, clean Benjamins." He fanned a wrapped bundle of bills. "One-hundred-thirty K."

"Yeah, okay." Gorya laid a hand on Alik's arm to stall any aggressive action. "But we want see Kruger."

"Not gonna happen." Derik nudged the duffel, which he closed. "You'll get your cash, and we're finished. You'll have no reason to come here again." His face morphed into hard planes, his eyes narrowed and lips pressed into a tight slit. "Get it?"

Gorya tightened his grip on his brother who looked about to explode. "Okay. We take money and leave. No trouble." He stepped forward and reached for the bag.

"Not quite yet." Derik drew a sheet of paper from a file on the desk. "This is a paid-in-full document. I'll meet you in ten minutes at the UPS store up the block. You'll sign and notarize this doc there, and we'll witness it, and then you'll get your cash." He nodded toward Chick, whom they first noticed, hovering in the corner.

"My partner will take care of this," patting the bag, "and your brother can watch him if you want. When this," waving the single sheet, "is signed and notarized, you'll get your cash." He again opened the bag and dumped the contents of wrapped hundred-dollar bill bundles on the desk.

"You stay back and watch." Derik stacked the money in piles of ten-thousand until he had thirteen and got a reluctant nod from Gorya. Stuffed back into the sack and zipped, Derik rose and shouldered the duffel.

"After you." He gestured at the door. Chick fell in behind, his hand resting on his re-holstered Glock, under his jacket.

The brother's looked at each other, and Gorya shrugged. "Let's go, Alik. Get this done. We got other work this afternoon." The larger brother grumbled as they exited the office, with Derik and Chick close behind.

Thirty-minutes later, the two Ukrainians had departed after signing the receipt, their lucre in hand. For lenders who'd just got their investment back, plus a thirty-percent profit in two months, they didn't look pleased.

Derik watched them go and turned to Chick. "Didn't look too happy, did they?"

"No. You get a sense they had something else in mind?"

"Yeah, that's what worries me." He shrugged. "Not much they can do now, though." He withdrew his cell phone and his auto-dial. It was answered on the first ring.

"Hey, Brita. It's done, and they're gone." He heard the exhale of tension from her. "So, c'mon back and let's get to work. We've got a new sports line to get moving." He listened, then disconnected. "She'll be here in ten minutes. You can return to the office, pard. I should be here for an hour or two to get started on our new business path, then I'll come in, and we can tie up any loose ends from our last deal."

"I'm on it, Boss," Chick said with a chuckle. "Nothing as tense as the last hour, for sure."

"Yeah, hopefully all back to normal, whatever that is." He turned toward Brita's office. "See ya then."

But Derik had a gut feeling all *wasn't* back to normal.

~ 22 ~

The brothers entered their black Hummer, and Gorya tossed the duffle bag full of cash onto the rear seat. Alik slammed his door and glared at his brother.

"Fuck! What was that, Bro? We came for her, not money. That blond bastard—"

"Nothing for us to do. The dame was AWOL, and guy and buddy were packing." He growled and started the SUV. "Kruger owed hundred-and-thirty-grand, and they paid off."

"So, we just pass on gorgeous cunt?"

"I didn't say that." He shifted into gear and pulled out of the strip mall's lot. "Need another plan. I want sexy bitch in our stable too. She'll make us plenty."

"Okay, good." Alik settled back and fastened his seat belt. "Just remember, I get first piece of her."

"You got it, Bro. We snatch her and hook her on H, you have as much as you want."

"Yeah, but gotta get her first. Ya got plan?"

"Working on it, but need lay low for a while." He gave a snort. "That blond guy no dummy. He be cautious for now, so we wait and let 'em cool off."

"Okay, I be patient, but not easy." Alik squinted and rubbed his jaw. "You get bastard's name?"

"Yeah, from paper we signed. Brand, Derik Brand."

"Good. I'll check him out. We take babe ... and *kill* Mr. Derik Brand. No fuckin' WASP makes fool outta me."

"Yeah, that bastard earned bed in hole with dirt on face, and we're gonna see to it."

"Right." Alik reached back, drew the sack onto his lap, and opened it. "Meanwhile, not so bad getting money, as long as not end of it. Thirty-K profit in two months don't suck." He fingered the wrapped bills, then rezipped the bag. "I'm gonna enjoy making guy pay, and not gonna be quick." The big brute's tongue swiped his lips.

"We get 'em, you take as long as you want. Me, I'm into putting babe to work for us."

They drove on in silence, each mulling their schemes for snatch and retribution.

No one screwed the Kolodenko brothers and lived to brag about it.

~ 23 ~

Brita and Derik hovered over her desk and studied sketches of her new designs. A week had passed since she'd paid off the loan sharks, and she'd finally relaxed and gotten into her work. They stood close, shoulders brushing, and electric tingles peppered her skin. She took in his face from the corner of her eyes.

Damn it! Am I the only one getting turned on here? No signs Derik felt anything. She stepped aside and pivoted to him.

"So, what do you think? These what you had in mind?"

"Exactly. What do *you* think?"

"I love them. After all, they *are* my designs." She chuckled. "We've produced some prototypes, and I'm already arranging for several TV ads, centered around tennis, golf, and pickleball."

"Sounds good. It's amazing how that paddleball sport is booming."

"Yes. The outfits are really crossovers to tennis. But it gives us an extra avenue to promote." Brita pushed up and bumped his arm, shivering at the heat that produced. She hoped she wasn't blushing. "Would you like me to model one for you?"

"Absolutely. You have them here?"

She nodded toward a door in the back. "In my dressing room."

"I didn't realize you had one in your office." His eyes

swept from her to the full-length mirrored door.

"Of course. I always try on my designs, and it's most convenient to do it up here." She glided toward the dressing room. "It'll only be a minute," and disappeared inside.

~ ~ ~

Derik watched her disappear behind the door and shook his head. His heart pummeled his ribs and desert dryness attacked his mouth.

Damn it, I'm falling for her, but I've driven her away, emotionally. She'd flinched at that brief contact. Chick often chided him for his candid manner with others. Tact was something he was usually good at, but other times, with no chance to consider his comments, he could be very direct. Likening her to a prostitute during that early meeting was probably a death knell for romance. His mulling was broken by the opening of that mirrored door.

Brita appeared in a red-accented, short white skirt and a sleeveless, V-neck white blouse with a small, red tennis racket and her logo emblazoned above the right breast. She pirouetted on long, athletic legs, the skirt swirling up, giving a peek at silken underpants.

"Wow!" His heart was in his throat.

"You like?"

"Gorgeous." He was referring to her as much as the outfit. "I love the accents." His voice hoarse.

"Thanks." She patted the tennis racquet image. "For pickleball, this will be crossed paddles." She brushed a hand over the skirt. "I've also designed short shorts to mix-and-match with the top, and belts, but I'm waiting on samples of those."

"Sounds good." Somewhat back in control. "So, the ads?"

"Scheduled to shoot in a few weeks. They'll run during both the LPGA and Women's Amateur Opens, and Wilson is sponsoring a mixed national championship pickleball week in three months." She settled on a chair next to him. "They're interested in private labeling the line with their logo, and they'll pay for the ad time."

She eased back in the chair, her grin igniting the air, sending his heart into full gallop. "How am I doing, partner?"

Derik ground his teeth. Her smile was warm but offered no promise.

"Looks like you've been doing what we discussed." He paused, his blue eyes on hers. "Despite our somewhat rocky start, I'm pleased at our partnership. And you?"

"Me too." She sighed and noted his passing stern look. Her brow wrinkled momentarily, then she continued.

"Getting out from under those loan sharks was such a relief, and with the money you've invested, I can be creative again. New life."

"Right." He shifted in his chair. "But it still pays to stay vigilant. Guys like that don't give up easily, and I know you sensed they had some other agenda, so be careful."

"Will do, but there's something else I want to discuss."

"Okay?"

"Must we totally cancel the couture line? It's how I built my reputation, and—"

"Look," he folded his arms, "I know change can be painful, but in today's environment, there's not enough market to go around to all the manufacturers." He studied her. Using feminine wiles again? He hoped not. "We'll keep the line open until most of the inventory is gone, but after that, it's finished ... unless there's another swing in the market place."

He rose. "Right now, concentrate on building up the sports and casual lines. I haven't seen anything on the latter."

"You're the boss, Derik. You've made that clear." She

struggled to tamp down rancor in her voice. "I'm working on them and should have samples ready in ten days or so. Okay?"

"Yes, and keep me posted on the TV ads, and be sure you stay inside our budget." All business now, he wondered if she *was* trying to use sex again to get her way. He hoped not, expecting more from her.

He gathered his briefcase and jacket and started for the exit, filled with swirling emotions. This was a woman he could love, but he was unsure if he could trust her not to be manipulative. Anyway, it didn't matter, because she obviously treated their connection as business only.

He shrugged as he departed the building. This was less complicated, but in his heart, he was deflated. The first woman he could care for in eight years, and it was ruined by circumstances.

~ ~ ~

Brita watched him leave and brushed away a tear. She could easily fall in love with that guy, but she'd driven him off. He couldn't even stand her touch, yanking away his arm from an innocent touch. Well, *mostly* innocent, anyhow. Her hope for a warm response was met by a cold shoulder.

Okay, they're business partners, and he's a great one to have, despite being so directive. She sighed, knowing he was right about their approach, but was a bit put out by his "I'm the boss" attitude. She turned to her design table, determined to create the absolutely best sports/casual lines in the country. That was who she was.

A winner.

~ 24 ~

Two weeks later, Derik stepped aboard *Martinique* and dropped his boat bag in the cabin. Back on deck, he cast off the bow line, and with his Perkins idling, scurried back to unfasten the stern tether. Under moderate power, the diesel engine drove the sloop away from the dock and into the channel leading to the ICW (Intracoastal Waterway). Once there, he motored north the short distance to the Haulover Inlet and access to the Atlantic where he could raise sail. The fifteen-knot northwesterly wind under a cloudless sky would hurry his trusty Choy Lee south, making about seven knots.

The white sheet billowed and crackled as it filled, the sloop listing to starboard under the strong breeze. Derik settled at the helm, his mind free for once, and sucked in the joy of wind at his back and the salty smell of misty spray peppering his skin.

His lips ticked up. In the aftermath of the Kolodenko payoff, three weeks were invested in getting Brita's new line up and running. Early results foretold a dynamite launch with preorders already piling in.

He shook his head and returned his attention to his yacht. It angled downwind, slicing through three-foot rollers as they overtook the waves. Sheets of spray were mostly cast ahead by the brisk wind, saving him a dousing. The Choy Lee 36 was a master at managing downwind conditions.

He glanced at his Rolex Mariner. He'd cast off from his

home dock at 7:10 a.m., and at this speed, he should make the little cove he favored off the east coast of Key Largo by mid-afternoon.

The boat was provisioned for a three-day weekend of fishing, relaxing, and diving. He had four fully charged SCUBA tanks, and that would lend authenticity to his next sunken treasure "find"—four, twenty-five-pound gold ingots. At the current price for gold, that was worth nearly three-million bucks, netting him about two-million-four at auction.

He chuckled softly as he adjusted his course more southerly and picked up a half-knot in speed. Would he even live long enough to judicially convert the full find into cash? More than two-thirds still remained, and he'd already netted over a hundred-twenty-million.

That afternoon, Sotheby's would sell four of his 1688 doubloons, the first he'd offered in eighteen months. He would follow the sale on his tablet. Better yet, subsequent to feelers he put out to a private site for high-end collectors, the gem-encrusted, solid-gold cross, with the etching scrolled on the back, *Para El Papa*— "for the Pope" —had received four offers, and he'd received a deposit from a billionaire collector against a bid of $2,000,000, which he'd accepted. No middle-man, nor the usual 15% or 20% "seller's fee" from an auctioneer.

Derik checked his GPS and confirmed he was now making a tad under seven knots. He grinned, settled against the rim of his helmsman's seat. This was the best he'd felt in weeks.

He enjoyed turning companies around, and making a nice profit as well, but he couldn't avoid the subliminal sexual tension of being around Brita. She was a gorgeous and unique woman, full of passion *and* compassion, with what seemed to be a high moral ethic, which didn't explain that tawdry attempt to influence him in their earlier meeting. Despite that, he was drawn to her, a magnet to pure iron.

He shook his head and sighed. Probably best not to mix business with pleasure. Brita already had several reactions to taking direction from him, and romantic entanglement could only make that worse. He gave a wry chuckle.

That this was best didn't mean he had to like it.

~ ~ ~

By four p.m. he'd arrived off Key Largo, and drifting over the outer reef, managed to snag two yellowtail snappers. An hour later, he was moored inside the C-shaped cove, largely hidden behind a stand of coconut palms on the small peninsula extending from its southern border.

Derik spent the next hour readying the sloop for living aboard. Clothes hung in the closet, he set up personal care products in the head, and then donned a swimsuit and took a dip, snorkeling around the sloop. Back aboard, he stretched out on the foredeck, drying in the late afternoon sun.

He awakened from a short nap and checked his watch. His doubloons should come up for bidding in the next fifteen minutes, so he went below, powered up his tablet, thankful wi-fi was available at this somewhat remote location, and found the Sotheby's website, where he could follow the live auction. He poured some Johnny Walker's Red scotch over ice, settled at the dining table, and logged into the live auction page.

Just in time. His coins were three items away. Derik clicked on their number and whistled as he saw pre-sale bids at $165,000. He knew from experience live or phone bidders were likely to run that up. So far, the most he'd grossed for a four-coin lot at auction was $195,000. Today promised to be better.

His lot opened, and the auctioneer, whom he could see on the live stream, announced absentee bids, raising the price to $215,000. Two phone bidders ignited a short but furious competition, and the lot closed out at $275,000. After Sotheby's deducted the 20% seller's premium and costs, he'd netted about $220,000.

Derik chuckled as he closed his tablet. So far, he'd sold a hundred-fifty-two coins via auction and direct to dealers, netting nearly eight million dollars, and he had over eighteen-hundred left. Plus, seventeen of the twenty-five-pound, twenty-four-karat gold ingots. Not to mention the diamond, emerald, and ruby jewelry, and loose stones. He shook his head and wondered how he could manage to vend it all, and keep coming up with plausible reasons where it came from.

When he returned to Miami, he'd talk to Chick about setting up a charity trust and start putting some of the funds to good use. They had thirty-million deposited in a half-dozen banks in South Florida, the Caymans, and one still in Martinique, way more than they needed to fund their operation.

Derik filleted the snappers and pan-fried them on the galley's stove. A sweet potato was baking in his small propane oven, and a pre-prepared salad sat ready in the fridge.

He poured a cold Pinot Grigio and dined at a small, portable table on the aft deck, enjoying a cooling evening breeze and the gentle roll of the sloop.

His thoughts drifted to Brita Kruger. How nice if he could share something like this with her.

I wonder if she likes to sail? A frivolous thought since he'd managed to sabotage any possible connection outside of business. Was there any way to fix that? He really missed a meaningful female relationship. He mused over the twins. He known them less than three days, but their magical connection seemed eternal.

But that was eight years ago, and he'd intentionally sailed away from something glorious. They're gone, and this was now, and Brita was the first woman to fire that kind of stirring in his heart—and he had to admit, his loins. The problem was, she seemed interested only in their business connection, and he thought again, that was probably best.

At least he now knew he *was* open to love again, and that was a good thing. He carried his empty dishes into the galley, rinsed and stacked them, and still in bathing shorts, went for an evening snorkel around the sloop. Then early to bed, and a sail down the Keys tomorrow for some scuba diving. Time to put more bone fides into finding the largest treasure haul "never" discovered.

The gold bars and maybe jewelry this time. He'd turn off his cell phone and Android tablet so there'd be no GPS trail for anyone to trace to his newest "find."

As he drifted toward sleep, the vision of a tall blonde beauty, clad in a short, colorful skirt and sleeveless blouse, gracefully smacking tennis balls filled his head.

He smiled softly at his physical response, then slept.

~ 25 ~

At his desk, Derik poised over his desktop computer as he completed his report on his latest treasure "find." He'd send copies to the *Miami Herald, The Fort Lauderdale Sun-Sentinel,* and *The Palm Beach Post,* all to validate his growing fortune. He also copied his accountant so he could begin preparing the tax ramifications from the various sales, including the two-million-dollar cross. He scrupulously paid his federal taxes, not wanting to encourage any more investigations than necessary.

He glanced up as Chick strolled in.

"Back to the grind, I see." He settled on a chair. "Tanned and relaxed. Good weekend?"

"Yeah." Derik tilted back and interlocked his fingers, stretching them. "I 'found' four gold ingots and some diamond and ruby necklaces off Key Largo in a small coral cave." He winked and rotated his monitor for Chick to read his report.

"No sign of wreckage." He grinned. "It was only thirty-feet, so I'm guessing some long-ago buccaneer swam down and stashed it there, and then lost track of where it was. At least, that's the tale I'll tell."

"Of course. And lucky you," he chuckled, "just looking for a fat grouper to spear, and there it was."

"Makes a good story, huh?"

"Yeah, but at some point," Chick rose and closed the door

before returning to his seat, "we're gonna run out of credibility."

"I know." Derik sighed and leaned forward. "Maybe I'm gonna have to sail back into the Caribbean and revisit the actual cay. A nostalgic voyage, and luckily, this time I'll discover the cave and chest." He sat back. "The two skeletons are probably right where I left them."

"What about the French and Martinique. Won't they grab most of it?"

"I checked an International Boundaries map, and the two cays actually sit in international waters, so no one will have a legal claim on it."

"They'll try," Chick chuffed, "but I guess as long as you don't make port at Fort-de-France, you aughta be okay." He studied Derik. "That be a problem for you?"

"What?" Derik was scanning what he'd written.

"Not stopping at Martinique?"

"Huh?" His eyes swept back to his partner. "Stopping? Oh," he shrugged, "no, I don't think so. I'm committed to being here right now. I'll make the stop at the cays, sail back home, announce the find, and give the location. There'll only be the tax ramifications, and it's all capital gains."

"Okay, sounds good." He pushed out of his chair "Got a time table?"

"Not before we finish up with Kruger." He plucked up a report from his desk. "Looks like things are humming over there. I'm gonna stop by this afternoon, after I clean up my desk." He rose. "I need some time with her to discuss where we are and where we want to go next."

He gave a small sigh. "I got a hunch she's got the bit in her teeth, and may be overeager to rush into the next phase." He made a soft grunt. "She won't be too happy if I rein her in."

"Well, good luck, then, pard." Chick chuckled. "Better you than me. I ain't got your patience for debate." They bumped knuckles, and Chick strode away.

Derik watched him leave, then sighed and picked up his desk phone and punched a button, answered on the first ring.

"Yes, Derik?"

"Hey, Ginny. Call Ms. Kruger and tell her I'll be by at two to discuss progress. Ask her to keep at least two hours open."

"Got it, Boss. And I love your tan. Nice weekend?"

"Quiet and relaxing, and it turned out, also profitable. Just what I needed. Now, I'm back in the saddle, ready to go."

"I'll warn Ms. Kruger." She chuckled and disconnected.

Yeah, I wonder how that'll go? He returned to his seat and started scanning e-mails before putting finishing touches on his treasure-find announcement.

He looked forward to whatever was coming, a glimmer of hope still simmering deep inside that, somehow, he and Brita might get together. He groaned softly. *Not likely.*

~ 26 ~

Derik pushed through the glass door of Allure Attire and approached the receptionist who looked up and smiled.

"She's on the floor, Mr. Brand," waving at the entrance to the factory, "checking production. Go right in."

Derik nodded and headed for the door, and once inside, immediately spotted the tall blonde, hovering over a finishing table. Radiant in pastel blue, silk slacks and an aqua-patterned, V-neck blouse, she straightened and turned at seeing him. Her smile lit up the room, and he flushed at the blaze it also ignited inside him.

Damn! What a gorgeous woman. No need for cosmetics to accent that natural beauty. Brita exuded a warmth he hadn't witnessed in any lady he'd dallied with in years. A smile tilted his lips and he waved and headed her way, struggling to tamp down the heat she fired in him.

"Ahh, so tanned and relaxed. You had a wonderful weekend?"

A nod, not trusting vocal response at that instant.

She gave a "follow me" wave. "Come, see what we have created."

Derik tailed her to another finishing table where shorts, blouses, and colorful skirts lay.

"These are the first of our new tennis and pickleball lines." She plucked up a sleeveless shirt and held it against her upper body.

"Beautiful." Sounding a bit hoarse, he was thinking more of her than the pretty tog.

"What is really beautiful," she folded and replaced it, "is the orders that are piling in, after only one ad campaign."

"I heard." His heart finally back in place, he sounded a semblance of normal. "They're really that good?"

"Better." She pivoted and started for her office. "Come up stairs and I'll show you everything."

Derik trailed her up the metal staircase, mesmerized by the sway of her firm butt in the form-fitting silk. A picture of all the things he really wanted her to show him spooled through his mind. He chuffed quietly and shook his head.

Quit it. You're acting like some lewd lothario. His stride broke as he was struck by an epiphany. Despite a plethora of brief, steamy encounters, he was starved for love and a real relationship. Managing his insanely huge treasure, the total devotion to building his business, and the specter of two redheads, made it easy to avoid any emotional commitment. What was he running from? Derik shook his head and joined Brita at the top of the stairs.

"You okay?" Her eyebrows arched.

"Yeah, yeah." A chuckle. "Just thought of something I need to take care of." *How lame is that?*

"Good. You look a bit troubled." She turned to her office. "Anyhow, come in and I'll show you what's going on." She glanced back at him. "I'm somewhat embarrassed that I needed an outsider to see where Allure Attire should be headed."

Derik followed her through the entrance. "That's often the problem with many businesses. It's the old "forest for the trees" axiom. Some very creative people get caught up in their dream and don't see the need to venture onto a new path."

"You're right, of course." She settled behind her desk and woke up her computer. "My whole career has been immersed in haute couture clothing." She smiled and rotated the monitor toward him. "It took a very bright outsider to help me create this."

"Wow." Derik leaned in, their heads inches apart. "Those are purchase orders?" The warmth from her face and a waft of intoxicating *"eau* d'something" sent flaming mouse-feet racing down his spine.

"Only the first of seven pages, you darling man." She pivoted slightly, her moist, pink lips inches from his, begging to be kissed. "We have a six-week backlog, and we just got started."

Derik gritted his teeth and edged back, not sure where this alluring closeness was going. She was a business partner and showed no signs of seeking anything else. He didn't want to create tension that might sabotage what they were building.

"Terrific!" The word forced through a constricted throat, he swallowed hard. "If this keeps up, we'll have to increase our capacity, but I won't rush into that until we verify this is a sustained surge."

"Not even two more Singers and another cutting table?" She glanced through the glass at her factory. "I have room for that out there, and we shouldn't—"

"I'll agree to that." Derik stood back, creating a safe space between them. "Summer is arriving, and vendors need sports merchandise. Order the sewing machines and whatever else you need to support them."

"Good. I know where to get two nearly new ones immediately." Brita studied him. "We've got another ad shoot next week, and magazine and TV time booked. In light of all this," gesturing at the monitor, "should we still run them?"

"Certainly." Derik shoved his hands into his pockets, still struggling to control his heart. "We want to sustain long-term interest, and that requires promotion." Grinning. "If that happens, then we can look to real expansion."

Brita exhaled a sigh of relief. "Have you seen the finished TV ad?" Her finger flew over the keyboard, and a YouTube video materialized on the screen. "Here's the one we've been running during the Miami Open tennis tournament."

She hit ENTER, and Derik was again drawn down, almost cheek-to-cheek, as he watched the action on the monitor.

Brita, playing tennis and pickleball in three different outfits, then posing seductively as she praised the fashion and quality of her new sports line. The outfits looked terrific, and so did she. No wonder sales were soaring.

Derik pushed back and rose, hands again in his pockets to conceal what had grown very close by.

"That's great stuff." Moving to the front of her desk, he perched on a chair. "Golf promo is next?"

"Yep. A LPGA major tournament in Texas, I believe."

"Swell." He rubbed palms together. "Looks like you're well on the way to recovery. Quicker than I expected, and that's a good thing." They both laughed.

"So, maybe we should have a celebration." Brita leaned back, a smile dancing on those delectable lips. "A short, happy break from the hard work it took to get here."

"What d'ya have in mind? *Joe's Stone Crabs*, or something fancier?"

"Actually, I make a great wiener schnitzel ... my mama's recipe. Why don't you come by my place about seven-thirty? It's probably inconsistent with the so-called super-model persona, but I love to cook." Her grin widened. "I'm very good at it, too. Cocktails and dinner?"

"You're sure you want to do all that work?" Derik's brow wrinkled. "After a busy day here—"

"Exactly. That's how I wind down. This way I can share it with you. I owe you a lot." She nodded at the computer. "Not just that, which in itself is special, but for rescuing me from those scary Ukrainians." She came out of her chair and stepped to his side. "My white knight. Without your intervention, I could be laying in a ditch somewhere." Her eyes held his.

Derik was again finding breathing a chore. "Okay," he croaked, followed by a chuckle.

"It's a date. Seven-thirty." Was she just relaxed at everything going so well? At ease with him, or was there something more there? Could she possibly want him after the brutal way he'd treated her on their earlier encounter?

Derik was at a loss, so opted for wait-and-see.

~ ~ ~

Brita studied him as they descended the stairs and out the front, unsure of exactly what, if anything, was going on between them. She was more powerfully attracted to this hot and complicated guy than any man she'd ever known. And she'd managed to drive a wedge between them with her shameless behavior that first day over drinks.

Derik seemed at ease and not at all withdrawn from her, but was that the actions of someone seeking romance, or just one who was a friendly business associate? She was unsure, so she'd play this evening carefully until she understood *his* intensions. The success of their partnership was more vital than any possible love affair.

She turned to him on the walk, outside her entry door. "So, see you tonight then, at seven-thirty."

"Right. Shall I bring a bottle of wine?"

"Why not. A Pfalz Dornfelder is an excellent, reasonably priced German red that will go great with the schnitzel."

"See you then." Their eyes locked for a moment, then he nodded, smiled, and turned for his white Jaguar F-Type sports coupe, parked in their small, off-street lot.

Her heart tumbled in her breast as she returned to her shop, and wondered what the evening held for her.

~ 27 ~

Gorya picked up his buzzing cell phone and glanced at Alik. "It's Oleg. Maybe good news for change." He pressed the green button.

"*Da?* Ya got something?"

"Yeah, Cuz." Gorya had the phone on SPEAKER, sitting on a side table. "Kruger met with blond guy, Brand. I pick 'em up on long-range mic when they on street."

"So? Get on with it."

"Okay, Okay. Sounds like gonna have dinner at her place tonight. She cooking, and he arrive about seven-thirty."

"Her condo on Key Biscayne?" Gorya rose and began pacing.

"Nah. She sold that. At house in Coral Gables. That's where she hangs bra, nowadays."

"Ha! Perfect. We hit 'em tonight."

"Ya want me along, Cuz?"

"Yeah, sure. Extra backup good. I think guy carries, so gotta take him out quick," settling on his easy chair. "Love ta see bastard go slow and suffer, but not worth risk." Gorya caught Alik's eyes, who nodded.

"Want him dead, and girl not injured. Alik'll have hypo ta put her ta sleep. I'll handle blondie, and you cover our six."

"Sounds like plan, Boss. When d'ya wanna do this?"

"About eight-thirty. Give 'em chance to get mellow.

Maybe we catch 'em in sack. Make life easy."

"I'd love to hit sack with that babe," Oleg said, "but—"

"Ya gotta wait turn," Alik rumbled, "I got first pick on that sweet piece of ass."

"Okay, Cuz. I'm patient guy, but it don't look like they got that kinda relationship. Good-byes seemed very—what's word—oh, yeah. Platonic."

"Whatever," Gorya cut in. "Pretty soon, all babe will be eager for is next fix." He gave his brother a hard look. "Don't overdose her, and when hooked, we gotta manage fixes so she don't look like strung out addict." Gorya picked up the phone.

"Meet us at storage locker on Calle Ocho at eight, Oleg, and we go together from there." Disconnecting, he turned to Alik.

"I know ya don't care how strung-out babe is when ya fuck her, Bro, but we gotta manage this dame right. Keep her hooked and scared, but not doped up, and she'll bring big bucks." Moving to his desk, he woke up his computer.

"See if she got people ta worry about, so she plays ball, keep 'em safe."

"Good idea." Alik glanced at his brother and licked his lips. "Whatever, I'm gonna love breaking her in." He grabbed his crotch. "I get hard just thinking of it."

Gorya chuckled and shook his head. *What an animal.*

~ 28 ~

Derik, cradling a liter of wine, exited his white Jag coupe in the drive of the mocha-colored, CBS ranch house. His eyes swept the lighted Coral Gables street, lined with a variety of single-story houses, neatly spaced on large lots. A quite upscale but understated neighborhood. He'd passed a public park and playground on the next street. This was a fine place to raise a family, thoughts that had edged into his mind recently.

That scenario never occurred to him during his three, passionate, sexually draining dates with Karen Matsu, an affair ending badly two-months ago. Karen wanted something serious, but Derik sought an emotional tie much deeper than what that hot little babe could offer.

A house filled with kids and love only really occurred to him since he met Brita. Derik sighed and shrugged. Hadn't seemed likely, but maybe tonight's "celebration" would offer an opportunity to repair the damage his sharp tongue had wrought. Hope, as they say, springs eternal.

He strode up the drive, mounted the small portico and rang the video doorbell. A moment later, a smiling Brita stood in the open entry, ever lovely in lemon-yellow silk slacks and matching blouse. Delicious aromas of cooking veal wafted past her, and Derik was unsure if his watering mouth was the result of that odor, or the sight of the blond beauty.

"Ah." Her grin widened. "Right on time, and you've

brought the wine." She leaned in, took the bottle, and ushered him inside.

"Couldn't find the one you mentioned, so I hope this works. It *is* a German red, however," following behind and enjoying the view, en route to her den.

Brita glanced at the bottle and nodded. "This is fine." She pivoted to him. "Have a seat while I open this so it can breathe." She moved toward her kitchen and looked back.

"The schnitzel needs another ten minutes. I have some mini-meatballs and warm Brie and crackers for appetizers on the table there. Scotch is your drink, right?"

"Yep." He settled on a velour armchair. "On the rocks."

"Okay." She disappeared through a doorway. "Be back in a minute with the drinks."

Derik gazed at the now empty doorway and wondered where this was going? It had all the markings of a date, but with none of usual anticipation. At the coffee table, he selected some meatballs and two crackers slathered with the warm, gooey Brie, all on a small plate. Cocktail forks were there for the meatballs which were warm and juicy.

Brita returned with a tumbler of iced scotch and a white wine for her. She settled on a loveseat to his right and helped herself to the hors d'oevers. "How are they? The meatballs are from Costco."

"Tasty." Derik sipped his scotch. "Looks like you went all-out."

"Not really." A small giggle. "I usually have these in the freezer, ready when needed." Brita tasted her wine, the rose. "The veal should be ready." She gestured toward the dining room. "Have a seat and I'll serve."

Derik stood, scotch in hand, and stepped toward the doorway. "Need a hand with anything?"

"Nope. It'll just be two plates. Salads are already on the

table." Carrying her wine, she disappeared into the kitchen.

On entering the dining room, Derik found a rosewood pedestal dining table that seated six, with two places set. He set his drink on the placemat and was about to take a seat when Brita called.

"Derik!" Her voice strained. "Can you come in here for a moment." A brief pause. "Quickly!" Harsher.

He stepped away from the table and strode into the adjoining kitchen. Brita hovered near a wall that sported an answer pad for her doorbell monitor.

"Look!" A finger jabbed at an image on the video monitor.

"What the hell!" His mouth screwed into a snarl. "Shit! That looks like one of the Kolodenko's. And there's another guy with him." Derik pulled back. "Not the brother, though. So, where's—?"

He held up a hand. "Listen. The back door," glancing at the connecting laundry room and the entry door beyond.

"Derik! What's happening? Do you think—?"

"They're looking for more than their loan." He grabbed her hands. "I think they're here for you, Brita. Damn it."

"What?" Her voice barely a squeak.

"I left my ankle gun at home."

"You carry a gun?" Her eyes flared

"Yeah. I'm a very rich guy, and there's lots of bad people out there. Never occurred to me I'd need it tonight." Eyes sweeping the room, he snatched up a large carving knife, and towing her behind, raced into the next room.

"You got any weapons?"

"A twelve-gauge pump, but it's in a gun safe in my garage."

"No good." They were in the family room, and he spied a trophy case. He hurried over and extracted a heavy cup.

"Make yourself scarce, Brita." There was a loud thump at the front door. "And call 911." Two steps brought him to the wall at the hinge side of the door, holding the trophy as a club.

Brita scooted into the dining room, dialing her cell phone.

~ 29 ~

The raised-panel door imploded with a loud boom, the door jamb splintered, and two men charged inside. Gorya Kolodenko lead the way, carrying a large pistol. Derik stepped out and swung his club, catching the Ukrainian across the temple, sending him tumbling to the floor. His gun skittered across the floor and into the den.

The second man whirled, a stiletto in hand. Derik snatched his arm and threw a flat hand chop at his throat, but it was fended off, just as the rear door burst open and Alik Kolodenko rushed in.

Derik pivoted, the guys arm still in his grasp, and used body leverage to spin him away as the glittering blade clattered away. A quick pivot to meet the bull rush of the bigger brother. No chance to grab the knife or gun, so he'd have to rely on his well-honed martial arts skills.

Derik sidestepped, ducked, and threw a chop at man's collarbone close to his neck. Alik turned and shrugged.

"You gonna need more'n that, fancy pants," advancing, fists balled, ready to punch.

Derik dance backward, seeking an opening, and hoped his martial arts training would work on a brute of this size. From the corner of his eye, he saw the third attacker regain his feet and stagger for the pistol. He gasped as Brita hurtled in and raced for gun, but he saw no more as Alik threw a punch, catching him on the shoulder. Derik bounced back, able to maintain his feet. He'd been hit as hard by a blitzing linebacker, but that was over a decade ago. Derik shook his head and struggled to clear his vision.

Eyes fastened on his attacker, he was still aware of a scuffle behind him, punctuated by a resounding thud, an "oof," and the thump of someone hitting the floor. Brita was down, and if he didn't finish this now, she may be gone. Stepping in, he tried to goad Alik into a charge.

It worked. The brute came hard, arms spread wide. Derik dropped and did a leg sweep while trying to deliver a kick to Alik's groin, but he only caught thigh. The hulk stumbled and dropped to his knees, but despite Derik's quickness, he managed to grab Derik's shoulder. Brute strength won out as he swept the smaller man into a bearhug.

Derik somehow kept both arms free. He gasped for breath from the pressure against his ribs, and slammed his elbows onto the collar bones, close to the neck. Alik grunted, then groaned as Derik repeated the blow twice more, and the crushing grip loosened.

Derik twisted and ducked, managing to slink free. He snatched Alik high on the bicep, spun around, and seized his other shoulder from behind, leaping onto his back. Both legs circled the big man's waist, his ankles hooked together as his arm sought a choke hold. Alik roared and bucked, trying to throw Derik off, but he was locked on and couldn't be shaken.

Alik staggered around snatching at Derik's arms but they remained secure, squeezing the breath from him. The Ukrainian slammed backward into the wall, knocking the wind from Derik and smacking his head, but he hung on and increased the pressure. The brute pitched backward, dropping hard onto his assailant's back as they hit the floor, but Derik gritted his teeth and still hung on, applying even more force.

Alik rolled back and forth to no avail, eventually scrabbling to hands and knees, bucking and pitching, but Derik hung on. Shielded by the bulk of the man and vision blurred by the beating he took, Derik couldn't find Brita or the third attacker. He had to finish this brute at get to her aid before she disappeared. His jaw clenched, driving past the agony in his ribs and back from the pounding he'd taken, he put all he had left into his choke hold.

Success, finally. Alik emitted a soft chuff and collapsed on the floor, with Derik still on top. Derik staggered free, lurched to a wobbly stance, and scanned the room. He blinked twice and swiped at his eyes, stunned at what he saw.

Brita sat on the third guys ass, binding his hands behind him with duct tape. Gorya's 9mm was tucked in her waistband, and that Kolodenko's hand and feet were already bound.

"Brita." Derik staggered toward her. "What the hell—?"

"Oh, Derik." She rushed to him. "Are you okay?" She peeked a the prone Alik. "I wanted to help you but had to be sure these two couldn't get back into the fray." Her voice now heavily German-accented. "I was terrified."

Derik took her hand and walked over to the third guy, still unconscious on the floor. He plucked up the roll of duct tape and squeezed Brita's hand.

"Not too scared to level this thug." A glance at her. "What happened?"

"My Tae Kwon Do training." She shivered. "A straight leg kick to his chin as he was grabbing for the gun." She leaned against him. "A haymaker, you Americans call it. Never actually used it in a fight, and it hurt like hell." She managed a shaky chuckle. "I learned the art mostly for conditioning."

"Well, it probably saved my life—and yours. If he'd got to

the gun while I was still struggling with the hulk over there
....."

Derik trailed off, no more needing to be said. He returned to Alik, still face down on the floor, and bound his hands and feet. Then he noticed something in his back pocket—a ten-inch plastic cylinder. Derik lifted it out and opened the cap, spilling the contents onto his hand.

"Son-of-a-bitch."

"What—what is that?" Brita touched the tube. "A hypodermic?"

"Shit! Now I understand." His head jerked up at the wail of fast-approaching police. "I knew there was more to this than just the loan."

"What do you mean?" She grabbed his arm. "What else?"

"They wanted to snatch you, hook you on dope, and probably turn ya into a high-priced hooker." She came weeping into his arms, and he caressed the back of her head as she shuddered with sobs.

"I dug into their background after we paid 'em off. Their main business is prostitution—probably human trafficking."

"Oh, *mein gott*." Her arm circled his back. "You saved me—again." She leaned her head back, eyes locked on his. "Twice you saved me from these—these monsters."

He continued to press her to him, savoring her warmth and the electricity prickling every nerve, as he held her eyes.

Those orbs now dry, she sighed. "Can we now stop playing these games, my White Knight. You are the man—" Her words were cut off by his mouth against hers. Lips parted and tongues dueled with growing passion.

And then the police charged through the door, seeking explanations. Romance would have to wait while things were sorted out and the three villains were dragged into waiting patrol cars for a trip to lockup.

~ 30 ~

Derik perched on the loveseat, Brita snuggled against him, her head on his shoulder. They'd just finished giving their version of what had occurred to a wiry little detective, Jack Harris, from Miami Homicide.

They watched as the Kolodenko brothers were marched off to awaiting patrol cars. The third hoodlum, apparently a cousin, was carted away by paramedics, not yet recovered from Brita's "haymaker" kick to his jaw. Their weapons had been gathered, along with Brita's track trophy from high school in Bonn, Germany. Not surprisingly, it was for high-jump. They rose as the detective approached, Brita still clinging to Derik's side.

"Okay, folks," Harris said, "I think I got all we need for the moment. We'll get outta your hair now. You might have to come down to HQ at some point if the Boss wants a formal statement." He glanced out the door and chuckled. "Those mutts got a lot more'n they expected. That'll teach 'em not to mess with a tough guy's girl." He shook Derik's hand and looked at Brita.

"You got quite a boyfriend here, miss, and you didn't do too bad, either." His eyes swept from one to the other. "You guys might want to go to a hotel or something, with both door jambs broken." Harris turned to leave.

"Anyway, we'll let you know if we need anything else." And he was out the door.

Derik drew Brita around to face him, both arms clasped around her waist.

"What d'ya think? Should I take you to a hotel?"

"Will you stay with me here?" Her eyes wide, her arms around his neck.

"Yes, if that's what you want."

"More than anything, my darling." She rose on her toes for a gentle, lingering kiss. They parted slightly, her eyes devouring his, her breath coming in small gasps.

"Yes." He held her tighter. "But I never thought—after the things I said that day—"

"Deserved," her voice breathy. "But all water gone under that famous bridge. All I've been able to think about—"

"Me too." The next kiss was filled with passion pent-up from weeks of denial. They lingered there, their mouths exploring each other's, then their eyes, their necks, and ears. Derik stepped back, panting, and glanced over his shoulder.

"Let me try to secure the doors somewhat, just to feel safe." The loveseat was dragged across the room and wedged against the front door. A heavy armchair went into the laundry room to seal that entry. Glasses from the kitchen were balanced on the arms of both seats. If someone shoved against either door, they'd fall and make a clatter. Then his hand in hers, she led him to her master suite.

As they reached the side of her queen-size bed, Derik spun Brita into his arms, tight against him, eyes locked. The kiss began slowly, one hand on his neck as the other slid up his cheek and into his long, blond hair. Derik drew her pelvis against his, already hardening there, and the kiss grew more intense. He groped her butt while the other hand slid under her blouse and found firm breasts unfettered by a bra. A tweak of her nipples drew a gasp and even more intense kisses.

Minutes slid by as their fingers and lips kindled one blaze greater than the last. Brita reached down, undid his belt, unzipped the fly, and his pants were gone. Seconds later her slack pooled in a pile on the floor, with his knit shirt and her blouse quick to follow. With only underpants remaining, he slid onto the bed pulling her atop of him, where they continued their oral attacks.

Derik rolled over, Brita beneath him and rose to his knees. His tongue trailed across a cheek, down her neck, and into the valley between two luscious mounds of flesh, lavishing oral pleasure on one, then the other, sucking and tweaking each erect nipple, along with a teasing trail of fingertips.

Brita moaned and writhed, breathless, but still managed to remove his Jockeys. Her silk Bikini quickly followed as Derik's mouth and skilled fingers ventured from her breast to her belly, and then further south. The warm lips of her pussy were open and wet, and he savored its sweet nectar.

"Oh, Derik! Oh, God, that's so wonderful." Panting hard, she touched his shoulder. "Flip around so I can do you too, darling." Her voice breathy with ardor.

He obliged, never stopping his own attack, and shivered as Brita's fingers trailed over his raging hard-on, as she licked and sucked on his "boys." Their erotic attacks continued— and then it was time to move on. Derik raised his head and did a one-eighty, hovering over her, his eyes searching hers.

"Yes, darling, yes. I need you in me—*now*."

"I don't have a condom." His eyebrows arched.

"I don't care." She grasped behind his neck, pressing him down for a wet kiss.

"Fuck me, Derik." Brita hissed and spread her long, lovely legs. Arching back, he entered her, and those strong gams locked around his waist, her arms circled his neck as they thrust together with ever growing urgency.

Ardor long delayed was too-quickly slaked, Brita

emitting a small scream and he a shuddering moan as they came, he seconds before her.

Bodies slick with perspiration, he laid atop her, his dick still encompassed in her pulsing pussy, sucking him dry.

They hung together for several minutes, fingers fluttering and mouths gentle adventurers.

"I was so terrified I'd driven you away that foolish day," she whispered. "I realized too late you were the man I've sought for years." She sighed and lifted her head for a gentle kiss.

"Me too, beautiful." A hand brushed over her askew pixie cut. "You're the first woman in many years that I've felt a connection to, other than sex." His lips brushed her eyes.

"But I'm sure you've seen women, even if only for mutual physical pleasure." She cupped his face in her hands. "I've been with *no one* since I started by business." She pulled him down, savoring the warmth and electric tingles that contact caused. "My life has been work, work, work. I avoided romantic relationships, because in the fashion industry, more often than not, they lead to ruin."

Derik rolled to one side and cradled Brita in his arm, holding her snuggled close, her head on his chest.

He chuckled. "So, you were waiting for me, huh?"

"Don't laugh." She raised her head, eyes on his. "You're *exactly* who I was waiting for. I just never expected you to be my White Knight too." She brushed his lips with hers.

"And you, Derik? Who were you waiting for?"

A sighed as he pulled free and rose to his knees to straddle her pelvis. "*You*, it seems, my love. Unlike you, I've *have* had many very brief, sexual flings ever since returning home after weathering that hurricane eight-years-ago, but nothing ever stuck. It was always two people enjoying sex together and moving on. But this is *very* different."

He leaned forward for a kiss that grew in intensity as his fingers revisited her body, rambling in a tantalizing voyage across her neck, breasts, and belly.

"Let me show you."

Lips trailed fingers until his tongue found a second set of lips, open, wet, and emitting an intoxicating nectar.

"Oh, *gott*." She trembled. "Yes, my darling, *yes*. Already, I am about to cum." Hands in his hair, Brita arched her back and thrust up to meet his attack. She shuddered, wailed, and pressed his face tighter against her pulsing pussy. Then she collapsed, and Derik slid up, body to body, for a tender kiss.

"I hope that was worth the wait," he murmured into her ear.

"Oh, yes, *Liebchen*." She giggled. "You've even made me revert to German again." She caressed his cheek. "But this is wonder I've never experienced. I hope I won't have to wait long for more." She kissed him. "You have many years to make up for. Let me help you get ready." Her fingers trailed down his belly and found a surprise.

"Oh, my." She laughed. "It appears you need no help from me after all."

He cut her off with an ardent kiss.

"You in my arms is all the help I need." Derik began another leisurely voyage across her lovely body, tweaking one erogenous zone after another.

"This is a Garden of Eden," he murmured, "and I'm tasting the forbidden fruit."

Soon he entered her, and they began another carnal dance of love, first a waltz, but climaxing with a frenzied tango.

They continued multiple passionate releases well into the night before sleep found them, wrapped in each other's arms.

Life had changed for both, but they had no inkling of exactly how much.

~ 31 ~

"Oh, Derik."

He lurched awake. "Wow!" Brita was wrapped in his arms, snuggled half atop of him, her face hovered inches above his.

A wry smile creased her lips as she closed the gap, those sweet, cherry-red cupid bows brushing his with a tender kiss.

"You were dreaming, my darling, and squeezing very tightly." She chuckled. "I liked it."

"Yes, we were aboard my boat, and you were drifting away. I dove in and grabbed you, and ..." A pause and a glance at his Rolex, still on his wrist.

"Geeze, it's after ten." Fingers through her short, pixie cut and he smiled. "We've slept half the morning away." He rolled up, but kept Brita perched on his lap, reluctant to part with her.

"Well, we *did* have a very busy night." She snaked her arms around his neck and delivered a more intense kiss. "We didn't sleep until almost four."

"Yeah, and it seems to me we managed an encore just at dawn." His hand skimmed across her velvety skin. "You finally exhausted me."

"I've ... I've never done anything like this before." Her eyes dropped, and a pink flush tinged her apple cheeks.

"What?" His finger under her chin lifted her face. "Make love all night? I know this wasn't your first—"

"No, no." She slipped off his lap, perched next to him on the bed's edge, and drew the sheet across her waist. "I didn't mean that. But I've never been so filled with—" she paused, eyes fastened on his, "—with such a *need*. It was my business that filled my life. Proving I was more than an empty-headed bimbo, sashaying down a runway, I guess." Fingers caressed his stubbled cheek, and a soft smile tweaked her lips.

"I had no idea what I was missing." She edged closer, her nipples teasing his breast, glistening eyes wide. The tender kiss quickly morphed into heated passion, one arm around his neck, the other hand in his hair.

Derik slid onto his back, pulling her glorious body on top of his, hands roaming cross her back and buttocks. They rolled over and he drew reluctant lips from hers to begin their stroll across her breasts, belly, and finally, between her spread legs. His tongue ventured through a gossamer forest of fine blonde hair and into opening lips, glistening wet and begging for attention.

Brita quivered and shook, her hands tangled in his long, curly locks, as she muttered soft moans of pleasure.

"Yes, *mein Liebling*, yes." She shuddered. "Oh, god, I'm cumming!" And she did, amazed at her fourth orgasm of their evening together.

Derik pushed up and licked the taste of her from his lips. "There's more to come, lover." He slid forward and she raised her legs to bent knees as he entered her. She locked arms around his back and managed to roll over with her now on top.

"My turn," she whispered, and with him still trapped inside her, wet and tight, she began her ride as he thrust up against her. She leaned down and began tongue dueling kisses as his hands caressed her breasts. Growls, moans filled the air as they surged into a frenzied dance of love.

"Mein gott," she panted, "I'm going to cum again!" She reared back and her fingers raked his chest as she squealed, her body shuddered, but she continued to surge, her slick, velvety glove pulsing around his turgid rod until he grunted with his release.

Brita collapsed against him, their sweat-slickened body hot with waning passion, his receding penis still trapped inside her.

"Wow, Babe," He murmured in her ear. "It's been ages since I got it up five times in a single night." A glance at the window. "Well, night and morning, anyway." Said with a chuckle. He kissed her cheek, nestled close to his, his hands gentle venturers across still-moist skin. "I'd almost forgotten the difference between having sex and making love."

"I guess I've never made love before." She lifted her head, eyes on his, and peppered his nose and cheeks with tiny kisses. "At least nothing that ever felt like *this,* and it's been a long time since I've known anything but my own fingers." Her cheeks turned rosy, and she laid her head on his chest. "That was embarrassing." She giggled softly, then rolled off to lay next to him, her head propped up on one hand.

"So, does that mean we *are* in love, Derik?" She sighed. "I've never been."

"I don't know." His fingers danced across her cheek and neck. "Love's supposed to take a while, but the only other time I've felt like this was just as quick. The fabled thunderbolt."

"Eight years ago, you've mentioned." She snared his roaming hand and kissed it. "What happened then?"

"It couldn't work the way things stood at the time—and I had to sail home." He pushed to his seat, back against the headboard. "It was in Martinique, and I lived in Florida."

"Martinique? In the Caribbean?" She sat up, legs

crossed, a blonde goddess. "You were sailing alone in a hurricane, weren't you?" She grinned. "I did some on-line research into my new benefactor."

"Smart move, darling." He chuckled. "And speaking of sailing, ever done it?"

"Oh, yes, many times on a sixty-foot ketch in the Med." She wiggled next to him. "Belonged to one of the European designers, and he frequently guested many of the girls and so-called important clients." She grimaced and shook her head.

"The clients were looking to party with the girls, and a lot of that went on in the two staterooms." She glanced sidewise at him.

"Not me, though. I was up by the helm, learning the basics of sailing, or just sunbathing on the deck." She chuffed. "Didn't make the designer happy, but screw him."

Derik rose and pulled her onto her feet and into his arms for a standing snuggle.

"I still own that sailboat." He kissed her neck. "Let's dress and get some breakfast and then go for a sail." Derik glanced at the digital clock squatting on the nightstand. "It's still early. Maybe we'll run down to the keys and spend the night on the boat. Shed the tension from yesterday and relax."

"Sounds wonderful," she leaned back in his arms, "but can we afford to get away right now?"

"Two days?" Derik nodded. "Don't see why not. I'll call my very capable partner to give him a head's up, and you can do the same." His lips tilted up. "Got an idea Chick will be very happy about that."

"Okay. I'm pumped." She wiggled free. "Let me retrieve an appropriate sailing outfit, and I'll whip up some pancakes." She gathered her clothes from the previous evening. "I've got fresh blueberries for that."

"Yum." He started to dress. "Don't forget to bring a bathing suit. Something I expect you'll look stunning in." Derik chuckled. "I'll get my things when we get to Bal Harbor." He followed her toward the kitchen.

"I'll have Chick arrange for someone to fix your doors while we're gone." A peek at his watch. "With any luck, we'll be on the water by one."

"Sounds wonderful." She pivoted to him and took his face between her hand for a tender kiss.

"This is the happiest I've been in—well, I can't remember when." She turned and went about making breakfast, filled with a calmness not known for many months.

~ 32 ~

The *Martinique*'s diesel drove her through the rolling swells of the Haulover Inlet, and once clear of the breakwaters, Derik deployed full sail and jib, quartering against a fifteen-knot northeasterly breeze.

Clad in swim trunks and a sleeveless tee, he hunkered at the helm, one hand on the wheel and his other arm tight around Brita's waist. He glanced at her, delectably decked out in a scanty black bikini.

"Wow!" she sputtered at taking a face full of cold spray hurled at them by the wind. "That was chilly." She giggled, her hand stroking his neck.

"Yeah, but refreshing in this heat." He scanned his Rolex Mariner. "Another ten minutes and we can tack more southerly. Put the wind on our aft port beam. A couple of hours to Elliot Key, and then three more to Key Largo."

"Sounds glorious." She kissed his cheek. "That where we'll spend the night?"

"Yep. Got a little, protected cove we can snuggle into. We'll stop over the reef and catch some snapper for dinner." The yacht was steered ten-degrees to starboard in a successful attempt to lessen the rain of salty spray dousing them.

"You sound pretty confident." Brita slipped free of his grasp and plastered herself against his back, both arms circling his chest, her cheek against his moist neck. "I thought fishing is always unpredictable."

"Not when you've got a block of frozen chum and a tub full of live shrimp." He reached back and patted her rump. "I know a spot loaded with yellowtails. Won't be a problem."

"Yum. Those are the tasty little critters I often order at Joe's."

"These will be even better. Nothing like snatching a fish from the sea and going directly into the pan." He studied his billowing sail, rippling in the quartering wind, and the roll of the following sea.

"Standby to come about to a starboard tack." Derik caught her eyes. "Watch for the swinging boom."

"Gotcha." She stood back and eyed the main sail boom, ready to duck when it swept across the deck as they came about to catch a more favorable wind.

The maneuver completed and now on a more weather-friendly reach, they hurried south, making a good seven knots. If nothing changed, they'd be anchored in safe harbor by late afternoon.

~ ~ ~

Derik furled *Martinique*'s sails and used its diesel to motor the last few hundred yards into his special cove on the eastern shore of Key Largo.

They'd spent a productive hour over the middle reef, a half-mile offshore, using spinning rods and live shrimp to snag six "flag" yellowtails and one ten-pound hog fish, often mistakenly called hog snapper. The latter inhaled Brita's shrimp near the surface, just as they were about to quit. It gave a spirited tussle on the light rod. He grinned, watching her squeal with glee as her husky prey dove for the bottom.

"It's heading for a cave to try to cut you off, Brit," Derik cried, one arm around her waist for support.

"Not on my watch," she growled through gritted teeth as she tightened the reel's drag a smidge. The light rod bowed double, its butt braced against her chest. Brita's determination won out, and six-minutes later, Derik netted the reddish fish.

"Woo-ee." She pumped her fist. "Gotcha!" She dropped the rod on the deck and leaped on Derik, wrapping him with her arms and legs, laughing and peppering him with kisses. "*That* was fun."

He staggered under her attack and stumbled backward to plop onto a portable deck chair, his lover still tangled in his arms. Kisses of joy soon morphed into those of passion, and ten minutes passed before they came up for air.

"I love this, *Liebling*," she panted. "The sea, sailing with you, this fishing—just *being* with you." They hovered, faces inches apart, eyes rapt. Her tongue trolled slowly across her upper lip, and she cradled his head between her hands.

"You are my White Knight, my Lancelot, and I am happily falling in love with you." She drew his lips to hers and pressed her scantily-covered breast tightly against his bare chest, the kiss more intense than hunger alone.

Derik slipped an arm under her legs and struggled to his feet, Brita cradled in his arms, their lips still busy. He bore her to the cabin's hatch, separating to climb down the small ladder and scurried across the lounge and into the one stateroom where they sprawled on the queen-size bed, bound together now by something more than passion.

On hands and knees, Derik loomed over her. "I wasn't sure I'd ever fall in love again, my darling, but you've changed that." He leaned in and placed soft kisses on her eyes and cheeks. "You've set me free to love again."

"Again?" she whispered, her eyebrows arched. "You've

been in love before? Martinique?"

"Long past. I'll tell you about it another time." Lying next to her, his fingers trailing over an arched neck and firm breasts, now magically bare of her bikini top.

"Martinique?" She repeated and sighed with pleasure, her hand sliding up his neck and into his hair.

"Yes, but another time, darling. Now, there is only you." His lips followed his fingers, tongue teasing behind an ear, down her throat, then venturing to a nipple standing tall atop a magnificent mound of flesh. Derik swirled, licked, tweaked, and sucked on it, drawing shudders and soft keening from his paramour. He teased across her lower chest, lapped for a moment at her bellybutton, then continued down through a soft forest of silky hair to moist lips, opening in welcome to his approach.

Brita quaked at the monsoon of passion engulfing her, more intense each time they made love. Her heart thundered against her ribs as electric tingles bombarded her skin. She snatched away Derik's trunks, and he straddled her head, his rigid cock inches from her face, while he continued his oral assault on her soaking pussy.

Pink polished nails trailed the length of his throbbing dick, and she raised her head to kiss and tongue-tease his balls, finally taking them into her mouth. She sucked and licked each, bringing moans and quivers from her love. Derik intensified his attack on her clit, sucking, licking, twirling his tongue, with one finger inside, questing for the legendary G-spot.

"Mein Gott!" Thunderbolts laced Brita's body, her pelvis arched and thrusted against him, and she came in a quivering torrent, fluids soaking his face, a fervid groan echoing throughout the cabin. Her arms circled his butt and she crushed him to her, slathering his cock with tongue and

lips.

"Oh, damn," he grunted, and ejaculated with multiple spurts across her chest, white puddles of semen pooling on her belly. He laid atop her for a moment, quieting his heart, then rolled off and rotated to lay beside her.

"Damn, Brit, that was intense." He stroked her cheek and traced her lips. "Don't think I've ever cum like that before." His head cocked at a "pat, pat, pat" coming from the cockpit. Grinning, he planted a kiss on Brita's smiling lips.

"I'd better snare that hog fish off the deck before he manages to jump overboard." Exiting the bed, he pulled on his trunks. "I'll get it on ice while you clean up." He chuckled. "I kinda made a mess there, didn't I?"

"It's a lovely mess." She giggled. "And I'm glad I was able to be its instigator."

"Me too." As he headed for the gangway.

~ ~ ~

Martinique, anchored well inside the protective cove, swung slowly to the breeze and quiet lap of gentle wavelets. Brita laid nude on the forward deck, savoring the last of the afternoon's sun, soon to disappear over the coconut palmed shoreline. The soft hum of his diesel generator and the far-off shriek of gulls were the only sounds breaking the still over the water.

Derik hovered over his skillet on the propane stove, tending four fillets of yellowtail snapper, sautéing in butter and his special blend of seasoning. Miniature red potatoes were browning on the other burner and frozen asparagus just finished in the boats small microwave. Two bowls of packaged mixed greens sat on the dining table adjacent to the galley. Derik flipped the fillets and smiled. Smelled as good as they would taste.

"Brita, dinner's ready." He spied her through a narrow window, sprawled across the front deck. "C'mon down and pour some wine." Derik sighed, comfortably tired, and very happy. He hadn't been so romantically consumed in over eight years, and was happy that at thirty-two, he wasn't "over the hill" yet in ability to perform.

Derik thought of how, after they finally got their act back together over the reef ... and what a glorious act it'd been ... they'd run the boat into the cove and anchored. Masks, snorkels, and fins donned, they went for a swim. The water was not yet summer hot, and the little bay was resplendent with colorful, small fish. Two large crawfish—lobsters to some—were spotted, nestled inside small crevices in the rocky bottom, but they had tasty fish ready for dinner and no large pot to steam the crustaceans in. If still there in the morning, he might try to take and ice them for later, back in Miami.

They'd floated leisurely across the surface and took in the scene, Brita excited at the crawfish, and then animatedly pulling his arm and pointing at a long fish sliding by.

"Barracuda?" she managed to bubble through the water.

Derik shook his head and gurgled, "hound fish," then gave a "safe" wave of his hand to assure it was harmless.

Derik chuckled now, thinking of that and the following minutes, when they swam up to a miniscule beach to lay together and suck in the pastoral ambiance. The next thing he knew, they were making love again, this time finishing more conventionally with her on top, his dick buried deep inside her pulsing kitty. Back on the yacht, she laid on the deck for an air dry as he started dinner.

He was drawn from musing as Brita descended the ladder of the hatch and paused, hands on still bare hips.

"That smells glorious." She sidled over and draped herself across his back, head hovering beside his, and surveyed the stove. The press of her breasts on his skin and her pussy against his ass sent electric shivers lacing through him.

"Behave, dammit," muttered with a chuckle, a hand reaching back to pat her butt. "Dinner is almost ready." He pivoted and wrapped her in his arms. "You might wanna put on a t-shirt and shorts. It's gonna get cool once the sun sets."

"Okay." She planted a kiss on his nose and wiggled free. "And I still have to pour the wine. Pinot grigio?"

"Yep. There's a bottle in the fridge." Derik turned back to the stove and lightly prodded the fish. Done. It should be a criminal act to overcook yellowtail, a true delicacy when properly rendered.

Ninety-minutes later, they laid nestled together on a blanket spread on the front deck, bathed by an ocean-cooled breeze, and gazed at the sky, an ebony canvas spewed with winking diamonds.

Brita turned to Derik, snuggled a bit tighter, and pecked his cheek. She chuffed and shook her head. "Strange that if it weren't for the threat from those Ukrainian mobsters, I might never have met the love of my life. And if I'd thought at the time to sell the Key Biscayne condo, I would never have needed their money, or you to save me from them."

"Life's full of 'if's,' baby." She was partially atop him, and they shared a gentle kiss. "Another one ... if you had done all that and didn't change your business plan, we still may have found each other."

"Lording that up over me, huh." She arched her neck and nodded. Her grin held no animosity.

"No," he chuckled, "but the facts are the facts. I gotta say,

I also owe those bastards a heartfelt thanks, because without them, I may have been mired again without real love."

"Again, you said?" Her sapphire eyes held his, a hand brushing his cheek. "You said you'd tell me about that."

"I will, but not now." He drew her lips to his for a gentle yet urgent kiss.

"Tonight, this place—it's all about you, Brita. About *us*." His arms tightened with a warm hug. "Just us."

Her heart skipped happily in her breast, and she succumbed to her love and the ambiance of the evening. Kisses became more heated, caresses more electric, and soon they again soared into a newly discovered realm of Nirvana.

Only *they* existed in that magical moment.

The world around them would be real enough tomorrow.

~ 33 ~

Derik stepped off the stern and onto his dock as Brita hopped from the front deck, each with a mooring line in hand. *Martinique* was quickly snubbed to sturdy cleats, firmly against three rubber bumpers, already hung in place.

"Good job, mate." He relished the sight of her in denim short-shorts, bare-waist below a red checkered half-shirt.

"Thankee, Cap'n." She grinned and tossed off a credible salute.

Derik took her hand, drew her into his arms, their lips quickly engaged in a gentle kiss. He stepped back and chuckled.

"Best crew I've ever had." He snickered as she swept into a curtsy. "But don't get cocky. Not too high a bar to fill, 'cause you're the *only* crew I've ever had."

They giggled as he hefted a large cooler, and they strode arm-in-arm down the weathered-teak-planked pier toward his home. Derik glanced at his watch.

"I'm gonna get these fish on ice, hose down the boat, and scrub the deck." They paused as they reached his yard. "Here's a key to the house ..." he studied her for a moment, "which you can keep, if you'd like."

She glanced at the key, attached to a pear-shaped plastic disc, and then back at Derik, her eyebrows arched. "Okay. I guess after this weekend, this makes sense."

"Me too," with a grin. "So, I'll be maybe a half-hour with

the boat. You can get your stuff from the house and head back to town. When I'm finished getting the boat cleaned up, I'll go to my office for a couple of hours, just to check in and see what's what." He paused and tugged at her arm.

"Look," both her hands in his "I'm not expecting you to move in. At least, not so soon. But it's there if you want to come over ... any time."

"How about tonight?" She squeezed his fingers.

"Works for me." His chuckle was filled with warmth. "Seems like I can't get enough of you, gorgeous."

"Likewise, Sir Lancelot." Her smile lit up the air. "I'll change and run down to my shop to check on a few things. Seven o'clock work?"

"Perfect. I'll grill some of that hog fish, and there's a nearby farmer's market where I can get whatever else I need."

She melted into his arms for several minutes of teasing lips and fencing tongues, more the warmth of love than blazing passion.

They separated, each surfeit with pleasure as they hurried onto their own tasks, filled with a heated glow and hungers not yet fully slaked.

They'd stepped into new worlds, unexpected but joyfully embraced.

~ ~ ~

Derik strode into his office reception area sporting white linen slacks and a white-collared, robin-egg blue polo shirt. Ginny Mendoza, perched at reception, was collating files.

"Hey, Boss," she waved, "didn't expect you 'til tomorrow."

He grinned and returned the wave. "Got back early and

thought I'd come in to see if you guys managed to stay outta trouble while I was gone."

"Looking mighty nautical there, Derik." She eased back and studied him. "Have a good time?"

"Indescribable, kiddo." Derik nodded toward the office. "Chick in?"

"Yessir. In his office, I believe."

"Okay. That's where I'm headed if you need me."

"Gotcha." Ginny tossed off a flippant salute and returned to her paperwork.

He pushed through the inner door, happy he'd created more of a family with his people than just a work environment. Besides Ginny and Chick, Charlie Akata, a financial wiz he'd met while getting his masters at Northwestern, was his controller, and Eli Adler, a seasoned legal assistant, wrote contracts and did whatever buying and selling was required. It was a well-oiled five-person team, all of whom shared in year-end profits and healthy bonuses.

"Hey, pard." He entered Chick's office. "Miss me?"

Radford lounged back in his executive chair, ankles crossed over a corner of his desk, scanning a file. "Not a bit." He glanced up from his reading.

"Wow! That's the happiest I've seen you look in years." Chick dropped his feet and rose. "I take it you had a good time?"

"The best." Derik perched on the edge of a chair as Chick lowered onto his. "I can't remember when I've been so happy."

"I'm guessing about eight years, and it's about damned time." Chick leaned across his desk. "I'm happy for you, Derik. You gotta have life beyond work."

"Yeah, well you and Leona set a good example." He grinned. "When's the baby due?"

"Ten weeks. Micki's excited at having a sister to boss around."

"I bet. She's four, right?"

"Yeah, going on twenty." Chick plucked a photo from his wallet and offered it to Derik.

"Nice family." Derik handed it back. "I gotta make time for a visit." He ran fingers through his long, yellow locks. "Haven't seen your wife and the pixie in what—a year?"

"Probably. Let's make a date for dinner." Chick studied his partner. "Wanna bring Brita?"

"Absolutely." Derik grinned. "The way things are going, she should get to know my best friend and his posse. See what family life looks like ... just in case we get that far."

"Sounds like things are moving pretty fast, pal." Chick pushed to his feet. "I'm glad you're getting serious about a woman, but don't let an eight-year lag rush you into things until you're *really* sure she's the one."

"Don't worry. Right now, I'm just having a great time. I feel really good, Chick," also rising. "So, how're things going? Anything I need to worry about?"

"Like the Ukrainians?" Chick shook his head. "They're still in the slam, awaiting a court appearance and trial date." He circled his desk. "So far, no bail has been granted, and the ADA is trying to keep it that way. So, no worries there for the moment. Businesswise, everything is right on track."

"Okay." They bumped knuckles. "I'm gonna check my desk for messages and then maybe bail a little early. Brita's coming over for dinner—a tasty hog fish we caught over the reef—and I gotta pick up some stuff at the market."

"Sounds yummy. Nothing here that needs your input right now, so go whenever you want."

Derik nodded and headed for the door. "See you in the morning, then."

~ ~ ~

Chick perched on the edge of his desk and watched his friend leave. He sighed, happy Derik had broken those invisible chains from Martinique, but he was also concerned where this was going.

Chick knew Derik like a brother and could see he was open to falling in love with Brita. He certainly was in lust for her, and he suspected Brita was in the same boat. Chick was concerned about their endgame.

Derik loved their business and really enjoyed helping people escape financial ruin. Though they made plenty of profits, that wasn't his pal's main interest, because money wasn't a problem for him. Their secret treasure provided more than they could spend in two lifetimes.

His concern was over what this new couple wanted from life. Derik had confided, more than once, he sought a big family—at least three kids. Chick was unsure if Brita shared that goal. The woman, who may well fall deeply in love with Derik, was, he sensed, more consumed with her business.

Would she allow that to sink an otherwise wondrous relationship with the best guy he knew?

Well, time would tell. There was nothing for him to do—nothing he *could* do—to affect that.

He sighed again, rubbed the back of his neck, and slouched back into the folds of his leather executive chair. Whatever occurred, it was his mission to stand with his friend, the rest of the world be damned. A task he would not fail at.

~ 34 ~

Brita sauntered into the kitchen clad in Derik's tartan flannel shirt, sleeves rolled up to her elbows, its hem covering her to upper thighs.

Her entry drew a smile. Adorned in the boxers and cotton t-shirt he slept in, he plated two scrambled eggs beside slices of Canadian bacon and some buttered, whole-wheat toast.

"Hey, sleepyhead." The plate set onto a wicker placemat at the kitchenette table. "Amazing how sexy you make a simple shirt look."

She smiled, pirouetted with arms raised and wrists crossed, then looked at the LED wall clock. "Eight-ten. I haven't slept this late in ages."

She stepped to the counter, poured two mugs of black Costa Rican coffee, and settled at the table as Derik returned with a second plate of eggs.

"You're more relaxed now that your business has turned around." He slid onto a chair and leaned over for a lingering kiss, her fingers lightly on his neck.

Brita eased back and tasted her eggs. "Yum. Just the way I like them."

Derik chuckled. "After cooking breakfast off and on for over three weeks, I think I've got it nailed."

"Definitely." She laid a hand on his. "I've never been so spoiled." She nibbled on a wedge of bacon. "I was lucky to find time for a bowl of Cheerios when I was on my own."

She swiveled toward him. "I would never have guessed our new sport lines would have boomed like this. Orders are coming in faster than we can fill them."

"Well, with their beautiful designer modeling them so fetchingly on those TV ads, how could we miss?" He ate a fork full of eggs and shook his head. "All kidding aside, I'm pretty surprised too, at the explosive response. I think we lucked into the perfect time for something new on the market."

"Maybe." She finished her eggs and started on the toast. "But it was more than luck that you saw where we needed to go ... *you*, someone *not* in the garment trade ... and I, supposedly an insider, didn't." Brita slouched back and dabbed her lips with her napkin. "I'm totally embarrassed."

Derik shrugged. "Sometimes someone's gotta stand *outside* the forest to see the trees, baby. That's where Brand & Radford Investments shines.

"I guess, but it's a good thing I don't have a fragile ego, my darling." She sidled over for a more passionate kiss. "I'd hate for hurt feelings to get in the way of this," she mumbled.

One arm snaked around her waist, he rose and drew her against him, the kiss becoming even more heated. His other hand found its way inside the shirt, tweaking an already aroused nipple. Now breathless, he scooped her up and started for the bedroom, one of her arms in his hair, the other around his neck.

"Oh *Liebchen*," she panted, "we'll be so late to work."

"I just checked with the boss," he whispered, "and he gave us the morning off." Kisses peppered her eyes, cheeks, tip of her nose, and lips.

"The boss? *You're* the boss." She giggled.

"I know. That's who I checked with." They were in the bedroom now, and flopped together onto the sheets.

"In that case," her voice raspy with passion, "we need to do this properly." She drew his shirt over his head, her perfect nails caressing his back and teasing his chest as he slowly unbuttoned her shirt.

Derik hovered above her, his eyes savoring a view he never tired of. Then his mouth began a venture designed to drive her wild, as her hands roamed down his back and stripped away his shorts.

Soon their bodies were tangled on a voyage that seemed new and more exciting at every passage, fulfilling needs neither knew existed until they'd discovered them together.

They hovered in a nexus undisturbed by time.

~ ~ ~

An hour later, showered and dressed, they gathered their things for an afternoon at work. Brita was headed for her factory, while Derik had a scheduled meeting with Charlie Akata to discuss the last quarter's earnings.

"I've got something I wanted to discuss, before we got so ... distracted." She grinned and touched his arm.

"Okay. What's on your mind, sweetie?" *Does she finally want to move in? This back and forth between my place and hers is a pain.*

"I was thinking of how well our new sports lines were doing. We're already back to making a profit." She nestled into his arms, her back arched, their faces a foot apart. "With production ramping up, things are only going to improve."

"Yeah." His lips brushed her forehead. "That's what we do for our partners. This," his mouth brushing her ear and neck, "is a first-time bonus, however."

Brita chuckled and kissed his cheek. "More than I ever expected, *Liebchen*. But seriously, now that we've turned things around, I'd like to retain at least some of my haute couture line. They've done so well—"

"That was in the past, Brit." He stepped back and took her hands in his. "That line requires more work than reward. Look, you *have* created some beautiful fancies, but now the company is focused on making profitable duds. Things that provide good ROI. That's gonna be our focus." His eyes held hers. "Allure Attire is becoming a profit-oriented, commercial operation and can no longer be coaxed along as an expensive hobby."

"How can you *say* that, Derik." She pulled free from his grasp. "This is my *life*. It's never been a *hobby*." Her eyes flooded. "I love making great designs—"

"And you do it beautifully," he folded his arms across his chest, "and I want you to use those talents to design something that actually sells and makes us money." He reached for her again, but she recoiled. "I think we should begin working on a youth version of our sports lines. Something for pre and early teens."

"And totally ditch the high-end goods?" She knuckled away tears. "I put my *soul* into those dresses. Those are who I really am! Not some purveyor of common, commercial goods."

Derik shook his head and sighed. "But it's those common goods, as you call them, that's turned your company around and is making you viable again. Look, this is why Chick and I are successful." Derik reached for her again, but she shook off his touch and looked away. "We're not emotionally tied to a company's past, something often riddled with bad judgements precisely because of those emotions. We make the hard decisions the founders can't."

"But it's *my* company. Don't I have a say?" She glared at him, arms akimbo.

"Actually, you don't." He studied her, then shrugged.

"We're the controlling partners. We'll gladly consider any suggestions you may have, but in the end, our decisions are final." He snagged up his leather attaché case.

"I broke a cardinal rule with you, and I should have known better."

"What?" She whimpered, fighting off sobs. "What rule?"

"Not getting personally involved with a client." He gave a hard head shake. "I couldn't help falling in love with you, but I shoulda known a moment like this might come."

"I don't know what you're talking about." Brita slumped onto a sofa. "We've been so happy these last weeks. What's wrong with that?"

"Because it creates Catch 22." He settled next to her. "A time comes when I have to make a decision that benefits either my lover or my company."

"Is that really so hard?" Now she took his hands. "Doesn't love conquer all?"

"Not when it puts the wellbeing of my partner and my employees in jeopardy." His eyes held hers. "I can't allow you to do something totally emotional that'll risk our business. Despite my love for you, the company comes first."

"So, you choose them over me?" She leaned away, her eyes hardening. "You veto my plea to keep my designer line?"

"Yes, and I do it for your sake as much as mine."

"All right." She rose. "As you've made abundantly clear, you *are* the boss." She turned toward the bedroom. "I'm going to collect my things, since I want to help you repair that *mistake* you made. I'll be staying in Coral Gables again." She glanced back as she entered the bedroom. "Please call first, if you wish to visit. Otherwise, I'll see you at work, whenever. Strictly business, of course."

"Brita." Derik lurched to his feet. "Please don't make this personal."

"I take it *very* personal," she returned with a small, wheeled suitcase, "when my so-called lover chooses his business over me." She headed for the exit.

"When you cool off, baby, see if that shoe doesn't fit *you* too." He sighed and started after her. "I hope you'll realize I'm doing this for you and your business, not just mine."

A soft, pained whimper echoed back as the door closed behind her.

~ 35 ~

Gorya Kolodenko burst through the Miami Courthouse's door, closely followed by his bearish brother, Alik. They paused on the steps, hands shielding their eyes from the afternoon sun, and scanned the walk below.

"There he is," Gorya grumbled, "Russian bastard." They started down the steps toward a small, wiry, balding man, lugging a large, leather briefcase.

"Took ya fucking long enough, Vasilev." Gorya gripped his attorney's hand. "We been in fucking lock-up for over month."

"Look, it takes three weeks to get an arraignment, and then two more to get in front of a judge for a bail re-hearing." The attorney turned toward his white Honda Odessey and they followed.

"Not so swift justice, under law," Alik growled.

"The courts are jammed, and frankly, you're lucky to get any bail at all." The buzzed key fob opened the sliding side doors for his clients. "A half mil for attempted murder is a song, even though it took your cousin, Oleg, four days to bring me the fifty K needed to cover it. Plus, another thirty for his honor's favorite charity so he'd grant the bail."

"What charity?" Gorya growled.

"Who's do you think?" The lawyer arched an eyebrow. "And Oleg had to find your passports."

"What the fuck?" Alik crawled into the middle row of

bucket seats, while Gorya settled in front. "Our passports?"

"Sure." He fired up the engine and pulled out. "Gotta pay your way, and be sure you don't flee the country, as if that'd stop you."

"We ain't going nowhere," Gorya mumbled. "We got things to do here."

"*Da*. Things I wanna do, personal." Alik's face was grim.

"Yeah," Gorya glance at his brother and gave a short head shake. "Business to take care of. Drop us home now."

"We've got a trial to prepare for and I got motions to make. This isn't going away just because you're out on bail."

He studied Gorya from the corners of his eyes. "You need to stay clean and out of trouble, guys. Nobody's gonna bother you if you just run your girls, but try to keep the heavy stuff down, at least until we get through this." He nodded toward Alik.

"Pull anything serious and bail will get revoked, despite your thirty K cushion, and you might sit in the clink for a year before we go to trial." The Honda entered their street and he parked outside their storefront.

"Think about it, okay?"

"Yeah, yeah." Gorya stepped out of the minivan and joined Alik on the curb. "We gonna be angels." He slammed the door and waved the man on.

"We gonna be Angels of Death," Alik muttered as they crossed to their front door. "I kill that blond guy slow and painful." He turned to his brother. "I get guns and we go."

"Not so fast, Bro." Gorya snatched the bigger man's arm. "We do this now, just after release, and we go away for life." He unlocked the door. "I make plan. Wait month, maybe, and find right way."

"You got idea?" Alik followed him inside.

"Working on it. Gotta case out blond babe's shop. Make

look like heist gone bad." He patted Alik's arm. "Patience, Bro. I know is hard, but we gotta do it right."

The big man groaned and slumped onto his office chair. "Okay. You always figure best, but I itchy to waste that guy and get hot piece of beautiful ass."

"I know, but is gonna taste better this way. You'll see." Gorya picked up papers from his desk. "Let's see how girls did while we were away. Oleg kept them busy."

"Okay." Alik retrieved his 9mm Beretta M9 pistol from his locked desk drawer and checked it was loaded. "So, we still need girl for airport. I go now Little Havana, find me hot chick." He pushed up from his chair and strode to their mini-fridge to retrieve a hypo filled with heroin.

"You got roofies?"

"Yeah. I got. Won't use this," waving the syringe, "'til get her to hooker pad." Alik glanced at his brother. "No worry. Won't over-med this one. I get back, you tell me plan for blondie. Itching ta do that bastard quick."

"I on it, but I told you, we not gonna rush this."

"Yeah, yeah. Be patient. I know, but don't like it." He lumbered from the room, a growl in his throat.

~ 36 ~

Derik hovered over his desk and scanned a six-page file, the final figures from their last completed project. The entrepreneur bought back his shares after a very successful four-year turnaround, and the 15% price/earnings ratio netted Brand & Radford a substantial profit.

He'd finished the review and was about to deliver it to Charlie Akata to plug into their P & L when his cell phone buzzed. A glance at the screen drew a grunt as he tapped the green button.

"Hi, Brita. I was just about to call you."

"Oh?"

"Yeah," settling in his chair. "We haven't talked since we got back from the Keys, so I thought I'd better check in."

"Yes. Well, a beautiful few days didn't end well, did it?" A pause and audible sigh. "That's why I'm calling ... to apologize for my attitude last Sunday."

"Ha." A soft chuckle in his voice. "You beat me to it. That's why I was gonna call you. I'm really sorry for coming off so brusquely. It's not like me to shove my authority down someone's throat ... especially since I seem to be in love with that someone." His turn to sigh. "I hope you'll forgive me."

"I'm the one who needs to ask for forgiveness, *Liebchen*. I knew the rules when I agreed to this partnership, and I was totally out of line. So, I hope *you* will forgive *me*."

Derik laughed. "So, I guess we are both forgiven. Right?"

"Absolutely." The tension bled out of her voice. "And per your instruction, *Boss,* I've been working on our junior sports line designs."

"Boss, huh? Now you're rubbing it in." Derik drew over his desk calendar.

"Just a little. Anyhow, if you want to come by to see my new designs, I'll be here every day. Production is booming but not as fast as sales, and we need to discuss that too."

"Okay." Flipping pages, he found the current week. "Seems I'm free tomorrow after lunch. How's two sound?"

"Works for me. Like I said, I'm here pretty much full time, except Friday, when I'm shooting a new ad in the afternoon."

"It's set, then." He scribbled a note on the date's page. "See you at two."

Derik disconnected, leaned back, and wondered how it would go when they saw each other after that rather nasty confrontation. Apologies made on both sides, but lingering tension was palpable. He'd fallen in love with this woman, but wouldn't push her if she weren't ready to resume their affair.

He rose, picked up the file he'd been reading, and headed for his comptroller's office. His feelings for Brita couldn't be allowed to impact the rest of his business, and he did have other projects going.

Still, he was looking forward to tomorrow afternoon.

~ ~ ~

Derik arrived at Allure Attire a few minutes early, and lingered at the doorway into the shop, watching Brita who hovered over a finishing table, examining shorts.

Clad in fitted, silvery silk slacks and a pale pink,

sleeveless blouse, divided by a wide, black leather belt, she set his heart fluttering to the beat of hummingbird wings. He marveled at her beauty, classically sensual, but never tawdry.

Derik sighed, filled with strange trepidation as he stepped inside and picked his way through a maze of sewing machine operators and the noisy clack of electric shears at cutting tables. Production flowed with an ordered urgency ... and a surprising amount of noise.

Brita peeked over her shoulder, sensing his approach, and turned, a delicious smile creasing her lips.

"Ah, you're here." She pivoted and swept an arm across the room. "Full-throttle production, and we're still falling behind." She laid a hand on his forearm. "And now you want to start a *new* line?" The following chuckle was strained.

"Start *designing* a new line, yes." Nodding as he scanned the room. "Clearly, if we can't keep up with what we've got now, an expansion seems in order." He took her hand. "Let's go up to your office where we can hear ourselves think."

"Of course. You go on ahead. I just need a moment to talk to a few of the girls."

Derik nodded and started for the stairs, while Brita moved to a woman working at a cutting table. As he reached the top, he looked back and saw her now with one of the sewers. It didn't look confrontational, and a pat on the woman's shoulder seemed to confirm that.

Brita turned, waved at him, and started for the stairway. He dawdled outside the door and awaited her arrival. Then they strode together into her office. The closed door substantially reduced the noisy racket of the shop.

They settled onto two armchairs, angled toward each other, and Brita exhaled an audible breath.

"Busy, busy, busy." She shrugged. "We're doing all we can to boost production without sacrificing quality." Her eyes locked on his. "Again, Derik, I want to apologize for my outburst the other day. I just get so passionate—"

"Me too," he interrupted. "I came across way too strong. I'm not usually so aggressive."

"I get it. You *are* the boss, after all, but I'm just not used to someone telling me what I can and can't do." She smiled and touched his arm. "I'll get over it."

"Okay, let's forget it. But now we need to discuss our falling behind on deliveries." He leaned in, forearms resting on his thighs.

"Allure Attire has earned a reputation of excellence, and we don't want to damage that by pushing production and sacrificing quality." Their eyes met, followed by a lingering silence.

"I think we should consider an expansion of your shop, once we're sure this surge in sales has legs." Derik brought his attaché case to his knees and flipped it open.

"You mentioned you've started on the junior sportswear designs?" A pad of paper was retrieved and he scrawled a quick note. "We'll have to consider a new line's impact on our capacity when you begin production." He sat back, hands folded. "I'll see what I can come up with. Maybe we can find something without having to move the shop."

"That would be great. We've got enough on our plate without having to fully relocate." She rose. "Let me show you my preliminary designs."

Derik stood and followed Brita to her drafting table, hovering close to her side as they leafed through eight pages of sketches. She seemed to avoid anything more than casual contact. Despite her repeated apology, was she still angry enough to cool their romance?

Dammit! That's twice I've been harsh with this lovely woman. Finally in love again, and I may have fucked it up.

He sighed. Whatever it was, he couldn't let it interfere with their business relationship. This company was about to boom.

~ ~ ~

Brita quelled the rush of tingles surging through her. Derik hung inches from her shoulder as she showed him her new designs, but clearly avoided contact. Despite her heartfelt apology, had her childish behavior cooled his passion? She'd always been so bad with men, determined not to be used solely for their gratification. She'd managed to drive them all off until this wonderful man, who seemed to relish who she was.

Damn, that's twice I've behaved like someone I'm not, and it may be driving him away. No, love is too important. *I've gotta find a way to repair this.*

Still, a mist of coolness hung over them as they talked and discussed the future of her business. It trailed after Derik when he left, leaving Brita weeping softly at her desk.

Her heart was in a vise as she pored over what had occurred during the last few days. Somehow, some way, this must be fixed. She just had no idea how.

~ 37 ~

Derik paused at Chick's door and rapped on the casing.

"Hey, pal." His partner, looked up from a file he was reading. "Nice profitable last quarter," waving the report.

"Yeah. Brita's sports line has really taken off." He leaned against the jamb. "I'm on the way over there now. She's finalized some designs for a new juniors' line, and it looks like we may need to expand her production facilities."

"So soon?" Chick rose and joined Derik at the doorway. "Isn't that pushing it a bit?"

"Normally, yeah, but despite adding two new machines and a cutting table, she can't keep up with orders. She's got no room for any more equipment." They strolled together toward the exit as they talked.

"Now's the perfect time to drop in her new junior line, with Spring in full swing, and her current sales continuing to surge. If we can't meet demand, we may drive away clients." They halted at the office's exit.

"Anyhow, she's got prototypes and new projections, and in the past her estimates have always been conservative." Derik shoved his hands in his pockets. "No worries. I'll bring it all back and we'll go over everything in detail before we make a move."

"Sounds good," Chick said, studying his friend. "How's it going between you two? Don't let a good thing like that sour, buddy."

"It's weird, Chick. When we're together, there's real electricity, but we both seem afraid of getting burned." He shook his head. "I *do* love that woman, and I'm not letting her get away because of a silly spat."

"So, get over there and make it happen." Chick patted Derik on the back as he turned to leave. "Keep me posted."

Derik gave a small wave as he hurried off.

~ ~ ~

Derik entered the shop and spied Brita, clad in fitted tan slacks and a beige sleeveless blouse, on the floor, inspecting new production. She was a hands-on manager, someone constantly in the trenches, ensuring her products continued to meet her standards. He loved that.

She glanced up and waived him over. A patterned skirt and a contrasting short sleeve blouse laid on an inspection table. Brita took his hand and nodded at the outfit.

"What do you think?"

"Lovely." running a hand over the fabric. "Wonderful material. Soft and lightweight."

"It's a sample from our new Juniors line." She rubbed the material between thumb and forefinger. "This is a new, breathable fabric, ideal for hot summers." She gestured at two women, busy at their Singer machines.

"They're making one sample each of eight new designs for the line you wanted. If we approve, we can be in production by the beginning of the month." She spun and carrying the sample, headed for her office stairway with Derik close behind.

"We can discuss where this is going," said over her shoulder, "in the office, where we can hear ourselves think."

He nodded, happy at the idea of getting away from the

persistent drone of twenty sewing machines and the clatter of cutting tables. And he had another reason to seek privacy.

The metal stairs ascended, Brita strolled into her office and Derik followed, closing the door behind, the factory's din now muted to a low hum. She stepped to her desk and plucked up a file which she opened to display sketches of the new products she'd designed at his direction.

"Five for girls and three for boys. I've found eight fabric combinations that should give us a complete catalog for buyers to select from." Brita handed him the packet, which he began leafing through.

"The problem is, we can't keep up with current orders, so how are we going do *this?*"

"We'll handle it." His eyes swept slowly over her. "But I have something else consuming me right now." He flipped the packet onto her desk and stepped close to her.

"What's going on, Brit?" He lightly grasped her upper arms.

"What—what do you mean, *going on?*" said in a little girl voice, her eyes wide and moist.

"Goddammit." Derik pulled her against him. "I love you, woman, and I think you love me." His fingers caressed her cheek and slid into her pixie cut. "Are we gonna let one little dust-up get in the way of that?" His eyes plumbed hers.

"I—I thought you were—you didn't—"

"Oh, shut up and kiss me already." Drawing her tighter, his mouth brushed across a cheek and onto questing lips. They shuddered with the release of pent-up passion, their bodies moving against each other, hands busy adventurers, lips tangled and tongues darting, sending cascades of fire trilling through their bodies.

After several moments, Derik broke free, panting hard, both hands on Brita's waist. "Wait just a moment, my love."

He hurried to the window and lowered the blinds, then locked the door.

Brita's eyes trailed him, then she took two steps to her desk, snatched up the phone, and punched a button.

"Hold all calls, please." She gulped and tried to steady her voice. "No exceptions. I'll let you know when we've finished our meeting."

She barely had the phone on its cradle when Derik spun her into his arms, lifted her, and strode to the sofa at the side of the large room. He settled on the plushy cushions, his lover on his lap, and drew her questing mouth to his.

Magically, her blouse was unbuttoned, as was his shirt. His lips traced across her ear, down the side of her graceful neck, his tongue dallying at the notch at the base of her throat, then left a fiery trail en route to a thrusting breast, its nipple at attention, begging for inspection from that moist adventurer.

He glanced up when his brow was peppered by tiny, salty droplets and saw Brita's eyes overflowing.

"Crying?" His eyebrows arched.

"From joy, *Liebchen.*" She cupped his face in her hands and drew it up for a kiss. "I feared I'd driven you away again. My heart was shattered."

"Well, we're repairing that this instant the best way I know how." Their mouths merged into a ravaging kiss, tongues and lips busy everywhere.

Brita wiggled free and slipped off his lap, her fingers stroking his side while her mouth cruised across his neck, down his chest, paused at his nipples for some delicious tweaking before continuing her voyage south. She opened his belt, and with one brisk tug, had his pants around his ankles, freeing his raging hard-on which stood at full attention.

Derik moaned and shuddered as her long nails caressed

its side before teasing and cupping his balls. Brita's tongue strolled along the rigid shaft, then licked and swirled around the glans before cupping it between her lips.

"My favorite lollypop," murmured before fully engulfing it, swirling her tongue around its hardness as her head bobbed in a slow but steady pattern.

Derik groaned and quivered, and met her action with small thrusts of his hips. The only other sound was the soft slurp from her busy mouth.

"Oh, Christ, baby, that's so-o-o good." Her face cupped his hands, he drew her up for a fierce kiss. "But I need to be inside of you—right *now*." As they continued the kiss, his hands roamed across her breasts and down her sides to the waist of her slacks, which he thrust down. Two shimmied kicks cast them aside. Her butt cradled with one hand, the other around her shoulders, Derik rose, kicking free of his pants as he laid her on the sofa.

His mouth skittered slowly across her moist skin, lips plucking, tongue tweaking, firing her body with trembling bolts of heat as she panted and heaved against him. Finally, he arrived at her engorged, open lips, oozing moisture, begging for attention. He met that need, lapping up sweet nectar, then hunkered above and slowly entered.

Brita moaned and murmured something unintelligible in German as she snaked her arms around his neck and locked her long legs across his thighs, crushing their bodies together. Sweat-slickened, they rhumbaed together in a frantic dance of love.

Their bodies quaked at the onset of massive orgasms, and Derik's mouth engulfed hers to smother a feral scream, muting it to a modest groan. The kiss continued as they remained coupled, Brita's fingers tracing delectably across his back and butt, her ankles still hooked across his calves.

Derik rolled to his side and peppered her face and breasts with tiny busses. She turned, caught the back of his head, and pulled him in for a more sensuous but still gentle kiss.

"You fill my heart, *Liebchen*. Never have I felt so complete."

"Yeah, this is pretty wonderful, but we gotta keep the noise down," he chuckled softly, "in case someone comes up here and peeks through the blinds."

She smiled. "I'm not ashamed to show the world how happy I am."

"Me too." Derik slipped off the sofa and gathered his clothes. "Let's get respectable, and then we can go over getting ready for the new sports line." He began to dress as Brita nodded, sat up, and slipped into her bikini panties and pants.

"With those awful Ukrainians behind us," she rose, fastening her belt, "we can concentrate on our expansion. I'll show you my designs for the full line, and we can discuss what we need to do to produce it."

Derik nodded and decided not to tell her the Kolodenkos were out on bail. He hoped they'd move on and leave Brita alone.

He worried, suspecting that wasn't likely, knowing who they were.

~ 38 ~

A rap on his door drew Derik's eyes from the papers he was reviewing as Chick entered.

"How's it going, buddy?" his partner asked. "Everything on track with Allure Attire?"

"You referring to the business ... or Brita?" He leaned back, fingers interlaced across his breast.

"Both, I guess." Chick settled on a chair and gave a wry chuckle. "I guess I'm mostly concerned about you and Brita. The business seems to be cooking right along."

Derik's lips spilled into a grin. "Well, in that case, everything is going super well. Both with Brit and the business."

"You guys made up, huh?"

"Oh, yes. Fully and completely. Right there in her office, with the door locked and the blinds pulled." A sigh. "All kidding aside, I'm in love, and it feels great." He leaned back to his desk and picked up the schematic he'd been studying.

"As for the business, I wanted to discuss this with you." Drawing Chick in, he gestured at the blueprint, now on his desk.

"This is the layout of the eight-unit office mall where Allure Attire is located. They're all condo-type units, each owned rather than rented." Derik pointed to the third unit from the right. "Number Three is her space, and with the additional sports line we want to deliver, she needs more room." He tapped Number Four.

"This one houses a carpet and tile retailer. I want to buy him out so Brita can expand without actually moving to a larger facility." Pointing to Number Seven. "And the guy doesn't have to move far, because this one is vacant."

"You think he'll go for it?" Chick studied the plans.

"I'm gonna offer him enough to cover his investment, the cost of moving which won't be too bad, and a nice bonus. He's really only gotta shuffle stock a few hundred feet, and his address stays the same except for the unit number."

"Uh huh. So, *we're* gonna buy it instead of Brita?"

"If you agree." Derik settled on his chair and studied Chick. "We'll rent it to her, with an option to buy if-and-when she decides to buy back our shares, any time after three years."

"And you're confident the new junior line will fly?"

"Absolutely. She's offered a teaser to some of her clients, and they've already committed with preliminary orders." He chuckled. "For guys with zero clothing experience, we hit the nail solidly on the head with this one." He rose. "Brita's smart, hard-working, and demands excellence. I believe she'll handle this, and become rich—an icon in this business." Derik perched on the edge of his desk.

"If things keep going between us like I think it will, and we're sure we're serious—"

"Like get married serious?" Chick's eyebrows arched.

"Yeah, maybe like that." Derik grinned. "But what I mean is, I'll know she's not there because of my money. She'll be wealthy on her own."

Chick drew him up into a bear hug. "Damn, that makes me happy, Derik. I was worried you'd never shake off Martinique."

"I know." He stared into his partner's smiling face. "I had to come to terms with that, and being with Brita's made that possible. Past time to move on, and I want the warmth of a home life with a wife and a passel of kids." Derik chuckled. "With our genes, the brats should all be world-beaters." Derik returned to his desk. "Anyhow," he rolled up the floorplans, "since you agree I'll go down there and discuss this with her."

"Okay, keep me posted." Chick paused. "You sure everything's safe now?"

"You mean the Ukrainians?"

"Yeah. I heard they made bail."

"Well, they got paid off in full, but I gotta admit, they still didn't seem happy. Especially Big Foot."

"So, stay alert. You're packing, right?"

Derik flared open his sportscoat, exposing a shoulder holster. "Got my buddy, Mr. Glock, right here, and his little friend, my S & W .380 on my ankle. Don't leave home without them, nowadays."

"Good. So, get going." Chick turned and left as Derik gathered his papers and punched the intercom on his phone.

"Ginny, please call Ms. Kruger and tell her I'm coming down for a visit. We've got some planning to do."

Derik gathered his papers and attaché case and headed for the door, thinking about the Kolodenko brothers. He didn't need them fucking up how well things were going.

~ ~ ~

"So, what do you think?" Derik stepped away from her desk as Brita continued pouring over the floor plan.

"Will there be a lot of construction required? If they're tearing walls down—"

"Actually, we can do this without too much disruption. I think just wide doorways into the next building will work." Derik marked three spots on the plan.

"Your girls can continue to work while we set up the next space." He folded his arms. "Once I complete the deal, you'll get a detailed floor plan so you can lay out work stations, etc. Then we can pre-install the wiring and get the new equipment into position, ready to rumble." He patted the schematic. "You'll have more capacity than you'll need at first, but it gives you the opportunity to expand as the new business flourishes. Number Four is 20% bigger than yours, so I think you could quadruple in size before you'd have to consider another move."

"But I won't own it, will I?"

Derik took her hands. "I thought it's better to keep your capital free to run the business. You'll need to buy equipment, material, and hire new staff, and that guy won't sell cheap. I'll give you a long-term lease, and the option to buy, when-and-if you decide to repurchase my shares at the end of our contract, when you should be better prepared to pay for it."

Brita nodded. "Makes sense. I'll start interviewing for new staff next week, and I've got to finish the designs for the new line." She cupped his cheek with one hand. "This is really wonderful, and very timely. There's a clothing designers' convention to be held at the Miami Beach Convention Center in a bit over a month. If we can get the new line up and running by then, it'll be a great time and place to introduce it." She grinned. "There'll be girls modeling new styles for many designers, and I plan to steal the show."

"Sounds great." Derik pulled her in for a warm kiss. "I'll get to watch my love look sexy for everyone to admire."

"I'm only interested in one man's admiration, my love."

The kiss became more heated, and soon clothing began to come off.

"I'd better lock the door and pull those shades again," Derik said, his voice hoarse with passion.

Brita had already told the receptionist to hold all calls.

Anyone outside, listened at the door, would wonder at the muted sounds coming from behind the walls.

Then a barely heard trill from Brita, filled with joy, would allay their curiosity.

~ 39 ~

Derik and Brita lounged against the railing of her balcony and watched as workmen suspended plastic drop cloths across the east side of her factory. Two sewing machines, a cutting table, and a finishing table were relocated to make room for the construction crew to begin opening the connecting wall to her new addition. Electricians were already working to install power for ten new Singers and three cutting tables, based on the floorplan she'd designed.

"How long do you think it will take?" She turned to him.

"There's nothing complicated about it. Everything should be ready to go by end of this week." He wrapped her waist with one arm. "How many new people are you going to hire?"

"Three sewers and one each for cutting and finishing, to start." She shrugged. "We're beginning TV and social media ads tomorrow. Demo outfits are ready for every item in the new line, and we'll cross-promote from the existing line as well." She leaned in and kissed his cheek.

"I see from out accounts that you've stocked up on cloth and supplies, so I presume you're interviewing for your new staff."

Brita nodded. "I've got open auditions beginning this afternoon. The phone's been pretty busy, so I guess there's still a lot of people looking for work. I'm not going to hire anyone who doesn't have tons of experience."

"Sounds good." Derik pushed away from the railing, turned Brita to him, and planted a kiss on her forehead. "So, I'll go down and check on the construction crew, then I've got a meeting at the bank." He pulled her in for a hug. "Looks like you've got all the bases covered here, and I'm really excited about premiering our new line."

Brita returned the hug with a fierce squeeze, her head nuzzled at the side of his neck.

"Derik, my love, I can't tell you how happy I've been since you've come into my life." She arched back, her eyes fastened on his. "You've turned my little shop into a roaring success beyond my wildest dreams, and as a fabulous bonus, you've brought me love and passion I've never known before" She reached up and their lips met in a gentle kiss. "I've never felt so complete."

Derik smiled and ran a hand over her cheek and into her hair. "I echo those feelings about love—and passion—my darling. It's been a long time coming for me, too."

"Those girls you mentioned in Martinique? You still miss them?"

"Rarely think of them anymore, and *never* miss them, now that I've found you." A kiss brushed her lips. "That was then, and this is now, and I love my now."

He drew her to him for another mutual hug, clinging together for several moments, each relishing the contact. Then Derik eased back, hands on her hips.

"Gotta run now, hon. Good luck with your interviews," turning toward the staircase. "Pick you up at seven for dinner?"

"Yes, that's fine." She touched his shoulder. "We're still planning to sail to the Keys again this weekend?"

"Absolutely." He paused at the head of the stairs. "Relax time, and fueling up for a busy next few weeks."

"Wonderful. I love our time at sea together." She watched him toss off a wave as he started down toward the shop's floor.

~ ~ ~

Brita sat at her desk and once more scanned the job application from the ninth woman she'd interviewed. Two applicants were exactly what see sought ... five- and seven-years experience sewing in the garment trade at casual clothing shops. This last woman had minimal experience, and Brita had a sense she wasn't reliable.

Oh, well, there was one more waiting. If she didn't pan out, she'd decided she await more applicants. Brita looked up at a rap on the door. A thirtyish, dark haired, slightly chunky woman stood in the doorway.

"Come in, come in." Brita waved at the chair across the desk from her. The woman smiled, handed Brita her resumé, and slipped onto the seat.

"I'm Alena Popov," she said, her hands folded in her lap.

"Russian?"

"Georgian, actually, although those miserable Russians claim us." She shrugged.

"Wasn't Khruschev Georgian?"

"Yes, but that was from another time." Her English was nearly without accent. "Anyhow, I'm American now. Eight years a citizen of this wonderful country." She gestured at her application. "As you can see, I received extensive sewing training at a trade school and have worked at Levi's for three years. Unfortunately, they closed our shop, and I refused a transfer to North Carolina." She sighed. "South Florida is home for me now."

Brita nodded as she scanned the woman's resumé, her

heart rate rising. This could be her third new worker. She leaned back and studied her: attractive, round face and long, tapered fingers.

"Well, as long as your references check out, and you pass a sewing test, you're hired." She rose. "There are two other ladies downstairs, and I've set aside some machines to see how you work. If you're as good as your references, you can start next Monday, eight a.m. sharp."

"You'll be ready by then?" Popov gestured toward the construction area.

"Yes, to be completed by Friday. We're introducing a new line this week and expect to be very busy." Brita chuckled. "I pay well, as you've already seen, but you'll earn every penny."

"I'm looking forward to it." They rose together. "I love creating beautiful outfits."

They exited Brita's office and she ushered Alena Popov to the main floor where two other new hires awaited their tests.

~ ~ ~

Alena slid into her blue Toyota Corolla, glanced at the entrance to Allure Attire, and withdrew her cell phone. She punched auto dial and was answered on the second ring.

"*Da*?" Gorya answered.

"I'm in," she replied. "Start on Monday. I saw the blond guy you mentioned just before I went in for my interview."

"Good. You know what to do."

"Yes, but give it a little time, cousin. I don't want anything you do to lead back to me."

"Da, so what you think, smartass?"

She chuckled. "That's why you asked me, Gorya, 'cause I'm smart. Give me time to learn their schedule." She paused.

"You know, I saw in the paper there's gonna be a designers' convention in about three weeks. She's sure to go, and I'm betting he will too. They'll probably be here the evening before, prepping. A perfect time for you to do whatever you're planning."

"Da. You smart cookie, Lena. You keep me posted."

"You got it, cuz." She disconnected and started her car. She knew Gorya and Alik could be nasty. She didn't want any part of *that*, but he made her a very lucrative offer for finding a way for them to get inside to do what they intended. She planned to be clear of that, when the time came.

She drove off, thinking of Kruger's guy. A very handsome man. She hoped her cousins didn't plan on messing up that pretty face, but she doubted that.

~ 40 ~

Derik adjusted his course ten degrees more westerly, legs braced and leaning into the sloops starboard cant. Brita clung to his back, arms around his waist, her head nestled cheek-to-cheek on his left shoulder.

The sturdy yacht surged down the front of a wave and plowed into the next, the brisk northeasterly wind driving the spray away from them. A glance at the GPS on his laptop, perched on the helm's utility shelf, showed a speed of 6.8 knots.

"I love this." She rubbed her cheek against his light stubble. "The wind at our stern, the briny smell, the warmth of the sun on our backs ... and *you*." She brushed her lips across cheek. "I especially love *you*."

Derik's left arm pulled her around to circle her shoulder for a brisk hug. "No place I'd rather be." He nodded at the sea. "Beautiful, isn't it?"

The sun, still low on the eastern horizon, sprinkled the rippled waves with sheets of glittering diamonds, as snowy balls of cotton hurried across the cobalt sky. Far to the south, tops of palm trees promised their destination awaited them.

He glanced at his billowed sail and jib, set full against the gusting wind, and then ahead at the sea.

"Probably about four hours to reach the reef to catch some dinner. Plenty of time for a swim."

"And maybe some fun on that lovely little beach." She

kissed his neck.

"Yes. A perfect place to make love." He caught her chin with his free hand, and their mouth's began a promise of what was to come. It took strong will to break away, returning his attention to the sloop. He sighed, happy and at peace.

Life was perfect.

Then a vision of the Kolodenko brothers wedged into his mind. He hoped life stayed that way, but *perfect* he knew, was often a short-lived condition.

They anchored just after three p.m. on the middle reef, a half-mile east of Key Largo. A block of frozen chum, deployed in a mesh bag, soon brough out swarms of snappers, and in less than an hour they'd kept four lovely "flag" yellowtails, and released anything smaller back into the sea.

With dinner provided for, Derik motored to his private little cove, and they were soon snorkeling over the sandy bottom, strewn with rocks, anemones, sea urchins, and phalanxes of colorful fish. Brita tensed and grabbed Derik's arm when a two-foot barracuda cruised by. He shook his head and gave a thumbs-up—nothing to worry about.

Forty-minutes later, they swam to the tiny beach they'd visited before. Sprawled on their backs on the warm sand, arms linked, they sucked in the peaceful ambiance. Life couldn't get any better than this.

Brita rolled onto her side, and her fingers began a teasing course from Derik's neck and across his chest and belly.

"You said you'd tell me about Martinique and your other love, *Liebchen*."

"Loves, actually." He drew her atop of him, her silken skin warm and moist. "Later, on the boat, but now I have something else in mind."

Her neck in the crook of his arm, he drew her face close, their tongues darting and mischievous.

She cleverly eluded his lips, tweaking the corner of his mouth, then darting away with him in pursuit. Brita gently bussed an eye and the tip of his nose and skimmed across his lips and onto the other ear, Derik's mouth in full chase.

Derik puffed and panted with delicious frustration. He locked both heels across her calves and trapped her head between his hands, her face finally centered above his.

Breathing hard, he gasped, "You're a witch, woman."

"One very much in love," she whispered, coming down for a heated kiss.

Both arms curled around her as their lips devoured each other. They nestled together for several minutes, silently pledging their love with their mouths, while somehow their swimwear disappeared.

Brita finally pushed up and slid down, her tongue trailing across his damp skin to find his perfect cock, steel-hard. She settled on her knees between his legs and drew in his balls to suck and tease. Then she released them to her fingers to twiddle as she licked slowly up the shaft to lap at the base of the glans.

"Ohmygod," Derik groaned. "You're driving me crazy. I need you—to be *in* you—right *now!*"

Brita slid forward, crouched over his groin, and slid him into her soaking pussy, voicing a soft gasp. She paused, and tried the Kegel motion she'd learned for an entirely different reason.

"Oh, geez, I'm gonna cum already!" Derik gasped, both hand busy with her incredible tits.

Brita leaned forward and started to rock. "No. No you don't." She planted a sloppy kiss. "You wait for me, darling.

I'm just getting started."

Derik, teeth clenched, thrust up against her motion, his hands caressing her erotic figure. They panted and wheezed in a building crescendo. "I can't hold it, baby," he gasped. "I'm com-m-m-ing."

"Oh yes. Me too. Me too!" Brita shuddered electric fire coursing through her as she orgasmed, her pussy pulsing as she soaked them both. She collapsed across his chest, his still surging cock buried deep in her, and they laid together, quietly winding down as they caught their breath.

"That was totally amazing," Derik murmured in her ear. "I love you."

"Good." She kissed his neck. "I'd hate to think you were just taking advantage of a helpless woman."

They chuckled, wrapped in each other's arms savoring everything about the moment. Eventually, she rolled off and Derik lurched to his feet. She took his offered hand and he drew her erect.

"C'mon." He stepped into the sea, his bikini suit in hand. "No need to put these on. We can swim them to the sloop, and all this work," he winked, "has made me hungry."

~ 41 ~

Ninety minutes later, the last of dinner dishes washed and dried, they settled on portable chairs on the yacht's cockpit, and watched night creep across the water. He swirled a Chablis in his glass while holding her hand, their forearms interlocked.

"As promised, I'm going to tell you about that hurricane, now nearly nine years ago, pirate treasure, and the DuMelle twins." He sipped his wine.

"Pirate treasure? And *twins*?"

"Yes, but let me start at the beginning." Ten minutes passed as he weaved a story about the treachery of the storm, finding safety ... and two long dead pirates bones in the cave, and eventually the chest of treasure that cost them their lives. And the map.

"So, all the treasure you've found was really from that one chest?"

"No," not ready to tell the complete truth. "Much of it, but also because of the maps. Small catches, hidden in caves or buried on a remote island." He lounged back in the chair, feet propped on the gunnel, comfortable at telling a small misdirection. "Always lots of gold, probably Incan, but also precious stones and magnificent jewelry."

"Diamonds?"

"Some." He lowered his feet. "And blood-red rubies, but mostly exquisite emeralds. I think Colombia is noted for those green beauties." He finished his wine and set the glass on the deck.

"I'm retrieving it, a cache at a time. So far, it's all been there as shown on the maps." Some instinct told him to cloud the real facts. "The hard part is figuring out where that island is on the old chart." He rose and brought out the bottle from below to refill their glasses. "Anyhow," he settled back on his chair, "after the storm passed, I sailed to Martinique to refit—both the sloop and me."

He chuckled. "I sold a few Spanish coins and went looking for some way to blow off steam after nearly dying at the hands of storm Chico. That's when I met the DuMelle twins."

"Wow. Twins." She squeezed his hand, refusing to be jealous over things nine years past. "I bet they were beautiful."

"Tall, redhead, gorgeous, and *French* ... *very* French." A soft chuckle. "Every man's dream to make it with twins." He studied her eyes and saw no envy growing there. "I'm not going to say a lot more about that. Despite being hopeless in love with you now, it wouldn't—"

"Don't worry, *Liebchen*, I think I know how we stand." She planted a gentle kiss on his lips.

"Good. Well, suffice it to say, we spent three very passionate days together—"

"With *both* of them?" Brita's eyebrows arched.

"Ahh ... I was a lot younger then, and somehow, I fell in love with both ... and I think, they with me." He reached out and caressed her cheek. "But how could I choose one over the other, and I really couldn't stay. I had to get my treasure out, and my home was Florida. It was the hardest thing I ever did." He shrugged. "I almost didn't make it, and those girls filled my head for years ... until I met you."

"You still think of them?" She had both his hands in hers.

"Rarely now, and it's mostly curious, never passionately, since we've been together."

"Tactfully done." She giggled. "I'd love to see some of that treasure though. You know, the designers' convention is next week. Anything in there I might wear to the gala?"

"What a thing to ask," he said as he drew her to her feet and led her to the cabin hatch.

"I was just kidding, Derik." They descended the small ladder into the lounge. "I'm not—"

"Shh." He pulled her into his arms and backed her against the small dresser. She crossed her arms around his neck and their lips met, the warmth of his love infusing him. He slid one hand inside a top drawer as they continued to kiss.

He arched his head back, fingers of his other hand caressing her cheek.

"I suspected when I revealed my treasure secrets, you'd be interested in seeing some. I *did* bring a little thing along to show you. Maybe to wear at the gala."

Brita's eyes flared, one hand covering a silent "Ohh" from her lips.

"Derik! Ohmygod. It's unbelievable." Her fingers skimmed lightly over the piece, hanging from his hands.

Long, brilliant-faceted, dark, bluish-green stones, linked together on either side of a larger, oval jewel, all set in 22 karat gold, with strands of more emeralds dangling in a tapered pattern, creating a shallow V.

"I've—I've never seen anything like it." Moisture filled her eyes as he fastened it around her neck.

Derik stepped back and regarded his love, her face still rift with shock. "Gorgeous deserves gorgeous, my love. You'll knock their eyes out at the gala."

"It must be worth a fortune." She turned to view herself

in a mirror above the stack of drawers. "I've got the perfect gown from my couture collection."

"It's thirty-three carats of almost perfect, fully faceted Colombian stones, set in nearly pure, 22 karat gold. It's appraised at 350 K. I suspect it was crafted as a present for royalty, maybe even the Spanish Queen."

"*Mein gott.*" Though Brita spoke perfect, barely accented English, she seemed to revert to German when excited ... or scared. "I'm thrilled you will let me wear this at the party."

"Of course." He chuckled. "But I'm not l*oaning* it to you, darling. It's a gift of love."

"You're *kidding!*" Her eyes even wider that before. "It's too valuable. You can't—"

"But I can. It's only a tiny fraction of what I've found."

She came into his arms and smothered him with kisses, their togs disappearing as they shuffled toward the yacht's one stateroom.

That night's sex was filled with consuming love and adoration ... more than mere passion, and its completion spilled well into the early morning hours.

They eventually found sleep, four hours before dawn.

~ 42 ~

Gorya's nap was interrupted when his cell phone did a jitterbug on the small table beside his reclined easy-chair. He stretched, yawned, then plucked it up and scanned the caller ID: ALENA.

Gorya popped his chair upright and answered the call.

"So, Cuz. Ya finally got something?"

"Yeah. I think you're gonna like it too." A short pause with the sound of crinkling paper. "There's gonna be that clothing designers' conference I told you about, next weekend at the Miami Beach Convention Center, with a big kickoff party on Friday night at the swanky Doral Country Club."

"How's that gonna help us get that broad? Big crowd of people."

"Sure, but you don't have to do it at the party." A small chuckle. "I heard Kruger and the blonde guy talking. She's got a new line of goods they're gonna feature at the show, so, they're gonna be in her office after the shop closes, preparing the samples."

"You know what time?" Gorya moved to his desk and pulled over a note pad.

"The party—a gala, the call it—starts at seven, and she's gonna close early. They should be up there between four and six."

"Perfect. We make it look like robbery." He settled on his desk chair. "You leave door unlocked?"

"Yes, the back door. If you're careful, they'll never hear you enter."

"I *always* careful, Cuz." He stroked his chin. "Gonna need some extra muscle. Oleg never made bail and still in slam. Better get someone not connected to me. You know guy?"

"Lemme think." Soft humming as she pondered. "Yeah, Dimitri Tomov is muscle for a Russian drug boss. He owes me one, but it'll cost you. Reliable guy, though."

"How much?"

"Two G's would make him happy and eager."

"Shit. Oleg's on payroll. Two G's, huh?"

"You want a pro, Gorya. He's a guy you can rely on."

"Okay. This guy, Brand, ain't no pushover, so like you say, I want best. Make contact and have him call me. We'll hit 'em Friday at five."

"Gotcha," she said. "I'll call him tonight. He should drop by before, so everyone's comfortable with each other."

"Okay. You keep job at shop so no one get suspicious."

"Will do. I actually like it there. Brita's a good boss." She sighed. "Won't be a job there after she's gone and the Brand guy's dead, I guess."

"Yah, but business is business, and we gonna do this."

"I get it. Good luck, Cuz." And she disconnected.

Gorya laid his phone on the desk and turned to Alik, who'd just entered.

"We hitting the Kruger babe at work on Friday. You can kill blonde guy and get first shot at that hot little cunt, but remember, no damage, or I get real mad."

"No problem, Bro. I give her little shot. Keep her calm." He grinned at Gorya.

"I can hardly wait."

~ 43 ~

Derik glanced up from reading text messages on his cell phone as Chick's black Suburban pulled into the parking lot and settled next to Derik's scarred, white Honda Civic. He pocketed his phone and joined his partner on the drive.

Chick nodded at the non-descript sedan and chuckled. "Still suspicious about being shadowed, buddy?"

"Usually only when I'm coming here." They headed for the door of their garage converted into a vault. "I'm pretty sure it's not paranoia. I'm certain I've been followed at least three times when driving the Jag." He paused at the door to punch in the code to the magnetic lock, followed by a scan of his eyeball.

"Really?" Chick's eyebrows arched.

"Yeah." The locks clicked open, withdrawing three deadbolts, and they stepped inside. The door closed and relocked behind them. "Different vehicles each time," Derik continued as Chick worked the keypad and eye scanner on the inner door to the vault room, set in the repurposed repair bays. As an ultimate safety, Derik's treasure couldn't be accessed without both of them there.

"I went through simple evasive maneuvers with lots of turns and doubling back, and all three stuck with me." They paused in front of their bank vault-type door. "They probably wanted to discover where I stored the treasure." He worked the combination to the vault, and then both of their eyes were scanned.

"That's why I bought that old, non-descript Honda and parked it in the garage, far from the Jag. No one looking for me would pay any attention to a beat up, white Civic."

The whir of the locks withdrawing, followed by three thumps, indicated the six-foot door was unlocked. Chick pulled it open and they walked inside.

"So, what's on the agenda today, Pard? More goodies for an auction, or do you have another private buyer?"

"Some of both. There's a guy in Virginia who's hot for that jeweled chalice. He's the high bidder off that private site, at a million-five."

Derik retrieved the fifteen-inch-tall, 22 karat gold vase, etched with a ribald scene of cavorting naked women, and encrusted with diamonds and rubies. He secured it in bubble wrap before placing it in a duffel he'd brought in with him.

"I'm also gonna sell two ingots to a gold merchant in the diamond district, and send four doubloons and some of the jewelry to Christie's for their next auction." He opened a drawer of one of six cabinets containing coins and jewels, and after pawing over an assortment of rings, selected one.

"Aha. Got it." Derk turned and proffered a ring to Chick. "Like it?"

"A Beauty." Chick rolled it around his palm: pure yellow gold centered by a large, brilliant cut marquise emerald, surrounded by small, faceted diamonds on each side. "Almost a shame to sell it."

"No. I wanted to ask your permission to keep it personally."

"You don't need my permission, Derik. This is your treasure, not mine."

"Yeah, but I made you an equal partner at the beginning.

I could never have gotten all this done without your help and discretion."

"Yeah, I know, and it was very generous of you. It's more than I coulda ever hoped for. Anyway, of course, take whatever you want. I suspect you're gonna give it to Brita, huh?"

"Good guess." A wide grin split his face. "It'll go with that neckless I gave her, and I plan a dual purpose."

"What's that?"

"We're going to that big designers' bash at Doral next week. She'll wear the neckless, and I'm gonna give her the ring there ... and ask her to marry me."

"Wow!" Chick drew his friend in for a warm hug. "I'm really happy or you, Bro." He studied his partner for a moment.

"And Martinique? You've put it totally behind you?"

Derik paused, a finger rubbing the crease of his nose. "Frankly, I can't really say, pal." He sighed. "Falling so hard for those twins ... I don't know. But that was nearly nine years ago, and I left knowing nothing could ever come of it."

He plucked a small, velvet box from a shelf, set the ring inside, and slipped it into his cargo pocket. "I guess what I feel is, that was then, and this is now, and Brita doesn't play second fiddle to anyone. I feel damned lucky she loves me the way I love her." He turned back to the cabinets. "I'm hoping she says yes."

He glanced at Chick. "Can't wait to start raising a family. Boys or girls ... doesn't matter," he chuckled, "they'll learn to sail, fish, and hunt."

"Sounds like a plan." Chick planted a friendly punch on his shoulder. "You ever talk to Brita about kids, though?"

"Can't imagine it being a problem." Derik shrugged. "She's young, fit, and comes from a family of five."

Derik selected four doubloons, two other rings ... one emerald and the other ruby ... and two jeweled bracelets, all from the cabinet drawers. Each were carefully packaged and slipped into a second duffel, along with two twenty-five-pound ingots. The jeweled chalice resided in its own tote.

As they exited the building, Derik scanned the surroundings, but saw nothing threatening. With so much wealth—more than anyone but the two of them knew about—he was always cautious and alert.

Back at their cars, the duffels were slipped into the back seat floor. Derik turned to Chick. "We're gonna have to make time to discuss what to do about the rest of the treasure. At this rate, we'll both be dead before it's half converted."

"I agree. You've already made me wealthier than I could have ever imagined." Chick laid a hand on Derik's shoulder. "My family and heirs are fixed for generations. Let's finish our contract with Brita, though, before we make any hard decision." His lips tilted up. "And you're gonna have a wedding to plan. The booty can wait until things settle down."

"Agreed." He opened his Civic's door. "I may not make it back to the office today. I've gotta get these ingots to the gold merchant and complete the sale on the chalice. He'll do a wire transfer into our Cayman account. And then I've gotta send off the coins and jewelry to Christie's." He slipped onto the driver seat. "So, I'll see you in the morning."

"Okay. Nothing special going on this afternoon anyhow." He leaned on the door frame. "I'm really happy you finally found love here, Derik. You deserve the best, and Brita seems to be high on that scale."

He stepped back as Derik fired up the Honda's engine and closed the door. "See you in the a.m.," Chick called with a wave as Derik drove off. Once settled inside his Suburban,

Chick lingered while the a/c cooled the inside. His fingers massaged his eyes as he thought about his best friend.

He was happy Derik was finally getting past the magical hooks redhead twins had snagged in him. It took eight years and one very special lady to break that spell, and Brita was the first woman Derik had dated that was really worthy of him.

Still, one question nagged at him. Chick had little doubt Brita would happily marry his partner. Their mutual love was clearly deep and undeniable. But Chick worried that Brita had an equal passion for her business. He'd rarely seen anyone so consumed with making a success.

Having kids could interfere with that. What would she put first? Derik, or Allure Attire?

He sighed. Derik would learn the answer to that soon enough.

~ 44 ~

Derik lounged against the hood of his white Jag sports coup and watched the stream of workers exiting Allure Attire. As planned, Brita sent her employees home early so they could prepare for the big designers' convention that would kick off that evening with an elegant bash and awards ceremony at the ritzy Doral Country Club. Brita was in the running for the Hottest New Line Award, and they had a lot of prep to do to properly display their sports line.

Derik pushed away from his car and carrying a garment bag, headed for the door as the last of Brita's people trickled out. Brita and he would go over those outfits they would demonstrate that night at the gala. Brita would also walk the runway, modeling her adult sport line, something she hadn't done in over five years.

He pushed through the door and seeing the lower floor empty, locked it behind him. Only Brita and he should be still inside. He glanced at her second-floor office windows, lights on and shadows moving. Brita was preparing for the evening. He climbed the stars and rapped on the door before entering, not wanting to startle her.

Brita hovered over her desk, studying sketches of her newest designs. She glanced up and smiled. "Hi, lover. Right on time." She nodded at his garment bag. "Your tux?"

"Yeah." He hung it on a coat hook. "Figured it'd be easier to change here and go directly to the Doral."

"Good." An impish grin creased her lips. "And that way, I get to see you nearly naked. Maybe I'll finally be able to have my way with you."

"You've been having your way with me for months, darling, and it's been wonderful." He perched on a corner of her desk and peered at the sketches. "These for tonight?"

"No, just some new ideas for additions to our junior line." She rose and reached over to cup his chin for a kiss. "Samples for tonight's models are downstairs on the tables."

Derik stood and drew Brita into his arms. The kiss was tender and lingering, savoring loves rather than igniting passion. They clung together, luxuriating in the heat of their bodies nestled close. The kiss broke, they arched necks back, grins tickling both sets of lips. "If we start this, we'll be late to the party." Derik caressed her cheek. "We've got prep work to do." He reluctantly drew back. "Let's go down and look at what you've prepared." He took her hand and started for the exit.

They descended to the main floor and Brita led the way to one of the finishing tables on which were neatly stacked four piles of sports clothes.

"You've arranged for teen models to walk the runway at the gala tonight?" Derik picked up a patterned short-sleeve blouse and a scalloped-hem skirt, and rubbed the fabric between his thumb and forefinger. "Nice material. Should be comfortable in hot weather like we have down here."

"Yes, and the blouse has a moisture-wicking feature to help with perspiration."

"Terrific. Looks like you've thought of everything." He retrieved a small, wheeled suitcase from under the table. "Let's pack this up. Anything else needed for tonight?"

"Yes, my love. Two of our adult outfits, tennis and pickleball, which I'll model myself." Brita gathered those items off another table and added them to the case.

"Will I be jealous at all the hungry looks you'll be getting?"

"I hope not." She chuckled, then glanced at her gold Piaget watch. She took his hand, twirled into his arms, and arched her neck, their lips inches apart. "I will only have eyes for you, *Liebchen*." Brita grinned. "I am *so* excited for tonight. Fortunately, we have plenty of time to dress before we must leave." She planted a warm kiss on his lips. "But I must get these outfits to our models early and fine-tune their presentations."

She wiggled free and caressed his cheek. "If all goes as I hope, we'll have plenty of time for a proper celebration afterwards."

"Yes, and I have an idea for something to make the evening even more special." He held both her hands, their eyes locked."

"What? Tell me." She stepped to the table and zipped the travel case closed.

"It's a surprise. Something I think you'll ..." Derik paused and cocked his head at the sound of three beeps. "A door-opening alarm?" He scanned the front entrance. "I locked that one."

"The back door from the alley!" She glanced at the entrance to her storage room. "But I always keep it locked."

"Brita, get upstairs and call 911."

"Derik, what d'you think ...?"

"The Ukrainians are out on bail."

~ 45 ~

Gorya parked his black Hummer in a small alcove in the alley, fifty feet from the rear door of Allure Attire. He glanced at his brother next to him and Dimitri Tomov in the back.

"Ready?"

They nodded.

"Okay. Alik goes first. He grabs woman. Dimitri, you next, go for big blond guy." His lips drew into a tight snarl. "Careful. He tough guy. Best to kill him quick."

He stepped from the driver side onto the cinder path, and his two cohorts followed. They gathered in front of the SUV's hood.

"I come last to backup, if needed. They busy getting ready for big party and don't suspect nothing, so should go easy."

"Yeah, Bro," Alik muttered, "that's what we thought in Coral Gables. This Brand guy not so dumb." He looked at Dimitri. "If you take him down but not kill, I want the pleasure."

"I get it," Gorya laid his hand on his brother bulky bicep, "But don't take chance. He can fight."

"Yeah, okay," Alik growled. "Do what ya gotta, Tomov. Him dead is good enough, I guess."

"Okay." Gorya pointed up the alley. "Let's get it done. I want blond bitch turning big trick for us soon." They paused in front of the metal door. He nudged his bigger brother.

"Remember, girl packs a big kick, but don't mess her up. Her looks are money." Gorya tested the handle and found it unlocked, just as Alina promised.

He glanced back at his cohorts, nodded, shoved the door open, and stood aside as Alik and Dimitri moved into the storeroom. The brute had a syringe of heroin out, and the Russian his Beretta 9mm at the ready.

Gorya cursed at the chimed triple beeps, signaling an open door, and followed.

~ 46 ~

Derik sensed Brita hurrying up the stairs as he scoured the factory floor for a weapon. He had his .380 Smith & Wesson ankle gun tucked into his belt for easy access, but he wanted a cudgel. If this were the Kolodenkos, he suspected there'd be hand-to-hand, and he'd need an advantage over the Golem-size brother.

He strode to a close-by cutting table, snatched up a nearly empty roll of material, and yanked off the remain few yards of cloth. The three-foot-long, five-inch diameter, thick rigid cardboard tube would make a serviceable club. He hurried back to poise beside the store room door, just as it began to open.

As Alik stepped through, Derik swung his club, catching the big man squarely on the bridge of his nose and across his eyes. The hulk staggered into the room and dropped to one knee, his arms flailing. A large syringe slipped from his grasp and clattered to the floor.

"Soneofabitch," he roared, his hands to his face, blood spewing from his nose.

Derik had no time to follow up his attack on Alik as a second, husky guy leaped in, brandishing a large pistol. Derik swung his makeshift bat and cracked him across the wrist. The gun discharged as it slipped from his grip, the slug embedding harmlessly into a far wall.

Undeterred, the second man spun and delivered a hard

karate kick to Derik's chest, driving him back. Then he charged, a five-inch switchblade flicking open in his other hand.

Derik staggered but managed to retain his feet, gasped for breath, and shuffled back. He ducked under a swipe of the blade and bunted the arm away with his elbow, then stepped in and delivered a fist hard into the man's gut, drawing a breathy "oof." He didn't go down and managed to head-butt Derik.

Derik blinked, but snatched the knife-hand's wrist, sensing the guy's other arm somewhat immobilized from the blow of his club. The Russian delivered an elbow to Derik's cheek, momentarily stunning him and bringing tears. The room filled with grunts and curses as they tussled, each trying to deliver a telling leg kick.

As they fought, Derik spied the other brother, Gorya, snatch up the hypo.

"Where's my hot little bitch?" he growled. The Ukrainian glanced at the stairs and then back at the two men grappling. He had a semi-automatic up but no clear shot as Derik twisted and turned as he wrestled with his assailant. Gorya cured and rushed to his brother who was trying to rise, his nose still a gusher.

"Alik, get it together and finish that bastard," he roared. "Dimitri needs help." He tugged his brother to his feet. "I go find girl. You finish guy." He started toward the stairs but paused and glanced back.

Derik found the leverage he sought and shoulder-threw the guy, hurtling him into a shakily advancing Alik.

The Russian's feet smacked into the bigger man's knees, sending him crashing back to the floor, landing hard on his butt. He snarled and snatched at a large pistol, secured in his belt.

"I kill you now, bastard," his voice a nasal squeal.

Derik dropped to one knee and drew his S & W. The other guy wiggled to his seat, and while Derik had no desire to kill one or both—Florida's Stand Your Ground Law would absolve him—he couldn't take them both on, despite their current shaky condition. He slid forward and brought the butt of his small pistol down hard on the Russian's head. He then drew a bead on Alik, who managed to fumble his own weapon, skittering a few feet away.

"Don't," Derik shouted. "I don't want to kill you, but I will if you make me."

The bigger man glared at him but hesitated. "Gorya," he yelled.

"Okay, I kill him first, Bro, then we get girl. He can't get us both."

Derik watch Gorya sidle to his right to get a better angle. He didn't think he could shoot the giant and still get off a shot at the brother, but if he didn't do something quick, it wasn't going to end well for him.

Gorya raised his weapon. "Now you die, you bastard."

Derik slithered sidewise, trying to put the bigger brother between them. Who to go at first and still have a chance to survive? He gritted his teeth as the hulk edged toward his weapon. A shiver coursed through him as a thundering boom echoed through the room, and Gorya, eyes flared, flew face down onto the floor.

Alik screamed and snatched up his pistol just as Derik squeezed off two shots.

~ 47 ~

A few minutes earlier

"Brita, get upstairs and call 911."

"Derik, what d'you think …?"

"The Ukrainians are out on bail."

She stared at him, momentarily frozen. She knew the nasty loan sharks were no longer in jail, but she never thought …. the sound of hangers sliding on rods shook her free, and she bolted for the stairs.

Brita paused at their foot and glanced back. Derik was at a cutting table, ripping cloth from a roll of fabric. He was apparently seeking the heavy cardboard core as a club. She hated to leave him to face their attackers alone, but he was her very capable White Knight. She gritted her teeth and bound up to her balcony.

Her cell phone was on her desk for the 911 call, once she was sure they were under siege. She hoped Derik could hold out until help came. She'd die if anything bad happened to him.

She grimaced. She might end up worse than dead if that happened. Derik thought they wanted to turn her into a drugged-up prostitute. She hit the landing in time to see her lover belt the troll-like brother across the face with his makeshift club. Sounds of men fighting followed her into her office. She grabbed her phone and dialed 911.

"This is 911. What is your emergency?" A calm voice over

the phone did nothing to cool her panic.

"We're being attacked at my business by two—no three—men. They want to kidnap me." She glanced at her closet. "Please hurry. I don't know if we can hold them off."

"I have your location. Police should be there in six minutes. Try to stay calm, and hide if you can."

"They're gonna kill my boyfriend if you don't make it in time." She panted, out of breath, her hand shaking.

"The police are coming. Hide and leave your phone on."

Brita clenched her jaw and swiped tears from her eyes. "Tell police to come through the alley. The front door is locked." She laid the phone, still connected, on the desk.

"I must go now." Shouts came from below.

"Alik, get it together and finish that bastard," shouted from below. Grunts and curses filled the air. "I gotta find girl."

Brita lunged toward her wardrobe. When she'd heard the Kolodenkos had been released on bond, she decided to take out her own insurance.

Now was the time for that to pay off.

~ 48 ~

Derik watched Alik slump back, a black hole in his forehead and his lower jaw shattered. He gasped, pent up breath whistling out between tight lips.

The big brute was dead, and his brother laid in a widening pool of blood. The third guy, probably hired muscle, seemed down for the count.

His eyes swept the suddenly quiet room, and the smell of gunfire lingered in the air.

"What the hell …" He looked for Brita and found her, standing on her balcony, her 12-gauge pump shotgun cradled in the ready position at an angle across her breasts.

"You brought your shotgun from home?" His voice cracked, and his eyebrows arched.

She nodded. "When I heard these scum were free, I thought it was a good idea. Just in case." Her voice a hoarse rasp as tears trickled across her cheeks. "I was right, wasn't I?" She stared down, eyes wide. "The only things I've ever killed before … was grouse, and lots of clay pigeons." She made a wobbly and unsteady descent down the stairs, the gun still cradled in her left arm, her eyes locked on the third guy, sprawled on the floor.

Derik struggled to his feet and limped to meet her as she reached the bottom. He gently pried the 12-gauge from rigid fingers, leaned at against the rail, and folded her into his arms for a protracted hug. He kissed her forehead, the corner of his lips tugging up.

"You okay?"

She nodded and swiped away tears.

"You've done some trap shooting, huh?" He thumbed moisture from her cheek. "Clay pigeons?"

"Yes." She sighed and laid her head on his shoulder. "Actually, I was a finalist for Germany's Olympic skeet team, but my career took precedence."

"Wow!" He glanced at the storage room's door and the sound of fast arriving sirens, cars screeching to a halt in the alley. "Thank god you know how to use that thing, or you might be short one lover."

She forced a chuckle. "Even Don Quixote needed a Sancho. And you maintain you reputation as my White Knight, now a third time my rescuer. How can I not love this man?" The lingering kiss was filled with much more than passion.

They broke apart at the thump of heavy feet coming through her store room. Seconds later, three men in blue burst in, weapons at the ready. They surveyed the couple wrapped in each other's arms and the three figures on the floor. The first cop, wearing sergeant stripes, waved his pistol as he advanced on Derik and Brita, still huddled together.

"What the hell went down here? The emergency operator said someone was being kidnapped."

Derik and Brita separated, but he still held her hand. He gestured at the figures on the floor.

"Those are two Ukrainian gangsters and probably a hired muscle. They were already under arrest for an earlier attack on Ms. Kruger," his head tilted toward his lover, "and it looks like they made bail and were trying for her a second time."

He sighed, released Brita's hand, and shuffled on aching legs toward the bodies.

"Luckily, I was here to defend her. We had a brawl, and I was forced to shoot the big guy, who was about to plug me, then Ms. Kruger, who happily brough her shotgun from home when she heard they were out, shot that one before he could kill me." He faced the cop.

"Classic Stand Your Ground defense. They broke into our place of business and tried to kill me and grab her." Derik grimaced. "They were big into prostitution."

The officer squatted next to the brothers, felt their throats for a pulse, and shook his head.

"Not any more, it seems." He rose. "Anyway, I got a call into Homicide and a detective is on the way. Everyone stays put until he sorts this out, but I suspect it is what it looks like, and you two are probably in the clear."

Derik handed him his pistol and nodded at the Remington 12-gauge. "These are our weapons. Is it okay if we go up to the office to clean up and change? We've got an important affair to attend in a couple of hours, and we need to collect ourselves and change our clothes."

The cop shrugged. "Forensics will want to swab your hands and clothes for blood and fibers, but since you're not contesting what happened, it may be okay." He withdrew his police radio. "Let me check with the detective."

Five-minutes later they had approval from a Detective Harris, who was en route. He was the same one who'd covered the Kolodenko attack at Brita's home in Coral Gables.

They ascended to Brita's office on the mezzanine and collapsed on her sofa, she on Derik's lap, crying softly into his shoulder. He held her close and stroked her head, gently kissing her cheek and neck.

"This was so terrible, Derik." She raised her head, salty rivulets trickling across her cheeks. "I've ... I've never ..."

"Killed someone?" He grunted. "Me either, darling, but it *was* them or us. What they planned for you was even worse than death, I suspect."

She shook her head and growled, "The bastards!"

"Yeah." He stroked her cheek. "Overall, I guess we did the world a favor." They started at a rap on the door, and looking up, saw Detective Harris in the opening.

"Detective." Brita slid off his lap, and Derik rose, waving the man in. "Is it too trite to say we've gotta stop meeting like this."

Harris entered, chuckled, and proffered his hand. "Yeah, well after today, I'm guessing it may not happen again." The wiry little man studied them. "You both okay?"

"I'm a bit battered but not down, Detective." Derik touched his bruised cheek and glanced out the door. "I'm guessing they were focused on grabbing Ms. Kruger for their sex trade. The big guy had a hypo full of what was probably heroin."

"Right. We've put that in an evidence bag. That's how they work. They make the girl dependent on them for the drugs, so they're forced to turn tricks to get a fix."

"Bastards!" Brita reiterated.

"Anyway," Harris continued, "there's no reason you can't get ready for tonight. We can wait until tomorrow to take your statements at the station." He pocketed his Android. "You're going to the designer's gala at the Doral? Some off-duty cops are providing security."

He turned at the sound of new people arriving below. "Hang on a sec, willya." He strode to the balcony, looked down, and yelled and waved before returning to them.

"CSU just arrived, so if you don't mind a short delay, let 'em come up and swab you for blood, GSR, and fibers, just to make 'em happy. So my boss has nothing to complain about."

"Not a problem, Detective." He glanced at Brita who nodded. "We've got a couple of hours, and we're still winding down. We certainly don't want you in any hot water with your boss." He chuckled. "We know how *that* works."

Harris studied them for a moment. "I know you got a shindig to go to, and that'll probably keep you too busy to dwell on what went down here, but you both should consider seeing a therapist, sooner than later." His eyes held Derik's. "Taking a life, no matter how deserving, can be a traumatic experience. You may feel okay now, but that might change as it sinks in."

He sighed. "Even cops, who see murder and mayhem every day, will see a shrink after a deadly shooting."

They all turned to the door as a man and woman entered, both wearing blue vests emblazoned with CSU.

~ 49 ~

Twenty minutes later Miami-Dade CSU departed Brita's office after they finished swabbing samples from them.

Derik followed them through the door and lingered for a moment on the balcony, surveying the scene below. The dead Kolodenkos were bagged and already carted off by the Medical Examiner's team, and the rest of the CSU crew were finished collecting whatever they thought they needed to tie up what should be an open-and-shut case.

Detective Harris waved as he and the rest of his people exited through the alley door. Derik gave a thumbs-up and descended to lock that entry behind them, then returned to Brita, still perched on the sofa, head in her hands. He settled next to her, an arm around her, and she nestled her head on his shoulder, emitting a soft sigh.

"Do you think those Ukrainian monsters might have henchmen who could still come after us?" She hugged him.

"I don't think so. At least, not in America. A deep Internet search I did showed no family here other than two cousins, Oleg and Alena Popov, and from what I could—"

"Alena Popov is his cousin?" She touched his arm.

"Yes. You know her?"

"She's one of the women I hired for the expansion." Brita wiggled around and took his hands. "Do you think she's the one who unlocked that door?"

Derik stroked his chin. "Probably." He fished out his cell

phone. "She'd certainly would know our schedule, and that the place would be empty today after four, except for us." He glanced at the card the detective left and dialed the number.

"Harris," was his answer.

"Hey, Detective. This is Derik Brand."

"Yeah. Come up with something we should know?"

"It seems so. I'd did a deep dive on the Kolodenkos after that melee in Coral Gables, looking for background, and learned he had a cousin here, one Alena Popov."

"So?"

"Ms. Kruger hired an Alena Popov as a seamstress during a recent expansion. She's still an employee here." He glanced at Brita, who nodded.

"Okay. The probable insider who unlocked that door. Good to know, and saves us some time in research. I'll have her picked up. In case we miss her, let me know in the unlikelihood she shows for work on Monday." Harris made an unintelligible comment to someone in the car, then, "Enjoy your evening. You guys deserve a nice break." And he disconnected.

Derik pocketed his phone and drew Brita to her feet. "C'mon, beautiful, we gotta shake this off, clean up, and wow 'em at the gala tonight." His eyes swept the room. "I'm guessing no shower anywhere on the premises."

She shook her head." Just my private bath up here, and an employees' unit downstairs."

"Okay. You've got towels and wash clothes, and that'll have to do." He grinned. "I'll wash you, and you can do me." He tugged her toward the bathroom door. "Time's awasting."

"Oh, nice." She chuckled. "That's going to be fun."

Minutes later, they stood naked on the tiled floor, wet, soapy wash clothes venturing across bare skin. As he swirled the cloth over her perfect breasts, her prominent nipples snapping to their full glory, her sudsy hand found its way between his legs, binging what lingered there to immediate attention.

Derik crushed her to him, their bodies molding, slippery hands in desperate journeys across damp skin, their mouths fused with a new urgency. His lips and tongue coursed across her eyes, her cheek, an ear lobe, down her graceful neck, and onto those two nipples, standing proud.

Brita shuddered and gasped, goose bumps exploding across her back and arms as she gyrated her already soaking pussy against his rigid cock.

Derik snatched handfuls of firm butt, backed her against the sink counter, and dropped to his knees, tongue lapping her juices, swirling and tweaking her erect pleasure button.

Brita shivered and arched her pelvis into his attack.

"Oh, Derik! *Mein Gott*, take me. Take me—now!"

Both hands under her taut thighs, he hoisted her onto the sink's counter, and was quickly buried inside her engorged lips, her legs locked around his hips as they thrust together.

Panting and feral growls echoed inside the room, their intensity more a release of pent-up emotions from facing near death than just a dance of love.

Brita's arms circled his neck, and she slathered his face with kisses, his tongue locked inside her lips, hers swirling his.

"Yes, my White Knight, yes!" Gasping for breath. "I love you. God, I love you."

"Cum, baby, cum." Long, deep thrusts accompanied his thumb, teasing her clitoris.

"Oh, *Gott*." She surged against him in a growing frenzy, her pussy clamping his cock in a tight, velvet glove, drawing a growl as he released in a gush. He continued to plunge into her, his thumb still busy, and she shuddered and came in a soaking spurt amidst a howl of joy, her legs and arms crushing their sweat-slickened bodies together.

Wheezing breath and thundering hearts waned as they clung to each other, trading soft kisses, he locked inside her still pulsing pussy, moving slowly as they wound down.

"*Mein Gott*, that was intense." She eased back and stroked his cheek. "I never felt so in *need* of your love as that moment."

He grunted. "I suspect having just surviving a fight for our lives may have ramped up the intensity." His fingers ventured lightly across her damp skin. "You are one incredible woman, and I'm blessed that I found you."

"No more than I finding you, my love. You complete me."

Derik eased back, exhaled a soft sigh, and peeked at his Rolex. "We've only an hour to finish cleaning up, dress, and get to the gala." His lips tilted into an impish grin. "I'm eager to see you all decked out in one of your fanciest gowns and sporting that emerald neckless" He chuckled. "You're gonna knock their eyes out."

Twenty minutes later, they descended to the main level, he in a white tux offset by a black cummerbund and bow tie, his two face bruises barely hidden by concealer makeup. She radiated in an ivory silk formal, backless and deep-vee in front, slashed to her navel. The two sides barely covered her firm, full breasts. Settled between those lovely mounds, circling her graceful neck, sat the glistening emerald and diamond neckless.

Derik suspected she'd be a show-stopper.

~ 50 ~

Derik pulled his white Jag up to the valets at the front of Doral Country Club's opulent clubhouse. He stepped out, accepted his ticket, and circled the rear in time to offer Brita a hand to exit the low-hung sports coupe.

He returned to his trunk to retrieve the roller bag and handed it to an attendant with instructions to bring it to the models' dressing area. Returning to Brita, they paused, hand-in-hand, eyes locked, their faces split by wide grins, savoring the relief of being there ... alive.

Her arm linked with his left elbow, and they strolled through the entrance, headed for the ballroom. The striking couple drew admiring looks from both sexes, the men for Brita's plunging neckline and long, shapely legs, and the women for her dazzling neckpiece. Derik drew scrutiny, as much for his unsuccessfully disguised facial bruises as his handsome profile and athletic stature.

They found their table near the end of the runway where fashion models would strut their stuff during the dessert course. Derik stood by as she laid her Judith Lieber jeweled clutch by her seat, gave him a brief kiss and a gentle caress of his battered cheek, and headed backstage to check on their teen models and the outfits they were to display.

Brita found Cindy and Carl already unpacking the items.

"These are really cool, Ms. Kruger." Carl, a six-foot, wiry redhead, held up on of their pickleball sets.

"I love how you blended the colors and patterns," Cindy, a five-six, willowy blonde, said.

"Yes, they'll look great on you kids." She helped them lay out and match each pair.

"Carl, you'll start with pickleball, and Cindy with tennis."

She picked up a pair of long, taper-legged pants and a collared short-sleeve, cotton-blend shirt. "Carl, you'll go with this golf outfit next, and Cindy, you find the scalloped golf skirt and matching top." She laid it down and stepped back. "Then finish off with Cindy in pickleball and Carl in tennis." She gestured at the suitcase.

The teens sorted through the outfits, setting up the sets.

"Everything is properly sized for each of you." Brita nodded toward six curtained off cubbies. "Those are the dressing rooms. You'll have to be quick between walks so not to hold things up."

She patted the sixteen-year-old girl on the back as she stepped over and drew aside a curtain and inspected the interior.

"There are three other designers displaying their goods, so you can work a staggered schedule so not to be too rushed." Brita withdrew two more outfits from the bottom of the case. "I'll also be modeling these—one for tennis and one for golf, so I'll be back here if you run into any snags." Her eyes swept from one to the other. "Any questions?"

Head shakes confirmed all seemed clear. They were experienced, despite their tender years. Brita took her two garments and hung them in a dressing room. After a quick scan of the area, she left to return to her table.

Derik awaited her, lounging on one of the chairs, a Scotch in his hand and a vodka martini by her seat.

"I think a stiff drink or two is called for to finish settling our nerves." He chuckled as he rose and held the chair for her. "This should be an enjoyable and memorable evening—

in more than one way, I'd say."

She nodded and picked up her drink without sitting. After two sips, she turned to him.

"That was needed. Now let's dance." She snatched his hand and towed him toward the open floor, which was filling up with glamorously decked-out couples. The music at that moment was an Ed Sheeran ballad.

Derik took her in his arms, and they began to sway to the beat. Her four-inch stilettos were enough so she could easily rest her head on his shoulder.

"We're getting a lot of stares, my love." He nuzzled, then kissed her ear. "You look amazing."

"So do you, *Liebling*, despite your battered face, but I think it's mostly for this incredible necklace you've given me."

"Don't sell yourself short, darling. You're a knockout, even if you wear nothing." He nipped the ear. "I can testify to that."

She giggled. "What a thing to say," and gave him a squeeze.

They danced next to a rumba and anther ballad, but when the band switched to something fast, Derik led her back to their table. The tune ended, followed by an announcement that dinner was about to be served.

~ ~ ~

Derik eased back in his chair and studied Brita, still sipping her second martini.

"The sea bass good?" His smile was filled with love.

"Delicious." She finished the vodka drink. "And obviously, so was your fillet mignon." She chuckled. "There's not a scrap left on your plate."

He gave a satisfied grunt and patted his stomach. The food was superb. The sides as well as the main courses: roasted red potatoes in garlic and onions, and string bean almondine. The delectable odor as it arrived had fired up his hunger.

The dessert, Baked Alaska, would come during the runway walk of the models, which was about to start. Brita patted her lips and rose.

"Please unclasp the necklace, Derik." She turned her back to him. "I'm going back to get ready, and I don't want to leave it in a dressing room."

"Of course." He rose. "Good thinking." He unsnapped the emerald piece and slipped it into his inside jacket pocket.

She pivoted and gave him a fierce kiss. "I love you more than I can say." As she strode toward the back stage, it was announced the fashion show was about to begin.

Cindy was second on the runway, to the announcement: "Junior tennis attire, by Allure Attire."

A ripple of appreciation ran through the room.

Fourth was Carl in the pickleball set, also gaining an appreciative murmur.

And so went. Brita's second walk, in her lady's golf set, wound up the event and drew the loudest applause of the show. Derik was unsure if it were for the togs or the gorgeous blonde wearing them. He was definitely in the camp of those voting for the woman.

He sipped his Scotch and awaited Brita's return, thinking of what else he'd planned for the evening. It was a big step, something he never expected would happen while the twin redheads permeated his thoughts. This was the final move to put them behind him ... he hoped. In any case, that was nearly nine years past, and this seemed right.

He had no doubts he sincerely loved Brita and could

think of nothing that would challenge that. He glanced at the door to the back stage, eager for her return.

~ 51 ~

Brita wended her way toward their table, a glorious goddess, clad in ivory silk, fielding numerous congratulations from both men and women designers. Derik sensed many of the compliments were shadowed with jealousy. He rose and held the seat for her. She scooted in, snatched up a spoon, and attacked her dessert with gusto.

"I'm suddenly famished." She chuckled. "Strutting my stuff on a runway always made me hungry, but when I was a full-time model, something like this was a no-no." She gulped down a spoonful of vanilla ice cream. "Now I don't care if I gain weight."

"Listen, babe, whatever weight you may have gained looks fabulous." He rose and replaced the emerald necklace around her neck.

She glanced back at him, grinned, and renewed her attack on the dessert. "It really went well, didn't it?" She licked her spoon. "The kids were great."

"Absolutely. Real professionals," said as he caressed the back of her head, "but the star was my gorgeous lover. You're so much more beautiful than the typical, skinny model."

"So," she turned to him, a sly smile tickling her lips, "that's why you love me? For my beauty?"

"And the really great sex." He chuckled, then became serious. "Really, beauty is always a first attractor, and on a scale of one-to-ten, you're a twelve ..."

She giggled and shoved him with her shoulder. "Cad."

"I didn't finish." He caught her chin, turned her face to him, and thumbed away a smear of chocolate sauce from the corner of her lips. "I've had plenty of sex with women who looked beautiful, but I never found loved with any of them."

"What about those redhead twins in Martinique?" Her eyebrows arched, lips ticking into a small grin.

He shrugged and shook his head. "That was nine years ago, my darling, and loving you has put them well behind me. I'm talking about now."

He leaned in and kissed her, one hand lightly on the nape of her neck. Easing back, his eyes held hers. "Your difference from all those other girls is that you don't just *look* beautiful, you *are* beautiful—in every way. Your beauty comes from *inside* of you, darling. That's what I fell in love with—the beautiful person you are."

Brita blushed, then laid down her spoon, swiveled toward him, and took his face between her hands.

"Derik, that's the most lovely and romantic thing anyone has ever said to me." She drew him to her for a lingering kiss.

They separated, faces inches apart.

"Not only are you my Sir Lancelot, but a poet too."

"I guess you inspire me, darling." He glanced at the remnants of her baked ice cream treat. "Now, if you've done enough damage to your dessert, how about a dance?"

He offered his hand, which she took, and they rose together. Moments later, they swirled across the floor, bodies molded together, swaying to a lovely old waltz. Derik guided them toward the band and paused to talk to the leader. They shook hands and he returned to his partner, who watched, fists on hips, lips pursed.

"What was that about?" she asked, once more in his arms.

"A small tip to keep them playing slower music as long

as we're on the floor." He nuzzled her neck. "I like you in my arms, not spinning around, almost out of reach."

"Works for me." She kissed his neck. "Nowhere I'd rather be than in your arms." She arched her neck back and searched his face. "A small tip, huh?"

"Just a C-note, so everyone's happy."

She chuckled. "You're something else, *Liebling*." The kiss was filed with passion.

They swayed to four more ballads: John Legend, two from John Mayer, and Nick Jonas ... before he led her off to the adjacent lounge.

They settled on a bench at a back table and ordered drinks, Chevis on the rocks for him, and a dirty vodka martini for her.

They nuzzled and touched, hands making surreptitious ventures under cover of the table top.

"Happy?" he asked.

"Over tonight's full moon. And you?"

"Very." He sighed. "I'm picturing us together, sailing into the sunset, with our kids rumbling around the yacht. I might have to get something—"

"Kids?" Her eyebrows knit. "You want to have kids, Derik? At our age?"

"Sure. Three or four. Sons for me to sail and play sports with, and daughters to take after their gorgeous mom." He searched her face. "You *do* want kids, don't you?"

"I thought, you know, at our age, maybe we were past that." She took his hand. "We'd be so terrific together, just you and me." She turned her head and stared into space.

"At our age?" He shook his head. "We're only in our early thirties. Women have kids into their forties, nowadays." He caught her chin and turned her face to his.

"Brita, don't you want kids?" His dark blue eyes held

hers. "This is important to me." He ran his thumb over the velvet cover of the small box in his left hand, out of sight under the table.

"We never talked about children, Derik. We were so busy falling in love—"

"I know. I just always expected you knew kids came with a family." He sighed again. "It's not a *family* without children. So?" He studied her face. "Kids?"

"I chide people who don't have children, asking what they do for aggravation." She shook her head. "I ... I don't want them." Tears welled in her eyes. "I *never* wanted them. My business and my lover are all that consumes me." She dabbed her eyes with a tissue. "Is that so terrible? That I want to share my life with you, and *only* you?" She dropped her chin.

"I don't know." He expelled a soft groan. "It's a choice, I guess." He lifted her face. "But it's not *my* choice." He brought the three-inch-square box to the table top.

"I was going to ask you to marry me tonight." He laid the velvet case on the table. "Now I don't know what I'm going to do." He slumped back on the bench. "I love you without question, Brit, but ... but I don't think I can marry you if you won't have kids."

"I tied my tubes when I was twenty-two, darling." Tears were in full flow now. "I knew then I never wanted children."

"Oh? I thought you never got pregnant these last months because you took the pill or something."

"No. Tied tubes." She took both his hands. "Can't we get by this, *Liebling*? Little ones would only get in the way. We could be so happy together, just the two of us. Sailing, fishing, working together. It'd be bliss."

"It would, except for a large hole, not filled with the chatter of our babies, making life both more complicated and fun." He slid out from behind the table and rose. He held out a hand. "Come. I'm ready to leave, and I need time to process this."

She took his hand and stood, coming into his arms, her head rested against his chest.

"I love you, Derik, and I want to spend my life with you, but it … it can't be with reservations. Somehow, we have to work this out."

He tilted her chin and they kissed, followed by a sigh. "I just don't know how we can do that, my love. I believe tubes can be untied, but that would mean you making a choice you don't really seem to believe in." He stroked her cheek. "That wouldn't be fair to you." He shook his head and groaned again, moisture creeping into his eyes. "Either way, it'd be a burr under one of our saddles, and that would spell eventual doom for our relationship."

He took her hand and started for the door. "We need time to mull this over, and then do what's right for each of us." He glanced at her. "Neither should do something because it's right for the other, but not for ourself."

She nodded, tiny rivers of salty water coursing across her cheeks. She knew kids were out for her, and that may be the end of their affair. Did he love her enough to change his mind?

But he was right. Doing that would always be a wedge between them, and she was determined not to let that happen.

A few minutes later, settled in his Jag, seatbelts fastened, she turned to him before he began to drive.

"Derik, please don't hate me." Her eyes pooled again.

"Hate you?" He shook his head. "I could never hate you." He laid a hand on her thigh. "I've loved you too much for that. You've made a choice that feels right for you, as I have for me." He sighed. "Unfortunately, those choices are at total odds with each other, and at this moment, I don't see how it can work out."

He straightened and began to drive. "Maybe, in time ..." He trailed off and concentrated on exiting the Doral property.

She hunkered in her seat, head back, eyes closed, mewing softly as tears continued to trickle across her cheeks.

Derik gritted his teeth, determined not to let her crying influence what was a core tenant of his life—a real family meant children.

"I'll drop you at the factory so you can pick up your car." He paused. "It may be best if you spend the night at your place in Coral Gables. We both need time alone to think."

He glanced at her, wedged against the door. "We've come to mean too much to each other over the past months to rush into hasty decisions about our futures. We're still partners in a very nice business, and this thing shouldn't damage that. Okay?"

She nodded and dabbed at her eyes, but avoided his.

They drove on in silence, both mired in angst.

~ 52 ~

Derik slid his coupe next to the curb in front of Allure Attire, shifted to PARK, and noted yellow Crime Scene tape crisscrossing the door. He turned to Brita.

"You okay to drive home?"

She nodded and unsnapped her seatbelt. "I'll come by your place tomorrow evening to pick up a few things, if that's all right." Her eyes were still wet, and mascara streaked her cheeks like war paint.

"I can bring them down in the morning, if you'd like. I planned on coming by to see things are getting straightened up after that donnybrook."

"That's okay. I'd like to do it myself. Of course, you should visit here tomorrow. We're still partners, aren't we?" She forced a weak smile. "I ... I look forward to your input."

"Right. And you'll need someone to clean up, once the police release the crime scene. Your shop will probably be closed for at least a day or two." He took her hand. "You gonna be okay?"

"Yes, I think so." She shuddered. "That's sure to haunt me for a while, though." She looked at her watch. "Too late to call Rolf tonight, but I'll get him early so he can at least get the blood scrubbed off, once I'm back in business, and before workers show up on Monday." She sighed. "Luckily, it's the weekend and only a few were scheduled for tomorrow. I'll have to try to reach them tonight, telling them not to come in."

"Good idea. You'll have to explain some of what happened, and that you'll let them know when to come back to work. Assure them it will only be a few days at most, probably Monday, and that their jobs are safe." Derik exited the Jag and circled to her door. "I'll walk you to your car and see you get off okay."

She slid out and took his arm, fighting off more tears. Moments later, she perched on her driver seat, and Derik leaned against the open window frame.

"You may have to replace some equipment that got damaged in the brawl. One cutting table for sure. Insurance should cover any damage. Anyhow, I suggest you inventory that first thing and get it ordered." He reached over and thumbed moisture from her eyes.

Derik leaned in. "Somehow, we'll get through this, my love. We just need some time to figure it out." He kissed her cheek, and then stood back as she rolled up the window and backed her BMW out of her parking spot.

As she departed, he wondered if that statement was pissing in the wind.

Well, they'd spend tomorrow together, and he'd see how that went. He returned to his car but lingered for several minutes before heading home.

Fuck! Love, finally, after eight years of empty affairs, and suddenly there's this wedge between us. He gnashed his teeth. One needs to be able to compromise to make any relationship last. He sighed. There was a lot he'd do to keep Brita, but he didn't think he could come around to not having kids. And he knew if he pressured her into changing her mind, it would be that burr under the saddle he'd mentioned earlier, that would surely drive them apart.

His thoughts drifted to Martinique, nearly nine years

ago, when the need to get his treasure home had somehow trumped what promised to be exquisite love with one of the fabulous DuMelle sisters. He barked a humorless guff. The specter of having to pick one and not the other if he stayed was probably part of what drove him off. A real Catch-22.

His brow furrowed as he pictured the gorgeous redheads, waving him tear-streaked goodbyes as he sailed from Martinique's harbor. He'd been so emotionally conflicted by his choice, he'd almost turned back. He'd been more stubborn then—more inflexible—unwilling to change an earlier decision, despite a new circumstance, so he sailed home.

Somehow, he'd managed to put it behind him and move on to his life in South Florida. Now he had a similar choice to ponder, and wondered why this one seemed a tad less stressful.

Maybe because he wasn't as fully committed as he thought? Was that about not having kids ... or not losing Brita?

That uncertainty bothered him.

He turned off I-95, just a few minutes from home. He was tired. He'd fought a physical battle for his life in the afternoon, and now faced an emotional battle for his lover.

He relished a good night's sleep, something that may not happen, considering all that swirled in his mind.

~ 53 ~

Derik drifted awake, his eyes fluttering open. He rolled over and reached across the bed, but found only cold sheets. No Brita, warm and nubile, to draw into his arms. To kiss. To stroke. To make passionate love to.

He groaned and pushed up, his back against the headboard. No Brita, because he broke it off last night. He scooped up her pillow and buried his face in it, savoring the lingering odor of her Black Opium perfume, then cast it angrily aside and slid off the king-size bed.

He showered in his en suite bathroom. The hot water pummeling his body didn't relieve tension as he ran the events of the previous evening on a constant loop through his mind.

They'd ended what had seemed a perfect relationship over one stumbling block. Unfortunately, it was a biggie.

With a heavy sigh, he dried, shaved gingerly because of his bruised cheeks, brushed his teeth, and headed for his office. Maybe Chick would have a unique insight. Derik shook his head as he entered his Jag, knowing there was little chance to fix his broken affair.

~ ~ ~

Derik pushed through the glass entry door of Brand & Radford Investing, tossed a wave at Ginny as he blew by, and headed for Chick's office. His partner, always the first to work, was studying files in search of their next investment. Allure Attire was well on its way to financial success and wouldn't require too much future supervision. Derik rapped on the door casing, and Chick glanced up, arched his eyebrows, and motioned him in.

"What happened to you?" Chick shook his head. "I thought you were going to a fancy party last night."

"We were, but the Kolodenko brothers and some hired muscle broke in."

"Jeez, again!" Chick lurched up from his chair. "What the hell happened?"

"An all-out brawl." Derik settled on a chair and spun the tale in detail, including Brita and her shotgun.

"She killed him?" Chick's brow knitted.

"Yeah." Derik nodded and sighed. "It was him or me." Derik held Chick's eyes for a moment, and he gave a small head shake.

"Then I killed the big lug."

"You—what? Killed him too?" Chick slumped back and massaged his eyes.

"Yeah." Derik hitched around on his seat. "Don't think it'll be a problem. Classic Stand Your Ground defense."

"Holy shit, what a fuck up." Chick rose again and came around his desk. "I sure in hell am glad my partner survived. And his woman, for sure."

"Yeah. This was really all about Brita. Looks like they wanted to snatch her, hook her on drugs, and turn her into a high-end escort. That's my guess." He rose and shared a hug with his best friend.

"So," Chick stepped back, "you guys got to the gala?"

"No, we went." He made a wry grin. "The outfits were a hit, and Brita was sensational." He slumped back onto his chair, face in his hand. "But then things went to shit."

"What d'ya mean? You said you were going to propose." Chick settled on the edge of his desk. "Didn't it go well?"

"Never happened. Told her how much I loved her and looked forward to our raising a family together." He groaned. "Then the big shocker. Turns out she doesn't want kids."

"What? You're kidding."

"I wish. *Never* wanted them. She actually had her tubes tied ten years ago." Derik massaged his eyes.

"So, now what?" Chick touched his arm. "You guys gotta figure it out, but it sounds like a pretty big hill to climb."

"Ya think?" Derik made a mirthless chuckle. "But it's a deal-breaker, so we've gotta end it. Not fair to either of us to be locked into something that's not going anywhere."

"Too bad, because you were so great together." Chick returned to his seat. "So, what's your plan?"

"Well, I'll go down there this afternoon. See she's getting the place straightened up and that everything's on pace for our new product line, and to be sure she's okay." He shrugged. "The detective said they should be finished gathering whatever they need from the scene by Noon. He also suggested the need for counseling after a deadly shooting, and that may be good advice." Derik turned toward the door. "We've agreed it's best to separate for the time being. We're still partners, and lovers or not, she'll always be a good friend." He paused in the entry. "You got any new prospects since Allure Attire seems well on the way to success?"

"Just reviewing some files," he waved at his desk, "but nothing's standing out at the moment."

"Okay. So, let's see if we can come up with one, and we've still gotta decide what to do about all the remaining treasure. It's getting tougher to keep parceling it out and avoid scrutiny."

"Right. I'll see what I can dig up on a new client. There're several packets I haven't reviewed yet."

"Good. Once we get settled, I may decide to take some time off, if that's okay with you. Get away. Maybe go for a sail."

"Works for me, pard. While I'll miss your beat-up face, I should be able to keep the fires burning here."

Derik nodded and chuckled. Chick caught plenty of passes from him as his tight end in college, and he wouldn't drop the ball here, either. He headed for his office to check for messages, then he'd visit Brita and see how she was holding up.

He hoped killing that bastard wouldn't haunt her.

He suspected she was tougher than that.

~ 54 ~

Derik parked his Jag in Allure Attire's small lot, killed the engine, and paused. He slouched on his seat and knuckled his eyes. Was there any way to rescue their love affair? Brita was the woman he'd been looking for ever since returning from Martinique. Can he afford to lose her because she doesn't want kids? Can he stay with her despite that fact, and give up a life-long dream? That'd be a prescription for calamity.

He sighed and exited his coupe. He won't learn any answers sitting in his car. The entry was unlocked, so he ducked under the Crime Scene tape and crossed the vestibule to the door, sitting ajar, to the shop. Pushing through, he swept the room and spotted Brita, clad in coral silk slacks and a flowered sleeveless blouse, struggling with a fallen cutting table. She glanced up at his approach, a tiny smile creasing her lips. Gorgeous as always, except for red-rimmed eyes.

He groaned, realizing she'd been crying. And why not, with their magical relationship in jeopardy. He took her hand.

"Everything okay?" His eyes swept the room. "Looks like you're getting things cleaned up. Any problems with the cops?"

"Not really." She sighed. "Said they'd be out of here this afternoon. I reached Rolf's Cleaning Service and they'll come early tomorrow." She gestured at the dark stain on the nearby floor. "They should have the blood scrubbed up before any of my workers show up on Monday. Canceled the skeleton crew scheduled to work today, but they know something happened."

"No way to keep it from them, was there?"

"Not really." She thumbed away a small tear. "One of the girls called this morning. She gets Google news and saw a story about it ... including that two men died violently."

"She get any details?"

"Like that *I* killed one of them?" Brita grimaced. "Not that I know of." She nodded at the stairs and they started up toward her office.

"Frankly, I'm less upset about that than I thought I'd be." She paused at the top, turned, and caressed his scraped cheek. "It was him or you, and I sure didn't want it to be you."

"Yeah, me either." He gave a wry chuckle. "Clever of you to bring your shotgun when you heard they made bail." He gave her a one-arm hug, and they entered her office.

"Yes, when I heard they were out, it sent a chill down my spine. They scared me, especially after you figured out what they intended." She shivered. "If they wanted me, they were going to have to deal with some double-ought buckshot."

He paused as they entered her office, and took her hands. "That's a pretty heavy load for a trap shooter."

"Right. I bought a box of the double-0 on the way in with my Remington." She sighed and shook her head. "If I needed the gun for self-defense, I wanted to be sure it counted."

"That couldn't have been an easy decision." He caressed her cheek.

"What?" She snorted. "Preparing to *kill* someone? No, not easy at all, but I've always taken care of myself." She cupped his face in her hands. "No one ever did that for me until you, my White Knight."

He curled her into his arms, her head nestled on his

shoulder as she planted a light kiss on his neck.

"So, now we must face the proverbial elephant in the room," she murmured. "Is our love enough to ..." She dwindled to a halt.

"To what?" He eased her back, hands on her shoulders. "To compromise something basic to ourselves." He held her eyes. "Is love enough for you to change your mind about kids?"

She shook her head, tears welling in her eyes. "I ... I love you madly, Derik, but I just *can't* have children." She sighed. "I'd be miserable."

"And, I'd be just as unhappy without a family full of kids."

"Nothing more needs be said." She kissed his cheek and drew away. "What we have is beautiful, but there has to be more. It's just not going to work, is it?" She settled on the sofa, face in her hands, sniffling through tears. "I'll come by your place this evening and pick up my things."

"Not necessary. I can bring them in tomorrow." He settled next to her.

"No, it's okay. I've got stuff scattered all over the place. I should be there about eight. That okay?"

"Sure." He rose. "I'll gather together what I can." He hung there, lost for anything else to say. A sigh, a shrug, and he reached out to pull her to her feet. She came into his arms, their lips and tongues seeking a frantic voyage against each other. One final kiss.

She arced her neck, locking eyes. "Oh *Derik*. I hate this."

"Me too, Brit," he emitted a soft groan, "but I don't see any way out." He kissed her again amidst a fierce hug, then turned and left.

Brita collapsed on the sofa, drew a throw pillow against her face, and bawled. She hadn't cried that hard since she was eight and her German pointer, Sigfried, had died after being hit by a truck.

She made no effort to stop until her eyes ran dry, then tottered into her bathroom for a facial repair job before returning to her factory floor.

"This is life," she muttered. "Fucked up, for sure, but somehow I'll manage to get through it."

She had her now booming business to occupy her mind, thanks to a wonderful guy, and at least she knew she could fall in love. Who knows? Maybe he'll never finds someone in time to raise a family.

She grimaced, uncomfortable at thinking (or was it hoping?) of that misfortune for the man who'd saved her from both herself and two gangsters.

She peered at her reflection in the mirror above her sink.

Time to get back to work, and set those thoughts behind me. She turned and headed out of her office.

Her lovely business would be her savior. Blank everything else out.

~ 55 ~

Derik, seated in his den reading a file, glanced up at the sound of a key in the front door lock. A moment later, Brita entered, sporting her usual silk slacks and sleeveless blouse, trailing a carry-on roller bag. He sighed as he noted her still red-rimmed eyes. She'd been crying again.

He rose and laid the folder on a side table. "Hi, babe." He strode to her side and took control of the bag. "Wasn't sure you were still coming tonight."

"Got tied up with a late delivery of material, and I wanted to get it labeled and stored for the morning." She sniffled. "I ... I thought it best to get this over with ... so we can move on." She handed him the key. "Here. I won't be needing this anymore ... will I?" Her eyes, shadowed with sorrow, found his.

Derik glanced away, pocketed the key, set the bag aside, and gently folded her into his arms. Her head found its familiar spot at the crook of his neck, and he felt the soft drip of tears pepper his skin.

"What can I say, sweetheart." He stroked the back of her head and neck. "I *do* love you, but ..." He paused and gave a small head shake. "but I think it's best making the break now, while we're still friends as well as lovers. Later, I fear, we'd be neither."

"I know you're right, *Liebchen*," she gave a small nod, "but I love you so, I ... I can't ..." She wrapped an arm around his neck for a fierce kiss, her body undulating against his as her other hand gripped his butt.

Unable ... and unwilling ... to resist, their passion soared. One hand was inside her blouse to tweak erect nipples, the other massaging her ass, her pussy pressed hard against his surging erection. The air filled with moans and gasps as fingers fumbled with buttons and zippers.

His lips slipped across her cheek, his tongue tantalizing an ear before venturing down her neck to lap at the notch of her throat.

Brita shuddered as his mouth found a breast, his tongue swirling the nipple before drawing it in. Her hand scrabbled at his belt, seeking that gorgeous cock.

Then realty seeped into their ardor. Derik took her upper arms and edged them apart. Passion reluctantly controlled, their eyes locked, he sighed and shook his head.

Brita gave a small moan, a hand caressing his cheek. "My darling, my darling. What are we doing? There is so much love here." She took his hands. "Is there no way to save it?"

He shrugged and sighed. "I don't see how, without one ... or both of us lying to ourselves." He retightened his belt.

Tears again leaked from her eyes. "But, where will I ever find love like ours again, *Liebchen?*"

"I don't know, babe." He drew her in for a gentle hug. "It's taken me over eight years to find you. We can only hope there's someone else out there." He arched his neck back. "We've gotta believe there is, and we'll find love again."

They separated. "Meanwhile, I still value you as a friend and business partner, and that's been pretty terrific."

"Yes." A small smile edged onto her lips. "My friend and White Knight." She kissed his cheek. "Without you, I wouldn't even exist now—financially, or even alive."

"So," he touched her arm, "we'll work through this?"

"Of course. We must." She knuckled away the last of her

tears. "We have no choice. Life will go on, and it'll be better with you in it as a friend than not at all."

"Okay, then. Friends." He held out a hand, which she shook, once again fighting back tears.

Brita readjusted her blouse and slacks, gathered her roller-bag, and headed for the master bedroom to collect her things.

Twenty minutes later, after a very platonic hug, Derik watched his now ex-lover, keening softly to herself, wheel her case out his front door. He resisted escorting her to her BMW, hoping to avoid another tearful farewell. Moments later, the powerful engine growled to life, and he heard her exit his drive.

He slumped onto his den's easy-chair, arms folded, head back, eyes closed.

What a turn of events in only two days. He'd been so eager to show her the ring and ask her to marry him. Then a battle for their lives, followed by that glorious ball ... and then reality! He never suspected she wouldn't want a family, and he couldn't imagine himself without one.

"Well, it's not too late," he muttered. "But where am I gonna find someone like Brita in time to have kids?"

He chuckled. He'd have to start dating younger women if he wanted to fall in love again and have a family.

One thing's for sure. I'm not gonna force it. I've been in love twice, so it can happen again.

He shook his head as he gathered up the file he'd been reading when Brita arrived.

I need a vacation.

Derik stared blankly into space, fingers stroking the back of his neck. He'd just lost what he thought was the love of his life ... and he was strangely calm.

"You're one fucking piece of work, Brand," he snorted,

and began reading the report.

Work was his balm.

~ 56 ~

Derik entered his offices just before 9:00 am and found his executive assistant, Ginny, at reception.

"Hi, Boss," She grinned at him. "Slept in this morning, huh?"

"Had an errand to run, wise guy." He chuckled at the camaraderie he and Chick had fostered in their business. Their people operated more as friends and family than just employees.

"Chick in?"

"Yep." She nodded toward the inner door. "In his office, vetting a new, potential client." She rose and stepped around the desk. "You okay after that melee at Brita's." She touched his arm. "I heard that was really hairy."

"Yeah, I'm okay. A couple of scrapes and an ache or two, but nothing serious."

"And mentally?" Ginny injected herself into his path, her brow knit.

Derik laughed and patted her cheek. "What are you, my mom?"

"Just filling in for her, sonny." Her eyes crinkled. "Someone's gotta take care of you. Really though, Derik. You killed someone in self-defense. That can't have been easy."

"Yeah, well, I'm not as bothered as I thought I'd be, considering who it was and what he was trying to do." He paused and shook his head. "Got other things on my mind, though, so I might take some time off." He chuckled and grasped her by her upper arms. "Any more third-degree, Detective Mendosa?"

She smiled and patted his cheek. "Just looking out for my favorite boss." She stepped aside.

A moment later, he tapped on Chick's open doorframe. "Hey, pard, you got a minute?"

"Sure. C'mon in." He laid down the file he was reading and gestured toward a side chair. "How're ya feeling, Derik?"

"A little banged up, physically ... and mentally." He sighed and settled gingerly on the seat. His rump ached from a hard landing during the scuffle.

"You gonna see a therapist, like the detective suggested?"

"I don't know. Killing that brute isn't the main thing bothering me."

"Brita?" Chick's eyebrows arched.

"Yeah. She came by last night to pick up her stuff ... and return my key." He knuckled his eyes and eased back.

"You couldn't work it out, Buddy? You two had something pretty special."

"Nothing that'd survive." Derik grunted. "If either of us gave in, it'd be the eventual death of the marriage. The proverbial burr under a saddle." He leaned forward, both palms flat on Chick's desk. "Better we remain friends and business partners. I think she'll be happier that way too." Derik studied his friend. "So, you got a new prospect?"

"Yeah. A small motor manufacturer who, for a change, has gotten too far afield with unsuccessful new product lines." He plucked up the folder and offered it to Derik.

After a lengthy scan, Derik returned it to Chick. "Looks like a guy who could use our help." He hesitated. "You think you can handle it alone?"

"Planned on it, expecting you to stay busy with Allure

Attire." He leaned back, hands folded across his belly.

"Brita won't need much help for a while. She's got her hands full with the kind of things she's good at, and getting the new junior lines into full swing will keep her busy." He ran a hand through his hair. "Think you can keep the fires burning if I take off for a while, buddy?"

"Sure." They rose. "I'll keep an eye on Brita too, if she needs anything." Chick held his partner's eyes. "You planning on going sailing?"

"Yeah. Early summer is perfect for the Caribbean, and a strong El Niño in the Pacific should pretty well guarantee no hurricanes this time." He chuckled.

"Gonna visit Martinique?" Chick's eyebrows arched.

"Yeah, maybe, but I don't expect anything." He rubbed the back of his neck. "It's been nine years, and despite what it seemed, it was still just a two-and-a-half-day fling. They were two pretty terrific women. I'm sure they've long ago moved on."

He started for the door, paused, and turned. "I think I'll stop by my little treasure cays, if I can find 'em again. See if anyone's discovered them. And we gotta decide how to claim the balance of the loot." He leaned against the door jamb. "Maybe claim I found it on this trip. Even after paying capital gains taxes on the appraised value, there could still be thirty or forty million left. Maybe even more." He chuckled again. "Think we can manage on that, partner?

"We'll struggle through somehow, Derik." He smiled. "We're pretty resilient."

Derik laughed as he left, feeling a bit lighter. Life would go on but first he'd to talk to Brita. Let her know his plans.

~ 57 ~

Derik arrived at Allure Attire an hour later and found Brita in her office, writing checks. She glanced up at his rap on the door's glass pane, waved him in, and returned to her check book.

"Hi," her voice a bit strained. "Have a seat 'til I finish these last two checks."

He remained silent as he slid onto a side chair and gave a small shrug. Clearly, the whole vibe had changed between them, and Derik accepted that as good, showing the intention to move on. Or trying to, anyway.

Brita set aside her pen, tore three checks from the book, separated them, and set them to one side.

"Supplier payments." She rotated her chair toward him. "Fully stocked now for our first surge of orders, mostly for the new line." Her lips ticked into a grin, followed by an eloquent shrug. "I must admit I'm amazed ... and *very* embarrassed ... that an outsider, with no real clothing experience, could see what was needed better than me."

She slipped out of her chair as he rose, and came around her desk, taking his hands. "Its's no wonder you and Chick are so successful." She sighed. "I'm going to miss what we had together, *Liebchen*. More than miss it, I'm afraid, but it's clear from last night that this is best." She leaned in and pecked his cheek. "I value our friendship ... and your amazing business acumen."

She turned away and moved to her window to view her very busy, now fully expanded shop floor. "That," she nodded toward her production lines, "is the therapy I need while the pain subsides." She chuckled mirthlessly. "I'll be too busy during the day and too tired at night to brood."

She spun back to him. "I ... I didn't expect you today. Is there something I need to know?" Her brow knitted and luscious lips pressed into a thin line. "The Ukrainians?"

"No, that's over and done with. They're not coming back from the dead." He joined her at the glass, an arm loosely across her shoulders. "I checked with Detective Harris before coming here. One family member, a cousin, Dimitri Tomov, has disappeared, and the girl who left the door open, Alena, is in custody. Apparently, she's giving up their entire organization for a plea deal and protective custody. Heavy duty human trafficking in women for prostitution."

Brita shuddered, her arm around his waist. "That's what you thought they planned for me."

"Yeah. A beautiful, classy babe like you could bring a grand an hour ... maybe even more." He gave a small squeeze and stepped aside. "But like I said, no danger there anymore." He chuckled. "The word's probably gotten around on the street: Don't fuck with Annie Oakley."

Brita erupted into a nervous giggle and thumbed moisture from her eyes. "Okay, good. So, was there some reason for this visit?"

"Well, I wanted to check to see if everything's okay. That *you're* okay." He took her face between his hands and held her eyes. "*Are* you okay?"

She nodded. "As much as could be expected, I guess. I'm a survivor, so I'll make out." She reached up and stroked his cheek. "And you, Derik? Are you also okay?"

"Pretty much." He sighed. "But if you have a handle on

everything here for a while without me, I thought I'd get away." He glanced down. "Maybe go for a sail, just to be alone and work through all the emotions tied to the last few days."

"Like killing that monster ... and our relationship." She slapped her fingers across her lips. "*Oh scheisse.* That came out wrong. Please don't think—"

'It's okay. I kinda feel the same, and that's part of why I need to get away, I guess."

"So," she stepped back, arms folded, "a sailing trip, huh? And without me as mate." She grinned. "I loved our time on that lovely old boat." She fastened her eyes on his. "The Caribbean, I suppose." Her eyebrows arched. "Martinique?"

"Yeah, probably, on both counts. It's the best time of year, and no storms on the horizon. But if you're thinking of the redhead twins, geez, that was nine years ago." He shook his head. "They were too good a catch to be waiting for me. We've never had a single contact since I left."

He drew Brita to the sofa and they perched, facing each other.

"I'm gonna search for the little cays where I hid from that hurricane. See if the caves are still intact and undiscovered by anyone else."

"Why? Nostalgia?"

"Partly, but I'll take photos this time, and maybe when I get back, use them to document a 'new discovery' I'll claim so I can disclose the balance of the treasure." He shrugged. "I wanna get it out once and for all. Pay the gains taxes, and stop all the play acting. I wanna put some of it to use for a few good causes."

"So, you aren't going to look for the French twins? After all these years of them getting in the way of you finding love here?"

"They didn't keep me from you, darling." A soft smile creased his lips, and he caressed her cheek. "You drove them from my mind." He pushed to his feet. "I admit, I'd be interested to see what's happened to them over the last nine years, but I expect nothing for myself. That surely has passed long ago."

He drew her up for a gentle hug. "Anyway, with things on track here and settled between us, I feel free to make the journey." He started for the door. "I'll probably be gone for a month. Maybe even six-weeks. But I'll keep in touch, with my phone on if you need me for anything."

He gave her a friendly squeeze and was out the door, down the metal steps, and headed for the exit.

"If I need anything?" she muttered. *I need you in my arms, my love. In my heart!*

But that wasn't going to happen now, so it was time to lose herself in her work, and maybe, in time, she'll find love again.

She gave a very unlady-like grunt.

Not likely!

~ 58 ~

Derik scanned his yacht and mentally ticked off his "list" for his upcoming trip. New sails and rigging installed, the auto-furl motor serviced, and the hull hauled, scraped, and repainted. The Perkins diesel was tuned and the fuel tank filtered for water. The previous month he'd hired a marine interior designer to refit the cockpit. A new mattress and bedding, updated cabinetry, and all new appliances. Much of what had been there was ten years old. After his breakup with Brita, he wanted to start this chapter of his life with everything new.

He glanced at his watch. Still ten hours of daylight, and the boat was fully stocked. Why wait until tomorrow to leave? He shrugged and headed into his house to pick up his documents and passport.

Twenty minutes later, *Martinique* motored away from his dock and into the Intracoastal, headed for Haulover Inlet. Once clear of the channel, he raised full main sail and jib to take advantage of a warm and favorable northwesterly wind. Under indigo skies, peppered by scuttling puffs of cotton, the Choy Lee surged south-southeast, slicing through two-foot waves, throwing sheets of crystalline mist.

Derik stood at the helm, absorbing the cool spray, and pictured Brita, plastered to his back, giggling with pleasure. He sighed and shook his head. That's what he as getting away from. This cruise was just what he needed to renew his spirit.

He glanced at his billowing main sail, then at his GPS. Making about six knots. He trimmed the sail a tad and adjusted his course three degrees south, and speed crept up to seven knots.

Derik settled in for the long reach to the keys. He planned to stop for the night at his usual little bay on the east shore of Key Largo. Maybe catch a few yellowtail for dinner. An easy first day to settle in. He figured to reach his treasure cays in about nine or ten days, so there was no hurry. The boat's interior was so comfortable now, he had no qualms about living aboard, even when in port.

He drove any disparate thoughts from his head and focused his mind on sailing the yacht. What would be on his arrival in the Eastern Caribbean, would be. There was plenty to keep him busy en route.

~ ~ ~

At two in the afternoon, ten days later, Derik cruised at half-mast, east of the Windward Islands of the Lesser Antilles, searching for the hills that would show him to the cays that sheltered him from Hurricane Chico, nine years past.

The island of Dominica loomed to his southeast port, a landfall he'd been unable to reach at that hectic time. The mountains of Martinique were barely visible on the far southeastern horizon.

He had no satellite position from that time, so he strained his nine-year-old memory, and tried to recreate where those hurricane winds had driven him. The two hills of his lucky little cays were small and easily missed, even during this milder weather. He scanned the horizon to his southwest but saw nothing but open waters. No wonder no one ever found those caves, if he couldn't re-find the isles.

Two-hours later, after an unsuccessful track, he beat back toward the northeast against an unfavorable northerly breeze. With the use of his GPS, he'd set up another pass, this time starting five miles farther northwest. In a sense, this had become a grid search.

He glanced at his Mariner watch. If this try was unsuccessful, he'd head for Dominica and anchor up for the night on the northwest side, in Portsmouth Harbor. Maybe go ashore for some restock of food and top off his diesel tank. It was a cruise ships' port, so there should be plenty of facilities.

Ninety-minutes later, with no success, Derik headed for Portsmouth Harbor. His search would continue in the morning.

~ ~ ~

His Perkins diesel pushed the thirty-six-foot sail boat out of Portsmouth Harbor on a northwesterly bearing as Derik studied the horizon. The early morning sun warmed his back, and the rippled sea sparkled like tiny bits of polished chromium.

After refueling his diesel the previous evening, he'd gone ashore for supplies, then supped at a beachside café. Tourists and natives frolicked in the surf, including several delectable young babes. He'd snickered softly. Been there, done that, but not again. The night was spent peacefully alone in his very comfortable cabin, bobbing gently at his anchored mooring. Clad in green shorts and a white cotton tee, he savored the ocean-cooled breeze, salty and fresh. He studied his GPS as he approached his newest start point. The satellite map he'd viewed prior to departure showed some indistinct irregularity that just might be the tiny isles he searched for.

His newly chosen path, an attempt to duplicate his mad dash seeking safety nearly nine-years ago, should take him right into that vicinity.

Derik glanced at the weather vane atop his mast. Unfavorable winds today would require several tacks to reach the area. If things got too difficult, he'd resort to the Perkins, but he preferred to make it by sail.

An hour later his binocular sweep of the horizon jerked to a stop.

"Ha! Gotcha." What he suspected was the eastern of the two isles hilltop peeked into view. He came onto a starboard tack, and five minutes later the second isle, a half-mile west of the first, loomed into sight.

"Wow. I found 'em." It took a pair of tacks before he furled his sails and motored into the tiny cul-de-sac where he'd secured *Martinique* from the storm. The current, mild breeze required no special rigging, and a few minutes later he motored ashore in his dingy.

After hauling the small skiff up ono the pebbled shore, Derik made his way to the base of the cliff and found the snarled bush, clinging to its side. It had prospered in that unlikely spot, even more thoroughly hiding what laid behind. He reached up, grasped a stout stem close to its roots, and clambered up the steep slope.

He shoved a hand through the dense foliage, snatched the edge of the hidden cave's mouth, and drew himself onto the narrow ledge from which the bush grew. He thrust aside the foliage, slipped behind, and crawled into the cave. Rising, he fished out a flashlight he'd brought.

A quick sweep across the interior spilled shivers and goose bumps down his back at the surge of memory of the last time he'd been there. Casting his light toward the rear, he spied a glint of white—the pirate' bones laid seemingly undisturbed. Derik edged closer, careful to avoid the large hole that had once held a chest of enormous wealth.

No surprise. Everything was as it was, nine years past— the hole, the flat rock that had covered the chest, the cutlass used as a ramp. Only the spade was missing, but it sat at the other island, used to dig up that second chest, and that's where it probably was.

He sighed and withdrew his phone, activating the camera. Several photos of the long-dead buccaneers, with the flintlock pistol and cutlass positioned as he originally found them. Then the hole, the rock, and a shot toward the mouth of the cave. The only thing missing was the actual chest, but Chick would photoshop that in when he returned.

A dozen pictures taken, he settled to sit, cross-legged, and just absorbed the scene. He'd scrabbled into this lucky cave to survive Chico, and it changed his life in more ways than he could have dreamed. He grunted and lumbered to his feet.

Nostalgia could wait. He would visit the second cave, take photos, and then move on. This would be the great reveal on the genesis of his fortune, and he had to make it look good. He started for the entrance, then paused and returned to the bone pile. He retrieved the flintlock and the cutlass to bring home with him this time. The one pirate's tri-corner hat disintegrated at his touch. No surprise, after over four-hundred-years. He eschewed the one remaining set of leather boots, still somewhat intact. They still harbored bony feet, and handling that was a bridge too far.

The pistol and cutlass went into a canvas sack he'd brought, and he lowered them to the ground with a long piece of light rope before descending to the beach.

Derik motored the dingy to the second isle, a half-mile east, which was easier than maneuvering it with the sloop, which required raising and then resetting an anchor.

Three hours after arrival, he had what he needed from the two little cays: photos to document his "new" discovery, credited to the so-called map he'd claimed he discovered almost nine years ago; and his souvenirs—the cutlass and pistol.

Back aboard his yacht, he raised anchor and motored away from the cay before setting sail, destination Martinique. He checked the wind and estimated it would require only two tacks to reach its eastern coast and the port of Fort-de-France.

He sighed, flooded with memories of his last visit there. He had no expectations, certain the twins had moved on. They'd never made any attempt to contact him after he left, nor had he them. Their unsaid agreement seemed to be, it was a wonderful adventure—far more than just a fling—but there was no future in it. They would move on with their lives. He snickered. Problem was, he was never able to do that—until he'd met an exceptional blonde. But now that was also gone, and it was time to start anew.

He doubted that would happen again on the lovely shores of Martinique, but that isle *was* the next logical stop on this voyage of regeneration.

~ 59 ~

Derik motored his sloop into Fort-de-France Harbor in the late afternoon. First stop was to top off his fuel tank and get a mooring buoy assigned. Once tied up, he went about a thorough cleaning of the boat and checking supplies. Those chores completed, he put his dingy in the water and headed for shore.

Clad in beige linen chinos and a patterned polo, he strolled the boardwalk, browsed souvenir shops, and scanned the activities on the beach. No redhead twins in sight anywhere. He gave a soft chuckle. What had he expected? The DuMelle women there, waiting for him? Fat chance.

He purchased a pair of coffee cups, emblazoned *Martinique*. They'd be a good fit for the boat. He ceded to nostalgia and ended up at the beach-side café where he and the twins first dined, so long ago. The southern lobster was just as big and very delicious, this time accompanied by a local beer instead of bubbly.

Derik lingered over a hefty slice of key lime pie and watched the beach activities—four-on-four volleyball, some attempt at soccer, and tossing a Nerf football. Looked like fun, but he had no interest in joining in. He'd put in a full day and would turn in early. He'd play tomorrow by ear.

~ ~ ~

Derik rolled over in his queen-size bed and plucked up his watch: nine-twenty. He hadn't slept that late in ... he couldn't remember when. Sporting his usual sleeping attire—cotton boxers and a sleeveless tee, he slipped off the bed for a visit to the head. After peeing, he splashed cool water in his face and studied his image in the mirror. He could use a shave, but put it off. What were his plans for the day?

He had none. He'd completed his mission to his treasure cays, and he had three weeks, more or less, to bum around the Caribbean. He could hang around Martinique for a few days, or take off to the south, along the Antilles. Aruba would be the last stop. He'd need maybe two weeks to get home from there, sailing hard with few lingering stops—maybe a Puerto Rican casino.

Oh, well. He'd go for a swim. There was a nice little reef off the point where he could snorkel. Even grab a lobster, if he found one, and no one was around to notice. They were out of season.

He headed for the galley and an awaiting breakfast, and then he'd plan the day. No agenda to attend to. Just have fun and relax, but hovering in the back of his mind, he knew reality would have to be faced, sooner or later.

~ ~ ~

Derik returned to his sloop just before five p.m. He'd spent the morning snorkeling off the nearby reef and managed to collect several interesting shells for display in the boat's cabin—mementos of Martinique.

He'd lunched at a boardwalk café and then strolled the beach. He was lured into a volleyball game by Inga, a willowy and very nubile brunette, visiting from Holland. After two hours of combat on the sands, it seemed pretty clear sex was on the table for the taking. He tactfully declined after some heated kisses and wandering fingers. She definitely turned him on, but he'd moved past short-term flings, especially on that island and the memories that still lingered there.

Settled at his laptop in the yacht's lounge, he scanned e-mails and sent off two, one to update Chick and to lay groundwork for his newly "discovered" treasure, and a response to Brita's missive, informing him on the surge of new business from their junior line.

He leaned back, hands flat on the small table and glared at the screen, battling indecision, then sighed and shrugged. No sense in putting it off. A few clicks brought up a list of local car rental companies. He selected one and reserved a four-by-four Jeep Wagoneer for the morning. He'd make a driving tour of the Caribbean gem—a typical tourist move, but he knew where it would end up.

Derik grilled a T-bone steak and roasted a sweet potato in the ships galley, the pleasant odors both igniting his hunger and relaxing growing tension. A half-bottle of Malbec red wine further soothed him as he finished the novel he was reading and turned in for the night. As he settled in his cabin, awaiting the Sandman's magic, he fielded dual emotions for the coming day—anxiety and anticipation.

He was unsure which of the two were stronger.

~ 60 ~

After a galley-cooked breakfast of three scrambled eggs and four slices of Canadian bacon, Derik mapped his route for the tour of Martinique. He'd covered the isle with the twins, nine years before, but it was a beautiful place, worth a revisit.

He shook his head, lips tipping into a grin as he scrawled out his final stop, Island Reality, although he still hadn't resolved to actually visit their office. After nine years with zero contact, would they really want to see him? An Internet search discovered they were still the proprietors there.

The women seemed more sad than angry when he left, but that may have morphed into ire over the years. Could he face them? And what would be the reactions—his as well as theirs? Well, he'd face that when—and if—he finally got there.

Derik glanced at his Rolex and realized he'd dallied too long, and his rental Jeep was already awaiting him at the foot of the wharf. He donned khaki cargo shorts and a matching safari shirt, collected his wallet and passport. and paused at the small, locked, built-in chest. He shook his head.

Let's not rush thing, buddy.

The ladder quickly mounted up to the cockpit, he locked the cabin door. A tip to the local security guard insured he'd keep an extra close eye on the boat. A C-note well spent, with what he carried aboard.

A moment later, he motored his skiff toward the beach.

He grimaced, not accustomed to the flood of tension coursing through him. The time had arrived to face a long-time dream.

He hoped it didn't become a nightmare.

~ ~ ~

Derik lingered in the Jeep, parked a half-block from Island Reality's lot, fighting indecision. A glance at his watch showed 2:40 so the office would still be open and the broker or brokers should be present—the DuMelle sisters.

He grunted and shrugged. What the hell was he scared of? Either they'd be happy to see him, or not. In either case, no one was going to get shot—he hoped. He chuckled softly and shifted the car into DRIVE. He'd already survived a gun threat over a woman, so he wasn't worried about *that*.

He pulled into the one vacant spot in front of the office. A year-old Toyota Highlander rested in a spot labeled BROKER, so it seemed at least one of the twins should be on site.

He paused, grit his teeth, exited his car, and strode purposefully toward the door. He pushed through and was met by a slim, tan, moustached man at a reception desk, who rose.

"May I help you, sir?" Voiced softened by an islander accent.

"I'd like to see the broker, Ms. DuMelle?" He shifted from one foot to the other, hands thrust into his pockets.

"Ah, you mean Mrs. Karlssen. Gisele is in her office." He gestured toward the rear. "Please, follow me." He slipped between two desks manned by young women, and headed for an open doorway.

Derik swallowed a lump in his throat and followed.

Apparently, at least one of the girls had married. Why should he be surprised?

His escort stopped and rapped on the door jamb.

"A gentleman to see you, Gisele."

"Of course. Send him in, Rafe."

The music of that voice sent goose bumps scattering down Derik's spine. It was a well-remembered sound that lingered in his dreams for many years. He stepped into the doorway and spotted the gorgeous redhead, almost unchanged in nine years, rising from behind her mahogany executive desk, her eyes still scanning papers on the desktop.

She glanced up at the sound of him clearing his throat and froze. Her eyebrows arched, and a huge smile morphed across her face as she stepped around her desk, arms spread in a clear welcome. "Derik. *Bon Dieu,* you're back!" She engulfed him in a bear hug and kissed his cheek. "Why, *mon amour,* has it taken you nine years, and without a single word from you?" She stood back. "We required an Internet search to assure ourselves you returned to America safely." Gisele sighed and shook her head.

He took her hands, a sheepish grin tugging at his lips. "I'm so sorry, Gisele. It just seemed best—"

"I understand." She nodded. "But we were first worried, and then I admit, a bit angry that we've never heard from you." She shook a finger at him, then smiled. "I got over it. You were twelve-hundred-miles away and building a new life, and after all, what we had only lasted three days."

"Yeah, but those three days had hooks in my heart for eight years." He sighed as they perched on her beige leather sofa. "It took that long for me to finally find love again." *She said "I." And what of Coline?*

Gisele's brow knit and pink-lipsticked lips pursed. She leaned back and studied his eyes. "So, are you married now, as you see I am?" She displayed her left hand, adorned with a gold ring and a two-carat diamond.

"No." He sighed again. "We were very much in love, but a major, unscalable cliff in life motives injected itself, and we've separated."

"That's sad," said, despite a bare upward tweak of her lips.

"So, you've found love again too?" He was unsure of the emotions roiling in him.

"Yes, a wonderful Dane who spent a year wooing me, two years after you left." A winsome smile as her fingers traced his cheek. "Took that long, I guess, to convince me you'd not return." She leaned back, arms folded. "I have two beautiful children now."

"No surprise that children of yours would be beautiful, Gisele." He studied her for a beat. "And Coline? Where is she?"

"Off today." She moved to her desk. "Supervising some house repairs." She scrawled something on a yellow Post-It. "Why don't you drive up and see her?" She handed him the yellow slip. "It's only ten minutes, and while I can't say for sure, she may be glad to see you." She chuckled. "Of course, we redheads can be quite volatile, so one never knows what to expect." She grasped his hands and drew him to his feet. "In any case, now that you're here, you must go." She led him to a wall map of the island. "Here, I'll show you. It's easy to find, and your rental probably has GPS anyway."

Five minutes later, after a hug and a kiss on the cheek, Derik was back in his car, following Gisele's clear instructions on how to reach Coline's house.

Derik's heart thumped with an uncomfortable beat as he navigated the hilly road. Something about Gisele's attitude in sending him to Coline smacked of unexpected consequences.

Was this second twin as forgiving as her sister? Well, he'd soon find out.

He was surprised at how tense that made him.

~ 61 ~

Derik drove slowly up the inclined road and scanned intersection signs for Coline's street, Rue Montmarte. And there it was, curling off to his right along the side of the hill, lined with burst of red from bordering bougainvillea. As he turned in, he glanced back at the Atlantic, sparkling under the western sun. Quite a view.

He paused, fifty feet onto the road, sucked in a breath, and tried to corral his thundering heart. His visit with Gisele had met a warm welcome, but also a pointed rebuke for his nine years of silence. What might he expect from Coline?

He sighed and massaged the back of his neck, stiff with tension. Memories of those glorious few days swirled through his mind, days filled first with carnal passions that morphed somehow so quickly into an abiding love. Love for both, but somehow, had he stayed, it was Coline with a tighter grasp on his heart. Having to choose only one was part of what drove him toward home. That and the treasure.

Derik shrugged and gritted his jaw. He'd come this far to make amends if nothing else, and with no other expectations. Love shunned for nine years could only wither. Shifting the Jeep into gear, he cruised slowly along the narrow street and read addresses until he spotted a mailbox at the foot of a serpentine drive: "DuMelle."

So, Coline never married. Or at least is not currently hitched. He turned up the lane and spotted the house, a large white Colonial, perched atop of the rise. As he edged closer, he spied two trucks in the drive and workmen on the roof.

And there stood the woman, back to him, her elegant shape clad in beige safari shorts and a short-sleeve, white blouse. Rich, auburn hair fell in gentle waves to below her tanned shoulders. With fists planted on curved hips, she shouted instructions to the roofers. The remembered throaty ring of that voice spilled a wave of goose bumps down his spine.

Derik pulled onto the grass, parked, and stepped from the Jeep. He hesitated by the SUV but went unnoticed, her concentration focused on the construction. He gathered up faltering determination and strode toward her.

"Coline," his voice a choked-up rasp while still thirty feet away. Apparently unheard, probably due to considerable racket emanating from the rooftop. Jaw clenched, he edged closer.

"Coline." Still hoarse but stronger this time.

She cocked her head, then slowly pivoted. A hand above her eyes, a shield from the afternoon glare, her emerald orbs widened, eyebrows arched.

"Derik?" Her face twisted by emotion—anger or joy, he couldn't tell.

"Derik!" She charged him, arms flailing, and he braced for what appeared to be an attack.

Three-feet away, she went airborne, her long, graceful legs circling his waist, strong arms wrapped around his neck, and they tumbled to the ground, she perched atop of his waist.

The pummeling he expected, from which he'd not defend himself, never came. Instead, she pressed against him, those delectable lips consuming his, her fingers snarled in his hair. Derik's arms circled her neck, drawing her closer, the remembered heat of that still luscious body against his, filled him with wonder.

They laid together as her tongue visited his eyes, an earlobe, the crease of his neck, and back to his lips, mouths engaged in a long-forgotten dance.

"*Mon amour, mon amour,*" she pushed back, eyes locked, "you've come back, my darling." She cocked an eyebrow and gave a small head shake. "But, what took you so long?"

She sat back, perched on his groin, legs astraddle. "And never so much as a single word from you, you naughty boy." Her loose blouse hung open at the neck, and the view inside brought strong memories.

Coline wiggled her butt and chuckled as she sensed a growing hardness there. "And I see, even after all these years, nothing has changed *there* between us." She leaned in for more intense kissing, four hands beginning a long-remembered voyage across bodies alive with forgotten fire. Then she rolled off, rose, and offered a hand to draw him to his feet.

They stood, wrapped in the other's arms, savoring the warmth. Derik arched his neck and studied her face. "The mailbox said DuMelle. You never married, like Gisele?"

"No, I never found another love like—"

"Mamá?" A young boy stood ten-feet away, eyes wide, watching them.

Derik's eyebrows arched. A handsome child with a full mane of auburn hair, soon joined by what was obviously his brother, an identical twin, his hair cut shorter. Coline pulled away and turned to the lads, a grin splitting her face.

"Derik Brand, I'd like you to meet Alain and Antoine ... my sons."

"Your *sons*, Coline?" He shook his head. "You said you never married."

"True." A rue smile creased her kips as she curled her arms around each boy. "But these wonderful eight-year-olds are the product of my one true love." She faced him, an eyebrow arched.

"Your one true—? Eight-year-old?" His eyes flared. "Coline? Are you saying—?"

"They are *your* sons, *mon amour. Our* sons." Tears crept from the corners of her eyes. "Two blessings left for me by you, after your departure."

"My God." He swept the three of them into his grasp. "You had twins?"

"It runs in our family, my love." She giggled and kissed his neck. "I knew you'd return some day. I just *knew* it!"

He ruffled the boys chestnut locks and kissed her moist eyes. "This is going to take some getting used to," said with a hoarse chuckle, "but I'm gonna love every minute of it."

He released Coline, but the boys continued to hug him.

"Papa, papa," they cried. "Mamá said you would come." The boy with the shorter hair looked up at him. "You will stay with us now?" His damp, blue eyes glistened. "We've missed you."

Derik struggled to swallow a lump in his throat. "This is all a shock to me...?" His eyebrows arched.

"Alain. I am Alain. I wear my hair shorter than Antoine, otherwise not even Mamá can tell us apart."

Derik nodded. "We'll work it out, son." He caressed the boy's cheek. "Having a family has been an important topic for me in recent weeks, and suddenly, here it is, ready-made."

He turned and took Coline's hand. "I couldn't be happier." His kiss filled with love. "Still in shock," he murmured in her ear, "but ecstatic."

"Boys," Coline pulled away and knelt beside them, "You'll have time with *le père* later. Now, off to your football practice, and don't come home for at least two hours." She rose and gave both hugs. "I want time alone to show your dad our house." She glanced at Derik, came into his arms, and smirked. "Especially the bedroom."

~ 62 ~

They were wrapped in each other's arms, standing next to her canopied king-size bed, their mouths ardent messengers of love. Derik's chest could barely contain his heart. It was as if he'd never left. They settled on the edge of the mattress, Coline still clutched in his arms, as he caught her dimpled chin in his fingers, their eyes locked.

"How did this happen, Coline?"

"What? The boys?" She chuckled and tweaked his nose. "A natural occurrence after sex, *mon amour*."

"I *know* that, darling, but why did you let it happen?" He pressed a finger to her lips. "Don't misunderstand me. I'm overjoyed, but ..."

"I *wanted* it to happen, Derik. Hoped for it." She caressed his cheek, a small smile tickling her lips. "Gisele and I both fell in love with you, but I more hopelessly than she."

She sighed. "Gisele took the Morning After pill each day we were together. But I knew in my heart you were going to leave us, and I desperately wanted to keep you here. Having your child was the closest I could manage, it seemed. That they were twins was a special reward, and they kept me pure, awaiting your return."

"Pure? You mean—?"

"I've been with no man since you left, *mon amour*." Her brow wrinkled. "But nine years was a long wait, so you must make it up to me, beginning this very instant." An arm snaked around his neck as she climbed onto his lap.

Her lips attacked his, then roamed to his eyes, his ear, his neck, as busy finger peeled away his shirt. Derik needed no urging as he stripped off her blouse and shorts. As before, no bra was required to support her natural magnificence. Soon all that remained were bikini underwear.

Coline straddled him, sprawled across the bed, as her tongue and lips ventured slowly across his smooth, muscled flesh, nipping, licking, teasing him into a roaring inferno.

Derik snatched a thigh, flipped her around, and tore away her panties, just as his also disappeared. Her dripping pussy hovered above his face, and he leaned up, lapping her flowing juices, his tongue tantalizing her very erect clit.

Coline shuddered as she slathered and kissed his iron hard cock, her tongue licking the glans, then taking it into her mouth. She panted and lowered her kitty closer to his face.

"Oh, *mon amour,* yes, *yes.* It's been so long. I'm going to cu-u-m-m, *now!*" Her body shook and his face was soaked with fluids as he buried his tongue deep inside her, his thumb busy with her bulging clit. She squirmed and shuddered.

"Again! *Mon Dieu,* I come again." She bucked and shuddered, then engulfed his cock deep in her throat, tongue swirling and head bobbing as her fingers teased his balls. The nipples of her firm breasts caressed his belly, and he cried out.

"Oh, Christ, me too." He thrust up his hips and exploded in her mouth. She took it all, sucking him dry, the collapsed across his body, slick with sweat.

"My God, Coline, it's as if nine years never passed." He drew her up and snuggled together, her head in the crook of his neck. His hands stroked her body, just as firm and sensual as he remembered, as they wound down.

"I love you, Derik Brand." She breathed into his ear. "I

don't know what magic you spun nine years ago, but in just three days you became the only man I could *ever* love." She raised up on her elbows. "Thank God you came back. I've really missed you—missed *this*."

Her kitty nestled atop of his dick, and she wiggled her hips and thrust her dangling breasts in his face. An impish grin creased her lips as she felt him begin to harden again. A nipple had found its way into his mouth, and his hands on her butt brought a tiny gasp.

"I've never stopped loving you either, Coline. There's been other women, but ..." he gasped as she drew slippery pussy lips back and forth across his now rigid cock, "with one exception, they were just sex. No one .... ahhh," as he slipped inside her pulsing pussy.

Arms braced on the bed, she began to rock and twist as he surged up against her. His mouth found hers, tongues dueling, and his fingers teased erect nipples as they continued the ultimate dance of love. Her pulsing grip of her soaking kitty drove Derik into a frenzy. Moans and panted breath filled the room as they thrusted together, and they came, he first, quickly followed be her, accompanied by feral growls.

Spent, Derik slumped back as Coline continued humping his still hard dick. Hands braced against his chest, she shuddered into a second orgasm, then slumped against him, slathering his face with kisses.

She chuckled, their breaths winding down. "I seem to be trying to make up for all those lost years." She rolled to his side and snuggled close. "You never disappoint me, my sex machine."

He snickered. "Look who's talking. I hope that at my advanced age, I can keep up."

"Advanced aged?" She giggled. "You're only thirty-three,

aren't you?"

"Yeah." He nodded. "But that's a good ten-years past a guy's sexual prime." He bussed her cheek with a gentle kiss.

She sighed and hugged him. "Good thing, then, that I have plans for us beyond this wonderful sex." Coline rolled up onto an elbow. "You'll stay the night, *mom amour*?" Her fingers drew a line across his forehead, around his ear, and across his lips.

"I want our sons to get to know you."

"Of course. I have nothing more important to do. And tomorrow we'll all go to the port and show the boys the boat that brought me into your life. Maybe go for a sail around the island."

She slithered atop of him and kissed his eyes and the tip of his nose. "The same sailboat from nine years ago?"

"Yep." He hugged her and kissed the top of her head, laying on his chest. "Too many important things in my life happened because of that Choy Lee. I bought it from the lease company, and named her *Martinique*."

"Sounds wonderful. The boys will love that." She cocked her head and glanced at her watch. "Still time for me to catch Gisele at the agency." She slipped off him and donned her shorts and blouse. "I'm sure she's dying to hear what happened this afternoon." A brief, passionate kiss, and she headed for the door. "Stay in bed. I'll be back shortly." She turned and gave an impish grin. "We have more catching up to do. We'll eat in tonight. A lovely mutton fish Alain speared this morning off the inshore reef." And she disappeared though the doorway.

Derik laid back, hands clasped behind his head and smiled. How things had changed in little more than two weeks.

Fighting for his very life and that of his second love, and

now in the arms of his first love, with a family already started. He knew exactly how he hoped tomorrow would unfold.

~ ~ ~

Derik steered the Jeep along the coastal road toward the harbor with Antoine, the older boy by four minutes, in the passenger seat, and Alain in the rear. Coline trailed in her Toyota because she needed the car for a real estate showing later in the day.

Derik spent the night with her in his arms, savoring her warmth. They'd coupled only once more, slowly and with a tenderness of love instead of flaming ardor. He'd never felt so complete, not even at his height with Brita.

After a breakfast of eggs, slices of ham, and buttermilk biscuits, they sallied forth en route to his yacht for a morning at sea ... and something special he'd planned.

His sons ... he loved the sound of that ... pointed out features as they drove, and soon they arrived at the quay. Four were a crowd in his dingy, but they made it safely to the Choy Lee, bobbing gently to a small swell.

Coline and the boys wore swim suits, she in a modest one-piece, possibly in deference to her sons. Derik went below to change into trunks, while the three DuMelles inspected the cockpit and steering gear.

Derik poked his head up through the cabin's hatch. "Coline, come down here, will you? The boys can stay up top."

She descended the ladder, backlit by the morning sun which set her auburn hair afire. Derik's heart pummeled his chest. Modest swimsuit or not, she was, even at thirty-six, a glorious creature, one of God's perfections.

He folded her into his arms for a gentle kiss.

"Easy, my hot stud." She chuckled and glanced at the

open hatch door. "The boys—"

"No worries, darling. But they *should* know that papa loves mama." He took her hand and led her into the cabin.

"Anyhow, I've something to show you." He paused in the salon, near a small, wall cabinet. "You mentioned you followed me on the Internet, so you know I'm wealthy, but do you know how that happened?"

"Something about treasure hunting, and you apparently run a very successful business." She touched his cheek. "Why is that important? You weren't rich when I fell in love with you."

"Actually, I was."

Her eyebrows arched. "Oh? You seemed well off, but—"

"I survived Hurricane Chico in a hidden cave on a tiny, uncharted cay about thirty miles east of here." He grinned and kissed her. "While waiting out the storm, I discovered buried treasure there. Pirate loot. An unbelievably huge cache."

"Really? Jewels and gold and—?"

He nodded. "Worth maybe a hundred million."

A gasp as her eyebrows arched. "Really, so much?"

"Let me show you." Cradling her with one arm, he slid open a drawer and drew her close.

"*Mon Dieu,* such beautiful things." Coline fingered the collection—necklaces, rings, broaches, and gold doubloons.

Derik plucked out the emerald ring he'd planned to give Brita, took her left hand, and slid it onto her third finger.

"Aha, fits like it was made for you."

"Oh, Derik," she gazed at it, eyes wide, "I couldn't—"

"Sure you can." He drew her close, their faces inches apart. "I've always dreamed of finding a love like ours, and having a passel of kids." They kissed, one hand in her auburn locks. He nuzzled her neck and murmured, "We've already got two of those. All I need now is for you to be my wife."

"Oh, *mon cher*. I never intended to pressure you." She arched her neck to see his eyes. "I'm hopelessly in love with you, but you must have a life in Florida—"

"It's been a hollow existence for most of the past nine years without you, Coline." He held her face between his palms. "Nothing is more important to me than our being together." He planted a brief, fierce kiss on her lips. "You, me, our sons, together. Nothing is more important." He held her eyes. "Will you marry me, my love? Here, now that we're together."

"Oh, *mon Dieu*, yes, of course. It is all I've yearned for." She crushed him to her for a passionate kiss, then spun free, snatched his hand, and leaped up the ladder into the cockpit. Her sons looked up as she grabbed her cell phone from her bag.

"*Quest ce qui, Mamá*," Alain looked up from the fishing rod he was holding.

Her face slit by a wide grin, she hit an auto-dial and held up a finger to her sons. Two rings before it was answered.

"Island Reality."

"Gisele! Pass off all your showings to our agents." She shook her head at the response.

"This is more important, *mon cher*." A hearty laugh bubbled up. "We've got a wedding to plan!"

Screams filled the air as the boys rushed in for a family hug, all dancing in a circle.

Heads next to each other, Derik whispered to her, "And more babies, to make it a real family."

"Oh, yes," she chuckled. "It's a task I *love* doing with you. We'll begin tonight, *mon amour*." And she caressed his butt.

The End

AFTERGLOW

For those of you with a critical eye, please understand that while this story takes place in real places, I may have bent the physical nature of certain environs to meet the needs of this tale. Effort is made to keep to reality, but occasionally, story takes precedence over physical facts. I hope such things hasn't affected your enjoyment of this tale.

ALSO

If you enjoyed this novel, please take the time to leave a review at Amazon and recommend it to your friends. I believe you may also enjoy my first two steamy romances, *Trapped* and *A 3rd Time to Die*. Both have many 5-Star reviews and are full of action, sex, and surprise endings, and while available as e-books and softbacks, they both are also available as Audio Books, for those who prefer to listen.

Turn the page to read the first few chapters of *Trapped*.
www.amazon.com/Trapped-ebook/dp/B00GLX1EKU

TRAPPED
~ Excerpt ~

Prologue

Turn signal flashing, she eases into the right lane in front of a large, battered pick-up, with less than a half-mile to the Old Orchard exit ramp. Jackee Maren rarely drove so aggressively, but first delayed by her two sons' late departure from school, and then navigating around a minor fender bender on Dundee Road, she is already ten minutes behind, and she's *never* late. The Northern Illinois Chapter of the United Way won't start its planning session without its chairwoman, and Jackee hates the idea of keeping so many busy people waiting.

Peeling onto the ramp, her two boys bickering and shoving in the back seat draw her attention. Glancing back at the road, a ridge of goose bumps cascades down her spine. They're hurtling toward a string of glaring tail lights, cars unexpectedly stopped by a red light at the first intersection off the expressway.

She jams on the brakes and is stunned when her big Mercedes slews sharply right, smack into the path of the pickup truck. It slams into the rear fender of her sedan, sending it careening off the road, the seatbelts gouging her shoulder, crushing the breath from her lungs.

"Hang on boys," she gasps.

Oh god! My sons! They can't die here.

They spin down the embankment like an eccentric top, ricocheting off a bridge column. The wheel torn from her grip, the air filled with the screech of rending metal and the stench of burning rubber, the car rears like a great angry beast, its hind legs hamstrung. Slamming down, it hurtles backward into the culvert, bucking and skipping along the steep embankment.

Despite seatbelts, Jackee is flung around like a rag doll in the jaws of some huge Rottweiler. The air bag erupts in the midst of their tumultuous downward plunge, rushing out at 200 MPH, just as frontal impact slings her forward.

Her face catches the brunt of the blow, skewering lips on her teeth, smashing her nose. A searing bolt of pain fires across her brain, igniting a burst of red heat behind her tearing eyes. A sharp pitch right crushes her left cheek against the window, knocking her momentarily senseless. The sedan teeters, enveloped in a cloud of dust, hunkering precariously on its haunches before crashing down on its wheels, coming to a thunderous, grinding stop.

Jackee awakens to wailing and blubbering from the two small boys in the rear seat.

"Mommy." The call gasped through ragged breathing.

"Mommy." Now a frantic screech.

"I'm . . . I'm here."

We're alive! Thank god, we're all still alive.

She sags against the seatbelt, every joint singed with agony, unable to will herself into action.

Help should be coming. She moans. *Gotta hang on . . .* She slips out of consciousness.

The continual bawling and moaning of her sons stir her, drawing her out of the fog of semi-consciousness. One of her eyes is swollen shut, but the other flickers open, glazed with shock.

Where the hell's Fire/Rescue.

She winces, her whole body racked by pain.

Seems like we've been trapped down here for . . .

The warble of a fast-arriving rescue vehicle answers that question. She closes her eye, struggling to control the thunder in her head and the molten bands of fire across her chest.

"Lady? You with me?" A hatchet-faced EMT materializes at the shattered passenger-side window. She strives to focus on the man, who is futilely struggling with the door.

"Malcolm, Bryan," the words slurred through bloodstained lips. "Sons . . . back seat . . ."

"Yeah, they're still strapped in. We're gonna take care of everybody, but it's you I'm focused on."

Jackee's head lolls forward, her one open, emerald eye fluttering closed as she struggles to remain conscious. The swell and ebb of her breast confirms that, while battered, she still lives. Her sons in the back continue their chorus of terror, though it's winding down to a pattern of whimpers as their surge of adrenaline burns out.

"Can't budge this damned door," the EMT, grunts. His thick-shouldered partner, hefting a crowbar, joins him.

"Move over and give me room to work." Forcing one end of the steel into the jamb, struggling to lever it open, he glances at his partner. "Those kids look okay?"

"Probably. All that loud wailing is a good sign, but we'll check 'em out once we get everyone free. The woman's obviously suffered some airbag trauma and . . . oh, oh, she's coming around."

Jackee's unswollen eye blinks, her head inches up, and she tastes the blood oozing from her nose and lips.

"Oohhh. What . . . what . . .?" She struggles to turn her head. *Oh! My sons. The brakes . . . bad crash . . . are they . . .?"*

"Mommy." Malcolm's voice a hoarse squeak. "Are you hurt? We're okay, I think." His voice and Bryan's whimpering through ragged breathing is reassuring.

Jesus. So close. Don't know how I could . . ." She sags, her thoughts fading again.

"We're gettin' nowhere with this bar." He looks back.

"We need the hydraulics down here, and in a fuckin' hurry,"

he screams up at the road.

"On the way. How 'bout a power saw now?"

"No way. Too dangerous."

Ten minutes later, a hydraulic pry bar dispenses with the door. Frantic minutes drag by as they disentangle Jackee from the air bags, and her two sobbing, shaken sons, from their seatbelts.

Jackee smells the fuel that continues to seep from the ruptured tank, pooling beneath the wreckage.

Fire—or worse—is an eminent threat.

She floats to full awareness. Her body is festooned with welts, and her face feels like she's gone ten rounds with Joe Frazier. Strapped to a gurney, her head and neck immobilized, one medic checks her vitals, which, despite her tattered façade, are surprisingly robust.

"Looks like you're gonna be okay, Lady. Got someone you want me to call?" he asks.

"Husband. Phil Maren." Mumbled with a thick lisp over a swollen tongue and lacerated lips. "North Chicago Printing. In city. My sons?"

"They're shaken and bruised, but don't seem to have any major problems. We're checking 'em out now. They'll come to the hospital as a precaution, and your husband can pick 'em up there."

Moments later the ambulance races toward Skokie Valley Hospital.

A freak thing. Was it the brakes? Phil just serviced the car.

She sighs.

How did it . . .?"

She slips off into a sedative induced slumber.

Chapter One

Five Months Later

Where am I?

Intense, deep-cave blackness envelops her . . . smothering, almost thick enough to touch. She seems adrift, suspended a pool of dark, still water.

A bath? That doesn't make sense.

Despite a shroud of absolute darkness, she senses herself rising, finally breaching the inky surface, floating weightlessly.

And she is awake.

What was that? A dream? It seemed so real.

Jackee Maren lay very still, confused by the eerie perception of bobbing gently on tepid, calm waters. Despite a sense of warmth lapping at her, she shudders.

What's happened to . . .? Oh, how stupid of me.

My surgery. It's finally over. Five months since the accident, and breathing hadn't gotten any easier. But why is it so—so dark in—where? A recovery room?

Why have they left me alone?

A pungency unique to hospitals floods her with unpleasant memories: Momma, Daddy, and her own last visit. Not a happy moment in the bunch.

Icy tentacles caress her spine, kindling a mountain range of goose bumps.

What's going on? Why . . .? Oh . . .

Voices murmuring, barely whispering, apparently close by. What are they saying?

Spooky, laying here in this—this black place. Why haven't they taken me to my room? Phil'll be worried.

Won't he? He promised to take time from work to care for their sons . . . to be supportive for a change, while she recovers from this reconstructive facial surgery he seemed so eager for her to have. She shivers, momentarily reliving that scary car accident.

Spinning, lurching, crashing down that embankment. The shriek of rending steel.

God, it was terrifying! The boys tussling in back, and I was distracted, worried at being late . . . and wondering about Phil's frequent late nights. He was seldom home evenings before the accident. But that changed after I spun the Mercedes into that ditch.

Whatever. That was then. Gotta figure out the now. Why I'm still in Recovery. Get someone's attention. If she moves, will stitches tear? An undercurrent of voices pulls at her.

Why are they whispering?

She shivers again, her skin peppered by an icy sleet of uncertainty.

Has something happened—something bad? No one's here. No one to check on me. Did something go wrong?

Oh damn, it must be terrible.

Her heart tumbles, skipping into high gear. This crushing darkness robs her of any sense of place.

Maybe I'm dead, locked away in the morgue, lying on a slab, waiting to be cut up. It's so black, and they . . . Oh, shut up.

Jeez, it was only reconstructive surgery after the accident. Dead people don't lie around, thinking. Always ready to worry if there's a little hitch somewhere. Nothing bad happened. Still, I've gotta get someone's attention.

Hey. Why didn't I see that before?

How had she missed what was right in front of her . . . two shaded windows, a bare sliver of light glimmering at their lower edges. Dare she move, seeking aid? Still stymied by the strange aura of weightless floating on a glassy film of water, she tentatively stretches out a hand.

Am I moving? Eerie. I can't really tell in this utter darkness. Her unseen fingers trip lightly across the base of the shades.

Success. Both spool noiselessly upward.

Finally. She winces, blinking at the glaring light, before her vision clears.

There, three men, standing in a small white room, two wearing blue surgeon's scrubs, the other, the tallest, a dark suit. No second bed, no moveable tables, no guest chairs anywhere. No outside windows, either. Stark illumination from flickering fluorescent fixtures cast demonic shadows across their faces. She shivers, unassured by the sight of the trio of apparent doctors.

What is this place? A recovery room? Suddenly their voices become clear.

"I spoke to her husband," says the one in the dark suit, fingering the stethoscope looped around his neck. "He said she occasionally took both amphetamines and tranquilizers."

He said that? It was just this one time, and he said . . .

"Damn," from the taller of the two, "that wasn't on the admitting form. We could've rescheduled. Drugs and anesthetics always cause problems."

Problems? God, I knew it. Damned hospitals. Damn, damn, damn.

"We're checking," the third man says. "I'm not convinced tests will tell us anything that will do us much good in court, if it comes to that."

What the hell are they talking about?

She is suddenly struggling to breathe, her heart pummeling her breast.

Oh Jesus, something did happen. Something bad.

Head spinning, her world lurches surreally askew. She shudders.

I'm so cold. Her little lagoon churns from comfortable warmth into a bed of ice.

Something's terribly wrong. Hospitals are supposed to fix

things, but I had the same scary feeling while waiting for Daddy's test results, and I was right.

Gotta find out what's happened. Sucking in a ragged breath, worried about damaging her facial surgery, she grits her teeth before calling out.

"Hey."

Don't panic. They'll see me in a minute.

But they *don't*. Are they deaf?

"Over here." Louder now, willing them to look at her.

"You, out there. Please help me."

The taller surgeon cocks his head and turns.

Thank god. He'll see me now.

He pauses, still as stone. Then his eyes flare wide, his jaw dropping. Snatching at the other doctor's sleeve, he thrusts an almost accusing finger at her.

"Look," he shouts. "Look."

"Her eyes! Her eyes.

"They're open."

Chapter Two

The three men rush to the two little windows, the sports jacket of the tallest flapping in his haste.

My eyes? What about my eyes? Why is he so damned excited?

The taller of the two surgeons pushes in front, very close to the glass, his head seeming to fill both openings. She winces, blinking, from a bright light shined into her eyes.

"Mrs. Maren, can you hear me? Are you all right?"

"Of course I hear you. You're standing right there, aren't you?" He squints, bushy dark brow creased, lips pursing, but doesn't respond.

Is he deaf?

"Mrs. Maren, if you hear me, please signal somehow." A furtive glance at the other men, then back to her, his brown eyes boring into her. "Can you move anything?"

Ohmygod. She shivers, the truth crashing over her, sending her heart on a rumba rampage inside her breast.

I wasn't talking. Were they—oh, god—they were only thoughts inside my head!

I didn't . . . Oh, Jesus. I can talk, can't I? Stomach roiling, she gags back rising gorge, acid burning her gullet. Another reality stabs her, freezing her mind. She gasps . . . or did she?

Did I actually swallow? Despite the bitter taste, she senses no connection to her throat, her tongue, her lips. She feels nothing. The sour taste of bile fills her head, not her mouth, as if everything is disjointed. She can sense, but can she *feel*?

No. There's only this ethereal aura of weightless floating.

What's happened to me? *Why can't I talk? Why can't I feel anything?*

"Mrs. Maren?" His voice breaks through the jumbled panic surging through her head. "I'm sure you hear me. I see your eyes moving. Can you do anything else? Please, try."

Struggling to clear her mind, she focuses on his face, so close to the two little windows.

Move? Yes, I must be able to wiggle something.

Oh, god. Oh, god. Why can't I . . . Something. I gotta do something. Twitch, finger. Nothing. *Move arm, move.* It refuses.

Wag a foot. Make a fist. Nothing cooperates. She grunts silently, straining at the effort.

Scrunch, toes. No luck there, either. No need to see them to know the results.

Nothing. She tries to shake her head. *Stupid. Can't do that either.*

Shit. Can't move. Can't talk. Can't do anything. Nothing at all. Her mind spins dizzily, whirling down . . . down . . . down, into a black, chaotic whirlpool of terror.

"No physical activity," the other man in blue scrubs says, glancing at an electronic monitor, "but her heart rate's way up. She's agitated."

"I'm not surprised." The taller man studies his patient. Shrugging, he reaches for her hand. It's beyond her vision, and she feels nothing.

"Can't you signal us somehow? Maybe blink your eyes?"

Jesus. What have they done to me? What have they done?

Only she hears the screams of terror echoing through her head.

Nothing works. Gotta do something. Gotta get control. Fix this, somehow.

Tenuously in charge of her fractured psyche, she concentrates on the simple task of shutting her eyes.

They close.

Thank god. At least that's something, and . . . What the hell?

Those emerald orbs fly wide, the "window shades" closing and opening at the same time.

Unbelievable. They're not windows. They're my eyes.

"She did it. She did it. Mrs. Maren, please blink twice if you understand me."

Ohmygod. It was simple surgery. What's gone wrong? This can't be happening.

Can't panic. These are good doctors. Gotta calm down and cooperate.

Her heart still jackhammering at her ribs, she musters fractured courage, willing her eyes to blink twice. The "shades" closed both times.

"Great," said the taller one. "She understands. Get an EEG

on her. Let's find out what's going on." The other doctor hurries away.

Oh, Jesus. She pants, her throat closing, choking her breath, crushing her lungs.

I'm gonna be sick. Gasping for breath, she struggles against rising gorge swamping her.

What's gone wrong? Why can't I even wiggle a finger, or make any sound? Not even a grunt. It's like a bad dream.

That's it. I'm having a nightmare. Wake up, Jackee. Wake up.

"Heart rate and BP are really spiking. She's panicking."

"Can't blame her," the dark suit says. Leaning close, he speaks with a quiet firmness.

"Mrs. Maren, I know you're scared, but you've got to control your panic. I don't want to be forced to give you a sedative."

No, this isn't a bad dream, is it? The scary truth is I'm living the nightmare.

"Now we know you're alert, we can take care of you. Try to calm down. We need to ask you some questions and do further tests on your condition."

My condition? You call this a condition?

"Blink once for 'yes,' and twice for 'no.' Okay?"

Oh, god. What did you bastards do to me? A banshee's wail echoes inside the soundproof vault of her beautiful, blonde head. Purged, she struggles to stifle her panic.

Gotta calm down. Daddy taught me to be tough. You can do this. Finally, precariously in charge, she blinks once.

"Good," says the doctor she labeled Number One.

"Now concentrate hard and try again to move something. Even a small twitch of a finger or a toe. Anything. Can you do that?"

Okay. Gotta stop acting like a crazy dog, chasing its tail. Take a slow, deep breath, just like Daddy taught me when I *was little and afraid from a bad dre*am. But this is no dream, and she seems unable to govern her breathing.

Another damned thing that doesn't work. Mentally gritting her teeth, she bears down on the minor task of jiggling a tiny digit. Her thumping heart slows as concentration supplants fear.

But controlling her emotions seems all she can do. No twitch anywhere, not even a millimeter. Closing her eyes, focusing her mind, she wills just one finger to curl. No success. She gives a mental sigh, as reality sweeps over her.

Gotta accept the facts, no matter how terrible.

Strangely calm now in the face of unassailable truth, Jackee's green eyes find the doctor's, blinking twice.

"No? You can't move anything except your eyes or eyelids? Okay, don't worry. I'm sure there's something . . ." The clippity-clop of fast approaching wheeled carts cuts him off. Several white-coated people, led by Number Two, burst into the room.

"I've got the EEG team and the head of neurology," he says. An efficient group of newcomers, a conglomerate of men and women in blue scrubs and white uniforms, bustle about, setting up their equipment. Number One nods, taking her hand.

"We're going to run some tests to see what's going on. Figure out how to get you well. You're our top priority."

Jackee supposes he's giving a reassuring squeeze or patting her hand. It's out of sight. No way to tilt her head to look.

God, how scary. I can't even feel that.

She "shivers," chilled, as if lying in a snow. How is *that*? Physically, nothing changed.

"I'm Dr. Hersch," he continues, "and this (gesturing toward Number Two) is Dr. Lambini, Chief of Surgery. Our boss, the man in the suit, is Dr. Markowitz. We're doing our best to figure this out. Get you better so you can go home."

What a jerk. If that were to be reassuring . . . well, it's not very convincing.

His hollow charade is ridiculous enough to fracture her dam of tension, spilling the frigid bath of panic and terror into the ether, leaving her slack and listless. She's again bobbing gently, sending ripples across the newfound watery cove of her mind, no longer cold.

His words sow no confidence. She senses nothing they can do will actually work.

She blinks once through welling tears.

At least I can still cry.